Re
Shepherd Avenue

15 Sept 2017

To the one and only Amy
with much love!

xx
Charlie

Also by Charlie Carillo

Raising Jake

One Hit Wonder

Shepherd Avenue

Return to Shepherd Avenue

Charlie Carillo

LYRICAL PRESS
Kensington Publishing Corp.
www.kensingtonbooks.com

LYRICAL PRESS BOOKS are published by

Kensington Publishing Corp.
119 West 40th Street
New York, NY 10018

All Kensington titles, imprints, and distributed lines are available at special quantity discounts for bulk purchases for sales promotion, premiums, fund-raising, educational, or institutional use.

Special book excerpts or customized printings can also be created to fit specific needs. For details, write or phone the office of the Kensington Sales Manager: Kensington Publishing Corp., 119 West 40th Street, New York, NY 10018. Attn. Sales Department. Phone: 1-800-221-2647.

Lyrical Press and Lyrical Press logo Reg. U.S. Pat. & TM Off.

First Electronic Edition: June 2017
eISBN-13: 978-1-5161-0255-6
eISBN-10: 1-5161-0255-X

First Print Edition: June 2017
ISBN-13: 978-1-5161-0330-0
ISBN-10: 1-5161-0330-0

Printed in the United States of America

Chapter One

The elevated train ride into Brooklyn was as rickety as hell, and I hadn't been this way for nearly half a century.

But my instincts told me I was on the right path, like an old dog returning to dig up a bone he'd buried when he was a puppy.

I was the only white person getting off by the time it reached the Cleveland Street station in East New York, walking down those worn steel steps into a much different world than the one I'd known in 1961.

The Italian grocery stores were long gone. The shops in the shadow of the elevated train tracks now had gaudy signs in Spanish. Latin music and rap boomed from the windows of passing cars. I made my way on timid feet, feeling suspicious eyes from all around.

Who was I, this sixty-year-old guy with gray hair and a thick middle? A welfare inspector? An undercover cop? What business did someone like me have on these streets?

I walked fast, lest anyone stop me to ask questions, making the turn down Shepherd Avenue like a man on a mission. Which is exactly what I was.

My heart raced and my legs trembled. This was the street that haunted my dreams, a street I thought I'd never see again, even though it was just a forty-minute subway ride from my home in Manhattan.

Once upon a time, I knew the people who lived in these houses. They were all gone. It was as if God had shaken an invisible blanket on the street and sent everybody flying—to Long Island, to New Jersey, to the cemetery.

The houses looked smaller, and seemed to be hunching with the strain of the years. Metal bars covered the windows, and some of the porches were enclosed in protective cages. People had become their own jailers, and as I reached 207 Shepherd I stopped for a long look at the red brick house I'd once called home.

"Still standing," I said out loud. Not that this surprised me. My grandfather had built it, and he knew what he was doing. The only changes were protective ones. A locked metal gate sealed the once wide-open driveway, and there were bars over the windows.

I climbed the three steps to the front door, and here was another change—the dark wooden door I remembered had been replaced by a white metal door without a window on it. There was no knocker, either—the doorbell to the left of the door was another new addition.

I pushed the bell and was jolted by the sound it made, a jangly noise you'd expect to hear during a prison break. I wanted to run, but it was too late. The lock snapped—two or three of them, actually—then the door opened halfway and I was looking into the face of a Puerto Rican man about my age, standing there in jeans and a sleeveless undershirt.

"What," he said flatly, clearly expecting bad news.

I couldn't speak for a few moments. I stared into his inky eyes, wondering how he was going to react to what I was about to say.

"Is this your house?" I began.

He actually chuckled, revealing a smoker's teeth beneath a fierce black moustache. "If it ain't, I'm in big trouble."

"So you *do* own this house."

His smile morphed into a scowl. "Hey. Buddy. What the hell do you want?"

"Well, I used to live here, a long time ago. May I show you something?"

He was still scowling but he was also intrigued. I took a small black-and-white photograph from my shirt pocket and handed it to him. He cupped it in his hand, holding it gingerly around the edges.

"The fuck am I lookin' at, here?"

"That's me and my grandfather in front of your house."

My grandfather looked like an aging leopard, lean and graying but still vital, braced to spring at the photographer if necessary. His menacing looks were deceiving. He was the kindest, fairest man I ever knew. I stood beside him in baggy short pants and a T-shirt, skinny and knobby-kneed as a newborn calf.

Who the hell had taken the picture? Who even had a camera, back then? I couldn't remember. But somehow this image I'd treasured for so long had been captured in front of the house, the two of us looking at the camera as if someone had just stolen our lunch.

The Puerto Rican said, "This kid is you?"

"Yup."

"They shoulda fed you more."

"I had plenty to eat. Burned it off fast back then."

"Man, I ain't callin' you a liar or nothin', but this don't look like my house."

"There were no bars on the windows back then. And the door was different. But look, you can see the two-oh-seven on the door."

He squinted at the picture before handing it back to me. "Yeah, okay, maybe that's my house. Maybe it ain't. So what's the big deal?"

"I want to buy it."

His brow loosened and his eyes widened. Clearly, I was a lunatic. He tightened his grip on the doorknob and pulled the door close to his hip, as if to prevent an attack dog within from getting to me.

"Are you nuts, man?"

"I hope not."

"*Buy* it?"

"That's right."

"Why?"

"Like I said, I used to live here when I was a kid. I want to come back."

A sad look washed over his face as he let it sink in. He rubbed his eyes, as if maybe I was a mirage that would be gone when he dropped his hands.

But I was still there, staring at him, trying to look as sincere as I could.

"Lemme see the picture again."

He examined it as if seeking clues that would explain my wild offer. Finding none, he gave it back to me, then made rubbing motions in midair with his hands, as if to erase a blackboard.

"So, lemme get this straight. You come here and ring my bell and say you wanna buy my house, just like that?"

"Just like that."

He sighed, shook his head. "This ain't the neighborhood you knew, buddy."

"I know that."

"No offense, man, but you don't look too tough."

"I'm not."

"This is a tough neighborhood."

"I'm sure it is. It was pretty tough when I lived here."

He waved my words away. "Ain't nothing, compared to now."

"Are you interested in selling me your house?"

He hesitated, relaxed his grip on the doorknob. "You a crazy man, or what?"

"Probably. But I have money, which makes me a little less crazy."

"You on drugs?"

"No."

"Huh. Maybe you should be."

"Does my offer interest you in any way?"

"You ain't made no offer, man."

"Show me the house, and we'll talk."

He nodded at me, then rolled his head from side to side, ticktock, thinking it over. What did he have to lose?

The door swung open, and I was inside.

At first it was like a dream, like being under water, and then I realized it felt like that for a good reason: *I wasn't breathing.* I wasn't breathing because the experience seemed as delicate as a soap bubble, and I feared it would burst if I allowed myself to breathe.

But it was no dream. These were the walls, floors and ceilings of a very special summer from my childhood. I started breathing again as I followed the man down the narrow hallway to the kitchen where my grandmother had prepared innumerable meals and endless pots of coffee.

Could it be the same stove? I could have sworn I recognized the white porcelain knobs, veined with tiny cracks.

I swallowed. "Was this stove here when you moved in?"

"Think so."

"Oh my God. This must have been my grandmother's!"

"No shit?"

"It's at least fifty years old!"

"Well, it still works good."

Down the hall we went to the bedrooms, three in all, including the one I'd shared with my Uncle Victor. They were all painted in flashy shades of orange, yellow, and blue, colors my grandmother would have dismissed as "real Puerto Rican."

I lingered in my old bedroom. It used to look out on a small dirt yard where my grandfather and I raised chickens. Now that yard had been paved over and painted green, as if to fool people into thinking it was a lawn.

I pointed at the green cement. "That used to be our chicken yard."

"No shit? It's illegal to have chickens now."

"It was illegal then. Why'd you pave the yard?"

"Nothin' grows out there, man. Too much shade. It was just dirt. Cement's cleaner."

"We grew tomatoes out there."

"Well, good for you. I don't like tomatoes."

I turned to him. "By the way, I'm Joe Ambrosio."

"Rico Valdez." We shook hands. "You still wanna buy this house?"

"May I see the basement?"

He led the way down the echoey wooden steps to the basement, the only part of the house that retained an odor from my childhood, a burny, bread-like smell like no other I'd ever known.

I didn't like it and I didn't hate it. I just recognized it, with a sensation so powerful that I literally went weak at the knees.

Rico was suddenly worried about this crazy stranger he'd let into his home.

"Hey, man, you okay? Not gonna puke, are you?"

I was leaning over, my hands on my knees. I needed to catch my breath. I lifted my head as I scanned the basement, once the heart and hub of the Ambrosio family.

Now it was the starkest, saddest room I'd ever seen. The walls hadn't tasted paint in decades, and the sink and stove were gone. Bits of pipe jutting from the wall and floor looked twisted, as if those appliances had been ripped away by an angry giant. A rusty bicycle with two flat tires was leaning against one wall, surrounded by cardboard cartons stuffed with junk. The built-in wooden table and benches my grandfather had made to accommodate whoever might show up were gone, and the shadows on the floor from the two windows facing the driveway were striped, thanks to the bars over the windows.

It was like an underground prison cell. Rico could sense my sorrow.

"I was plannin' to fix it up down here, but my wife got sick.

Hadda drop everything, and then she died . . ." He hesitated and sighed, annoyed at me for raking up his sorrows with this impromptu real-estate showing.

"I'm sorry for your loss, Rico."

"Yeah, well, shit happens . . . still wanna buy my house?"

"You got coffee?"

"Instant."

"Make me a cup, and let's talk."

We sat at the kitchen table, sipping black coffee. Once I had him relaxed, Rico was a talker. I learned that he'd recently retired after a career with the Department of Motor Vehicles, lost his wife the year before after a long illness, and that his two grown children lived in California.

"All of a sudden, I'm by myself," he said, as if the thought were just occurring to him as he spoke it. "Ain't like I planned it this way."

I shrugged. "Nobody really plans their life. It all just kind of happens to us, don't you think?"

He stared at me, a funny smile on his face. "What are you, a fuckin' philosopher?"

"No. I write children's books."

"No shit? You can make a livin', doin' that?"

"I get by."

"You know, man, you look familiar."

"Yeah, I get that a lot. Don't know why."

He rubbed his face, pulled on his moustache and suddenly slapped the table, making the coffee cups jump.

"Whoa, whoa, what's wrong with me?" He pointed to the ceiling. "You ain't even seen the upstairs! You want to see the upstairs?"

"I don't have to see it. My grandfather built it, I'm sure it's holding up." Truth is, the roof could have been missing and I still would have wanted the house.

But Rico couldn't stop selling. "It's a moneymaker, man! Two-bedroom apartment, rent it out, you get fifteen, sixteen hundred a month!"

"Is somebody living there now?"

"Couple just moved out. I was gonna look for a new tenant."

"Don't. I want the whole house for myself. Let's talk price."

William Wallace
13th Century Scotland
1307 Edward deed

Edward 2nd. morried Isabella
Piers Gaveston Hugh Despenser

Edward 1347. King. 3rd.
Windsor Castle.
Prince of Wales. never King

Henry 3rd
1245. Rebuilding
Wsl Minsli Abbey
Simon - De Montfort
1264. Ruled. Henry
only a name
Edward Killed Simon
1st. Longshanks-
Captured Wales built
Castles.
Morgana of Norway died

He sank down in his chair, staring at me in wonder. "Are you for real?"

"Absolutely."

"That's a lotta rooms for one person."

"I like space."

He took a deep breath and held it with pursed lips, thinking things over. If I didn't plan to take on a tenant, it meant I had money. If I had money, he could gouge me on the price.

"Half a million!" he suddenly blurted.

I couldn't help laughing. At most, the house was worth something in the mid-threes, maybe four hundred thousand, tops. But not half a mill.

"Come on, Rico. My grandfather built this house for six thousand!"

"Yeah, and he had a pet dinosaur, didn't he?"

"Four hundred and fifty."

His eyes widened at my offer but he held strong.

"Half a million, buddy." He clearly enjoyed rolling that massive figure off his tongue, a rare experience for a retired civil servant. "That's my price, and I'm sittin' on it."

"Four seventy-five."

"Yeah, and then I gotta wait for you to get a mortgage, and by then it's summertime, and who the fuck wants to move into East New York when it's ninety-eight degrees out? Maybe you ain't so nostalgic when the street tar is melting. Maybe you wanna cool off in the Hamptons, think it over until September."

"I don't have a house in the Hamptons. Four seventy-five, and remember, this is just you and me, so you won't be losing six percent to an agent."

"Goddam bloodsuckers! And I *still* want half a million."

"Four-eighty, and you won't be waiting for my mortgage. I'm paying cash, Rico."

He forced a chuckle. He was trying to be cool about it, but he was impressed—I could tell by the flash in his eyes. "You sayin' you got four-hundred-and-eighty grand in the bank, ready to go?"

"The check won't bounce."

He smiled, oh-so slyly. "If you say you got four-eighty, then I know you got half a million. Which is still my price."

"But—"

He held up a hand to silence me. "You say *four-eighty* one more time, my price goes to five-fifty. Think hard, my man, if those coupla words comin' outta your mouth are worth an extra fifty G's to you."

We stared at each other, not blinking, for a full minute or so. This wild scheme I'd cooked up when I boarded the train in Manhattan an hour earlier was actually coming together, unless I blew it now.

"We got a deal, Joe?" Rico calmly asked.

"Look, I—"

"All I wanna hear from you now is 'yes' or 'no' for half a million."

I sighed, shrugged. He had me, and he knew it.

"Yes."

Rico smiled like a poker player whose bluff has paid off. We shook hands, long and hard.

"Congratulations, bro. You got yourself a house!"

We arranged to get together for the paperwork, figure out my move-in date. It was more real to me than it was to Rico, who sat there like a stunned boxer.

It was just now hitting him: He was selling his house! He started talking about moving to California to be near his children. Suddenly he was crying, and doing nothing to try and hide it.

"You okay, Rico?"

He nodded, wiped his eyes. "My poor wife always wanted to see California. She ran outta time."

"I'm sorry, man."

"You got a wife?"

"Never married."

"You gay?"

"No. Just unlucky."

He walked me to the door, assuring me that the roof was sound, the boiler powerful, the walls solid, the plumbing first-rate.

"I know all that," I assured him. "My grandfather knew what he was doing."

It was beginning to dawn on me—207 Shepherd Avenue was all mine! Unless this was all a dream, or maybe Rico didn't actually own the house . . . could that be? He'd answered the door, but had he shown me the deed?

"You okay there, Joe?"

"Yeah . . . we just made a deal here, didn't we? I mean, we have to draw up the papers and all that, but you *did* just sell me your house, right?"

"Hey, man, if you got half-a-million bucks, you got a house." He crossed his heart, then held up a hand. "Scout's honor . . . listen, you want a little free advice?"

"Shoot."

Rico looked left and right before speaking, even though we were the only ones there. "Never tell a Puerto Rican how much cash you got, 'cause he's gonna know you got a little more." A sly wink sealed this proclamation, which would have done me some real good about ten minutes earlier.

"I'll remember that, Rico."

I went out the front door and down the brick steps. Rico watched me go, then called for me to come back.

Jesus, had he changed his mind about the house already? Was this slam-bam deal we'd made in less than an hour too good to be true? Reluctantly, I returned to the front door, where Rico stood jabbing his finger toward my face.

"I *know* you, man," he said. "Don't I know you? Why the fuck do I know you?"

"I don't know."

"You famous?"

"Well . . ."

Suddenly it came to him, his eyes widening as he shook his finger at my face.

"Holy shit, I got it!" he cried. "You're the crazy guy on the bridge, right?"

My stupid smile told him he was right.

Yeah, that was me. The crazy guy on the bridge.

Chapter Two

It was too easy, and that's pretty amazing, considering how little planning went into my admittedly crazy mission.

It was a beautiful spring day, perfect for a walk across the Brooklyn Bridge, something I'd done a dozen times before. I was wearing shorts, a black T-shirt and green Keds sneakers. The small backpack I shouldered had the silver canister in it, and nothing else.

Nothing especially odd about a just-turned-sixty-year-old man crossing the bridge that way. I was dressed a little young for my years, maybe, but the city is full of characters, and I looked like just one more, walking from Manhattan to Brooklyn across that glorious span.

Until I stopped just past the middle, hoisted myself onto one of the suspension cables and began climbing toward the tower at the end of it.

"Hey, look at that guy!" I heard someone shout. I was moving fast, hand over hand in a crouching crawl, and whatever else that person had to say was blown away by the wind as I climbed higher and higher.

A gate blocked the way about twenty feet up but I was able to climb around it, scraping my chest on one of the protective spikes in the process. After that, the path to the top was unobstructed.

Car horns blared below, but I didn't look down. I had no particular fear of heights, but I'm a clumsy man even on flat ground, and the last thing I needed was any kind of distraction.

When the wind gusted I hugged the cable and waited for it to die down. The cable seemed to stretch straight into the clouds, but I knew that was an illusion. All I had to do was keep moving, and I would get there.

Now a helicopter hovered overhead and I knew it was a news copter, recording live shots of the deranged bridge guy. Was I a jumper, or just a climber? They'd know soon enough.

A hard voice of authority from behind—just the word "Hey!" I peeked back through the gap under my arm, like a jockey checking for rival horses, and saw four cops on the cable, inching their way toward me.

The lead cop yelled again, but I couldn't hear what he said. It might have been "Stop!" but I ignored him and kept going, suddenly aware that this cable I climbed was not a stationary thing. The higher I went the more it seemed to hum and sway with the wind, which is probably why it had stood strong for more than a century—give and take, give and take. It was like ascending something ancient and alive—the long neck of a Brontosaurus, maybe, and I had to reach the top before the creature turned his head and flicked me away . . .

They say it took eleven minutes for me to reach the top. It was good to be off the cable, standing on the flat surface of that stone tower. It was caked with a thick white-brown crust that turned out to be pigeon dung, and I remembered what Neil Armstrong said as he walked on the moon: "The surface is fine and powdery . . ."

I looked back at the cable, where the cops were making their way toward me, moving a lot more slowly than I had. Now the helicopter blades were loud as the craft hovered at eye level, capturing my every move, which so far was the removal of my backpack from my shoulders. I unzipped the bag and took out the canister.

"Don't do it!"

I turned to look at the lead cop, ten feet below, who straddled the cable with his legs while imploring me with his hands. Blond curls peeked out from the sides of his helmet and his bulletproof vest looked snug on him. The other three cops took his cue and stopped moving.

"Whatever that is," the lead cop commanded, "put it down!"

"It won't take long!" I replied. I unscrewed the cap on the canister and the cops drew their guns. Time for a split-second decision from the lead guy, who held up a hand and shouted over his shoulder, "Hold your fire!"

That was the break I needed to fling my father's ashes as high and far as I could into a dancing wind. The cops ducked their heads. The ashes seemed to hover in the air, forming a powdery white ghost that swirled around my head before spreading far and wide over the waters of the East River.

My father, Salvatore Ambrosio. A showman to the end.

I was suddenly exhausted. I thought about chucking the canister over the side, but I didn't want to hurt anybody, and it was beginning to dawn on me that I was already in enough trouble. I screwed the lid back on and waited for justice.

The lead cop was suddenly in my face, breathing hard. He had the gun trained at my nose, but he was calm. He was twice my size and half my age, one of those guys who looked like he lived at the gym.

"Let's have the can," he said softly. I handed it over. He shook it to feel its emptiness. "What was in here?"

"Ashes."

"What?"

"My father's ashes."

"You mean, his . . . remains?"

"Yeah."

"Not anthrax? Nothing toxic?"

"Unless it was in my father's body when they cremated him, no."

He turned to speak to the other cops, who had finally reached the top. One of them ordered me to get to my feet for a fast frisking while another plundered my backpack, finding nothing. The lead cop spoke into a shoulder microphone. I couldn't hear what he was saying, but I knew it was something to the effect that I was crazy but harmless, and I had no poisons or weapons with me.

"All right," he said to his fellow cops, "I got this guy."

They were dismissed and headed back down the cable. The lead cop packed the canister into the backpack, zipped it up and shouldered it. We were face-to-face. He had bright blue eyes that bulged a little and a face as smooth as a baby's. He was breathing hard, but I wasn't. He took off his helmet, ran a hand through a head of lamb's-wool curls and put the helmet back on.

"You saying you came all the way up here to scatter your father's ashes?"

"Right."

"You realize you've broken the law."

"I figured I did, yeah."

"Anything else you planned on doing up here?"

"Like what?"

"Like jump?"

I spread my hands. "Do I look crazy to you?"

"You want my honest opinion, or the one the shrinks tell us to give you?"

I laughed out loud. So did he. He put his hands on my shoulders with a touch that was surprisingly gentle.

"Ready to go down?"

"Sure."

"Can you handle it?"

I shrugged. "I have to do what I just did, only backwards."

He smiled. "You're a fuckin' genius. I'll go first."

He straddled the cable and waited for me to do likewise, right in front of him. Hundreds of people jammed the walkway below, gazing upward. We inched our way down the cable.

"What's your name?" I asked over my shoulder.

"Billy."

"I'm Joe."

"Pleased to meet you, Joe."

"Am I under arrest, Billy?"

"You will be. For obvious reasons, I'm not cuffing you 'til we get down."

"Billy, I just want to say I'm really sorry for putting you through this."

He chuckled. "Aaay, forget it. We can slow down if you want. I could use the overtime."

Chapter Three

When I was ten years old my mother died and my father flipped out. He sold our house, quit his job as a copywriter at an ad agency and took off on a summer-long cross-country journey, but not before dropping me off at his parents' house on Shepherd Avenue.

It would have been the same if he'd dropped me off with strangers, because that's what my Italian-American grandparents were to me. This was a completely different world from the gentle one I'd known in the leafy-green suburb of Roslyn, Long Island, and the transition wasn't easy.

Nothing accelerates maturity faster than a tough neighborhood. In that motherless summer of 1961 I learned how to fight and swear and survive. I became a vandal and a schemer. I even fell in love and had my heart broken.

Through it all, I developed a shell that would prevent me from ever, ever trusting anyone completely. It's a permanent thing, that shell, and it never cracks.

Mine didn't, anyway. And people have pounded on it pretty hard.

By the time my father returned from his journey a lot of things had happened. His kid brother Victor, then eighteen years old, was a high school baseball star who was drafted by the Pittsburgh Pirates, failed to cut it in the minor leagues and took off on his own journey. And my grandfather, a plumber named Angie, died of a heart attack—he actually breathed his last while seated beside me on a Ferris wheel.

Those are just some highlights from that adventure-packed summer. My grandmother, Connie, was worn out from it all. She was weary beyond her years, a lady with a heavy body and a failing heart that was never going to get any stronger, and when my father returned he realized that dumping me off in her care had taken a toll.

He moved into the house on Shepherd Avenue—he had no place else to go!—but he didn't get his old job back. Instead, he tended to the domestic chores around the house by day while pounding away on his manual typewriter at night. He had half-a-dozen marble-backed notebooks he'd filled with writings during his cross-country journey, and now he was tying them all together.

Connie watched him work with a fishy eye. "What are you writing?"

"A book, Mah."

"A book? All of a sudden you're an author?"

"I don't know what I am anymore."

"What's it about?"

"The things I did to make money."

She made a snorting sound. "Who's gonna read a book about that?"

"Probably nobody."

"So why write it?"

"Good question, Mah."

"Ain't you gonna get a job?"

"If I have to." He gestured at his notebooks, splashed open all around him. "First, this. I still got a few bucks stashed."

He continued typing. She slapped him lightly on the back of his head, as she'd done to me so many times when I drove her to the limits of her patience.

"A head like a rock," she declared.

"Got it from you," he replied, his fingers never once breaking their rhythm as he continued working. It sounded like gunfire when he typed. He struck those keys as if they owed him money.

I went to school at P.S. 108, which both my grandmother and my father had attended, while the two of them struggled to stay out of each other's way in the house. At breakfast they were already on each other's nerves. I was never so happy to get out of the house and go to school, even though I hated it.

My grandmother was a sweet savage who'd never expected to outlive Angie. She was always mumbling vaguely about her "bad ticker," and then her trim, muscular husband suddenly cut ahead of her on line to the cemetery.

She wasn't prepared for that. I think she felt there was something rude about it. In a bizarre way, my grandfather had stolen her thunder, but not for long. Connie was slowing down like a watch in need of winding, only who can wind a human being?

One night my father and I came upon her sitting on the kitchen floor, dazed and confused, like a boxer who'd been caught by a sucker punch.

"Mah! What happened?"

She shook her head to clear it. "I'm tired, Sal."

"Let's get you to bed."

"No, no, no . . ."

We each took an elbow. "Up you go, Mah. Come on."

"Turn the flame down under my gravy . . ."

Her breathing was shallow and she was as pale as the sheet against her cheek. I'd never seen her so vulnerable. My father was worried.

"Mah, I'm calling the doctor."

"No, no, no, just let me rest . . ."

She got her way: no doctor. But an hour later we heard a thud and found her facedown on the kitchen floor.

"Gotta check on my gravy . . ."

We bundled her up and took her to Brooklyn Hospital. It was the first time in her life that Connie had ever been to a hospital. She'd never had an operation or a checkup. She'd been born at home, and her sons were both born in the house on Shepherd Avenue. Not a doctor in sight.

But the medical roulette wheel we all ride finally landed on Constanzia Ambrosio's number.

Her eyes were wide with fear as she was placed in a wheelchair and pushed through the doors of the emergency room to meet her destiny. They put her on a drip to rehydrate her, but the doctor told my father she was in severe heart failure and it was only a matter of time—she might not even last the night.

My father held her hand. I would have held the other one but the drip needle was taped to the back of it and I didn't want to hurt her.

She jerked her chin toward the IV bag. "What's this for?" Her false teeth weren't in, so her words were mushy.

"You're dehydrated, Mah."

"Yeah? They can't just give me a drink of water?"

My father chuckled, but I think he was disguising a sob. "Jesus, Mah, you're too much."

She turned to me. "Joseph."

She'd never said my name so gently. I took a step toward her, and she inhaled deeply.

"You're a good boy," she breathed.

I was stunned. It was the first time she'd ever offered an opinion about me. I also knew it was the kind of thing she never would have said, had she expected to live to see another sunrise.

Which she didn't. I left the room to go to the bathroom and by the time I got back, Connie was dead. Weeks would pass before my father would tell me her final words, issued in an angry growl as she clenched his hand:

"I don't want to die!"

Remarkable words from someone who'd never seemed especially happy about being alive. But I was wrong about that. She grumbled all the way, but nobody loved life more than Constanzia Ambrosio.

Just before Thanksgiving my father delivered his manuscript to a literary agent in Manhattan. The Monday after Thanksgiving the agent called him, begging for exclusivity.

The book was all about the advertising business. My father called it *Creating Envy*, because that's what he said he did for a living: Make people jealous of each other.

It was a sensation when it was published in the spring of 1962. My father caught one of those cultural waves in which people are eager for the truth, or think they are. He told all about the campaigns he'd worked on, the truths they'd stretched, the clever thinking that went into ads designed to—what else?—make people buy things they probably didn't need.

Nobody had ever written such a book, and of course my father was burning his bridges on Madison Avenue, but *Creating Envy* made so much money that he'd never have to hack the nine-to-five routine again.

That was the good news. It was also the bad news, because it meant that Salvatore Ambrosio was not tied down anywhere. The house on Shepherd Avenue was sold, and we were off—around the world. Literally.

Until I turned eighteen, we never lived in any one place longer than six months. On my eighteenth birthday I announced that New York City was going to be my permanent home, that I was through living out of suitcases.

I thought that would upset my father. Instead, he seemed relieved, as if he'd just set down a heavy piece of luggage. Now he could follow his restless impulses a lot more easily. We happened to be living in the city at the time, in a two-bedroom apartment on Charles Street in Greenwich Village my father had bought for cold cash.

"Okay," he said. "Fair enough. You stay here. You okay on your own? What about college?"

"I have other plans."

He sighed. My student records from a dozen schools, American and international, were a hopeless mess. He was in no position to lecture me about my future.

He wished me luck and took off to wherever he was going, leaving me with a substantial bank account. I worked a string of dead-end jobs before eventually hitting my stride as a children's-book author. I was a double-threat, because I could draw and I could write. I also had no problems working within the constraints of the severely limited vocabulary available to storytellers in my trade.

Once I had good money coming in I moved to an apartment of my own, a studio on the Upper East Side. I was there for about three years before moving to another studio on the Upper West Side.

This was my pattern—a few years in one place, always a studio, and then on to the next apartment. Over the years I lost count of how many apartments I had all over Manhattan Island, from Tribeca to Morningside Heights. Always studio apartments, always rentals. I was a moving target. I dreaded the commitment of a mortgage or a marriage. The women came and went. Mostly, they went.

The only consistency was my work as a children's-book author. I was a big hit in this deceptively tough racket, maybe because one thing made me uniquely qualified for the work.

Despite all my crazy adventures, I had never really grown up.

Which is probably why I was in no shape to handle my father's death, and failed to dispose of his ashes in what you might call a rational, adult fashion.

Chapter Four

When we reached the footpath on the Brooklyn Bridge I was handcuffed and taken to One Police Plaza. It was a hell of thing to get through the crowd that had gathered, including three TV news crews, and that's where Billy the cop's brawny shoulders came in handy.

"Let us troo, please, let us troo."

I was fingerprinted and photographed, full face and profile. I was given the right-to-remain-silent speech by Billy, whose last name was Debowski. He took the cuffs off and told me I was going to be charged with criminal trespass, among other things. I told him I didn't want a lawyer. Then I was taken to a little room with a table and two chairs. I sat there alone for about ten minutes before the door opened and a short man with a beard, rimless glasses and the world's worst comb-over entered and introduced himself as Dr. Philip Rosensohn.

We didn't shake hands because he didn't offer. He sat across from me and folded his chubby hands together on the table.

"So," he began, "how are you?"

"You a shrink?"

He winced, very dramatically, as if he'd just been jabbed with a needle. "I'm not fond of that word."

"Sorry. Are you a psychiatrist?"

"Yes. Are you aware of what's happening here, Mr. Ambrosio?"

"Well, I'm under arrest."

"Right. Anything else?"

"Like what?"

"Is there anything you want to tell me?"

I shrugged. "I like your tie."

He forced a smile. "I guess you think this is funny."

"No, not at all."

"You're treating it lightly, wouldn't you say?"

"Do you see me laughing?"

"You risked your life, not to mention the lives of others, to do what you did."

"I didn't ask those cops to follow me. I was doing fine on my own."

He pulled a small notebook from his jacket pocket and read from it before saying, "Did you love your father?"

I laughed out loud. "Congratulations, Doc. You made me laugh. I guess I'm treating it lightly, after all."

"You climbed to the top of the Brooklyn Bridge to scatter his ashes. This indicates powerful feelings about the man, one way or the other."

"You think?"

"Mr. Ambrosio, please. Why did you do this thing?"

"Because the ashes had to fly as far and wide as possible."

He blinked at me. "I'm not following you."

"Look, my father was a restless soul. He couldn't stay put. Wherever he was, he wanted to be someplace else. He literally lived on every continent in the world, Doc, so when I got his ashes in the mail—"

"Whoa, whoa." Rosensohn held up a hand, palm out. "You received his ashes in the *mail?*"

"Right. He died when he caught a fever while hiking through an Amazon jungle and was cremated that same day. At least, that's what the letter from the local police claimed. You can't hold a body in that tropical climate."

Rosensohn sat back in his chair. "Well. That must have been quite a blow to you."

"Better believe it. The ashes arrived postage due."

Rosensohn's eyes widened. "Wild guess here—you and your father weren't close."

"Sure we were, when he was around. He was okay, my old man. Why do you think I climbed the bridge to scatter his ashes? I wanted them to blow as far and wide as they could. Wanted him to be in death as he was in life—all over the place."

"Bullshit."

That jolted me. Shrinks are always so neutral in movies and TV shows, and this guy was giving me attitude. I was starting to like him.

"Excuse me?"

"My instincts tell me you're not being truthful."

"Well, they're right on the money. I *don't* like your tie."

Ignoring the smart-ass remark, he plowed ahead. I admired his balls.

"You're a man of means. You could have hired a small plane to scatter his ashes. Instead, you went to the Brooklyn Bridge, knowing exactly what would happen, the attention you would draw in our current climate of terrorism. You wanted it to be dramatic, didn't you?"

"Seemed appropriate. My father was a dramatic guy."

Rosensohn hesitated. "Is your mother living?"

I wasn't expecting that. "Long gone. Died when I was ten. Buried in the ground, out on Long Island, when cemeteries were in style."

He leaned forward. "You realize you could go to prison for what you've done."

It was my turn to say "bullshit," so I did.

"I'm afraid it's not. Criminal trespass, endangering the general public—"

"Oh, come on. I didn't hurt anyone, my record's clean and I have money. Save it, Doc. Let's finish this formality so I can pay the fine and go home."

He stared at me and swallowed hard. "I have a feeling your mother's death has more to do with what happened today than your father's death. Could I be right?"

I actually felt dizzy, having just climbed to the top of the Brooklyn Bridge without feeling dizzy. I don't know if the shrink was right, but I couldn't say he was wrong, either.

I shut my eyes and covered my ears with my hands.

"Give me a break, Doc. For Christ's sake, I'm sixty years old and I just became an orphan."

I was released without bail, but only if a relative would come to take me home. I'd called my uncle Victor, who entered the police station in his usual state of dress: blue jeans, a black pocket T-shirt stretched tight by his belly, white socks and sneakers. His fists were jammed into the pockets of his blue windbreaker, and he looked exactly like what he was: a retired New York City bus driver who'd been jolted from an afternoon snooze by an emergency call.

I saw him before he saw me. He was pushing seventy, and his hair had whitened but his eyebrows remained jet-black, exactly the way his father's hair had gone. It was like seeing Angie's ghost walking toward me.

What a phone call that was, to Vic's home in Queens. He'd answered with classic Ambrosio nonchalance, not "Hello?" but "Yeah?"

I was relieved to get him and not his machine—if he had a machine, which wasn't likely.

"Vic, it's Joey."

"Hey!"

"Think you could pick me up from One Police Plaza? I'm in a jam, here."

A funny sound—he actually yawned! "You kill anybody?"

"Nah. Put on the news, you'll see what's going on."

"All right, let me put my pants on."

He hung up before I could thank him.

And now, less than an hour later, here he was, in all his unshaven glory.

"Over here, Vic!"

I was seated on a bench with Officer Debowski, who'd been ordered to stay with me until my relative arrived. Vic heard me and ambled over, as if this were a chance meeting in the aisle of a supermarket.

"See the news, Vic?"

He nodded. "Congratulations. You're the top story on New York One."

"This is my Uncle Victor," I said to the cop. "Vic, this is the man who brought me back down to earth."

Vic shook Billy's hand. "About time somebody did that," he said.

I laughed out loud, remembering how much I loved this peculiar lifelong bachelor—guess it takes one to know one, right? I'd always thought of Vic as a cheerful pessimist. He'd do anything for me, and I couldn't think of anything I wouldn't do for him, and so why the fuck did it take my arrest to bring us face-to-face for the first time in more than a year? I'd phoned him when I'd gotten my father's ashes a week earlier and we'd promised to get together, but something in the Ambrosio gene code seemed to prevent promises from jelling into realities.

(Lightbulb! Maybe that's why I did what I did, Dr. Rosensohn! Maybe I got myself arrested to make sure I would see my uncle!)

Vic patted my shoulder with his right hand, the way you might pat a dog who's just retrieved a stick. His left hand remained in his windbreaker pocket, clutching something.

"He's gonna be all right," Billy assured Vic in an overly-sincere voice.

Vic shrugged. "I'm not worried."

"Okay, then." Billy shook my hand hard enough to pop my knuckles, then gave me his business card.

"Call me if you need me," he said, and he was gone.

Vic watched him go. "A cop with a business card," he murmured. "How times have changed."

I hugged this uncle of mine, more like a big brother than an uncle. He didn't really hug back, but gave me a few awkward pats on my back.

"Thanks for coming, Vic."

"Forget it. Who do we pay?"

"What?"

"Bail. How the hell does it work?"

"There's no bail. They just want me to walk out with a family member."

"I guess I qualify."

He pulled his left hand from his windbreaker pocket. Clutched in his fist was a roll of bills thick enough to choke a pig.

"Jesus, Vic!"

"Took out as much as I could from a cash machine, and it's all twenties," he grumbled.

I was too choked up to say anything, but Vic wasn't.

"What the hell, Chinatown's right behind us, ain't it? Whaddaya say we go eat some chinks and drink a farewell to my brother, your father, like we promised we would?" He shook his money fist. "Come on. I'm buyin'."

We walked to the exit together. "Aren't you going to ask me why I did it?"

He chuckled. "What for, Joey? You probably don't know yourself. I'm just glad you didn't jump."

"I was never going to jump."

"Aaay, I know that. Ambrosios cling to life, no matter how shitty it gets."

Hours had passed since my arrest. The sun was setting as we got outside, and one lone pesky photographer followed us, snapping away.

"Shit," said Vic, rubbing his face, "is this gonna be in the paper? I didn't shave today."

"Mr. Ambrosio!" the photographer shouted at me. "Why did you do it?"

I ignored him. Vic and I increased our pace. The photographer kept up.

"Sir!" he shouted to Vic. "May I ask who you are?"

Vic ignored him, but when the photographer was right at our heels Vic turned and went nose to nose with the kid.

"You can go away now," Vic said in a deadly calm voice. Remarkably, the kid obeyed. We watched him trot away until he turned the corner, then we headed into the heart of Chinatown.

"That showed him," Vic said with pride. "Screwed him up good, not saying who I was."

"Unless he's with the *Post*," I said. Vic seemed puzzled. I held my hands up, as if to support a billboard.

"*Mystery Escort For Deranged Children's Book Author.*"

"Aw, shit."

We went to Wo Hop's and ate and drank as if we were both taking the fatal needle in the morning. There was very little conversation, though Vic did ask a delicate question through a mouthful of egg roll.

"Taylor know about this?"

I shrugged, felt my neck tingle. "Haven't heard from her." For the past two years, to be exact, but I didn't want to get into that.

Vic swallowed, jabbed the air with his fork. "You ought to call her."

"Maybe tomorrow."

"Don't be a dick. Do it before she reads all about it."

"I will, Vic, I will."

Taylor is my twenty-seven-year-old daughter, as she'd be the last to admit.

The fact that I was a fairly well-known children's-book author and illustrator gave my story that little bit of oomph it needed to jazz up the front pages. The *New York Daily News* had a great shot of me hurling the ashes skyward, under a headline reading DUST IN THE WIND: STORYBOOK ENDING FOR CHILDREN'S BOOK AUTHOR'S DAD. Not bad, but the *New York Post* took the prize with SEE JOEY CLIMB! over a shot of me high on the cable. And of course the *Times* showed its usual pizzazz with CHILDREN'S BOOK AUTHOR, APPARENTLY DISTRAUGHT OVER FATHER'S DEATH, ARRESTED AFTER CLIMBING BROOKLYN BRIDGE TOWER TO SCATTER ASHES.

The really crazy thing is how that climb filled my pockets. I had twenty-two children's books in print, and all of them surged in sales on Amazon as a result of my Brooklyn Bridge climb.

The money would come in handy, because a week later my penalty was finalized, with the help of a lawyer who charged me two grand: I would pay a $5000 fine, and attend twice-a-month therapy sessions for the next six months at my own expense. Two hundred bucks a pop for a total of twelve sessions with the psychiatrist of my choice, from the Police Department's stable of shrinks. Missing any of those sessions would count as a parole violation, which could send me to prison for six months.

"Couldn't you get rid of that prison threat?" I asked the lawyer.

He chuckled. "Are you kidding? You're lucky you're not behind bars right this minute! Hell, you're lucky they didn't shoot you! Just make sure you show up for the sessions."

I decided to stick with good old Dr. Rosensohn. Why not? Anybody who could tell me I was full of shit was all right by me.

Hell, if I'd had a few more people like that in my life, everything might have been different.

Chapter Five

I didn't call my daughter. I figured she had to know about my escapade, if she was anywhere near a television or a newsstand where she lived on the Upper West Side. And even if she wasn't, one of her friends was certain to tell Taylor about what her crazy father had done on the Brooklyn Bridge.

Then again, maybe not. She never took my last name, and it's not likely she told people I was her father. She went by the last name of her mother, a woman I dated for a month in 1984.

What can I say? It was a crazy time in New York City. To guys like me, fatherhood just happened.

Things moved fast after the ash-scattering. I put my father's Charles Street apartment on the market and it sold in two days for almost a million bucks. There was no mortgage on the place, so even after paying for the Shepherd Avenue house I'd still have half a million, plus the money my books continued to bring in. And Social Security was just two years away. In other words, I was set for life, provided I didn't break any records for longevity.

The biggest battle I had was with my accountant, who could not believe what I was doing. "I am strongly—and I mean *strongly*—advising you against this purchase," said Myron Rushbaum, CPA, a dramatic little man who had a hard time keeping Drake's Coffee Cake crumbs out of his moustache.

"Duly noted."

"It's a dreadful idea, all around."

"I heard you the first time, Myron."

"Nobody with reasonable means and a good home buys a house in the city's worst neighborhood. *Nobody.*"

"I won't have a mortgage and I'll have a fat bank account."

"Wonderful. They can mention your fat bank account at your memorial service."

"Myron—"

"Think of your daughter. Is this what you'd want her to inherit?"

"She can sell it."

"To who? Someone like you? Have you run your grand plan past her, by any chance?"

"We're not exactly on speaking terms these days."

Myron sighed and shrugged. "Well, I'm guessing this move of yours won't do much to improve the lines of communication."

"The good news is, they couldn't get any worse."

The Taylor situation wasn't entirely my fault. Her mother, Moonchild Parker, was an avant-garde art critic I met at a Soho loft party. (Was Moonchild her real first name? I was never able to find out, but believe me when I say it truly fit the woman.) We had a whirlwind courtship that stopped whirling after a month, but in that time she fell pregnant and seemed delighted by the prospect of single motherhood.

So she had the baby, and I did everything I was supposed to do in terms of finances and seeing Taylor on weekends. But when my daughter was two years old Moonchild moved to San Francisco and of course, the child went with her. Thus began my life as a weekend-phone-call dad, a four-flights-per-year to San Francisco dad, a who's-this-man-in-the graduation-picture-with-Taylor-and-Moonchild dad.

So it wasn't my fault, but at the same time, I let the situation make it easy on myself. What could I do? Move to San Francisco? No way.

So the years passed, and Taylor went to college for a degree in business before making her way back to New York City with some kind of job in finance that allowed her to have a nice apartment on West End Avenue.

And the last I'd seen of Taylor was at a Starbucks in her neighborhood soon after she'd moved to the city, two years earlier.

When your daughter's last words to you are "I never want to see you again," you have to be an idiot not to get the message. It really hurts, especially when you know you deserve it.

I broke my lease, rented a moving van and packed up everything I had from my latest Manhattan apartment on West Fifty-Seventh

Street. It wasn't much: a bed, a couch, a kitchen table and chairs, pots and pans, a few lamps, my clothing and my books. Some people who live alone save everything. Others keep it light, treating a home like a lifeboat that could sink under the weight of too much stuff. I'm a lifeboat guy.

My father's apartment was practically barren. He'd basically used it as a crash pad between his adventures, the last of which took his life.

He always called me to have breakfast with him at the Bus Stop Café in the Village before he took off anywhere, and his final trip was no exception. His canvas bags were packed and at his sides like a pair of faithful hounds while he ate his omelet, jiggling his foot throughout the meal.

"Why the Amazon, Dad?"

"Why not? Never been to a real jungle. Think I'll need a machete to hack my way through?"

"I'm sure they'll provide you with one."

He finished his omelet and refused my help to carry his bags out to Hudson Street, where he hailed a cab to JFK.

"Water my plants," he said as he hugged me good-bye, and that was the last I saw of him, an eighty-two-year-old man in what appeared to be perfect health, eager to swing a machete on his way to whatever it was he was after.

That bit about watering his plants was an old joke. He never had any plants. Too big a commitment.

The new owners of his apartment wanted some of his furniture, and I gave the rest of it to a charity shop on West Tenth Street.

My last link to the island of Manhattan was officially broken.

When I got to Shepherd Avenue I was lucky to get a parking space right in front of the house. I climbed those steps and rang the bell.

A weary-looking Rico let me in. How different it looked empty! Most of Rico's stuff had been shipped to the West Coast. He would be leaving for the airport in a matter of minutes, as soon as he handed over the keys. This he did with great solemnity, as if enacting a sacramental rite in a church.

"These are for the front door . . . the back door . . . the garage . . ."

His voice echoed off the bare kitchen walls and his eyes were wet. I don't think he liked the house, but its history was in his bloodstream, as it was in mine, and now he was saying good-bye.

"How are you getting to the airport, Rico?"

"Eddie Everything's taking me."

"Who?"

"Cuban guy, lives down the block. We call him Eddie Everything, 'cause that's what he does. Little bit o' everything. Good guy for you to know, Joe."

As if on cue the doorbell rang and a lean fortysomething man with wild eyes, bushy hair and a graying goatee let himself in. His denim overalls hung on his lean frame like laundry on the line.

"Rang the bell, then I saw that the door was open so I came in," he said. He shook my dry hand with his damp one. Something about him made you think he was being pursued, but he was friendly enough for a fugitive.

"Eddie Martinez, at your service. You movin' in? That your van outside?"

"Yeah."

"I'm early. You need help unloading? Twenty bucks."

Rico laughed, then I laughed. As a matter of fact, I *did* need a hand unloading, and with Eddie Everything's help all my stuff was piled up in the kitchen in a matter of minutes. I gave him a twenty and he gave me his card, which contained his name, the handwritten words *I CAN DO IT* and a cell phone number. Then he clapped Rico on the back. "All right, my man, let's get you to the airport."

Would Rico and I hug each other as we said good-bye? No. It didn't come to that. Instead, we stood face-to-face and gripped each other's forearms, like an outgoing mayor welcoming an incoming one to the leadership of a troubled city.

"Good luck, Joe," he said, leaving the words *you're gonna need it* unsaid but fully understood. Then Eddie picked up Rico's bags. They went out the door to a rattletrap blue station wagon parked behind my van, loaded the bags in the back, got in and drove away without a backward glance or a wave.

207 Shepherd Avenue was all mine.

Chapter Six

Like a giddy child I walked the rooms, my footsteps loud on the creaky wooden floors. The floors had been swept but the windows needed washing and everything cried out for a coat of fresh paint.

I went upstairs to check out the apartment Rico had urged me to rent out. Back in 1961 a lonely old bachelor named Agosto Palmieri had lived in these upper rooms, paying what was certainly a pittance in rent to my grandfather. I remembered his opera records and his big, sad eyes, which always seemed to be brimming with tears. When my father and Vic sold the house after my grandmother's death they agreed to give the buyer a break if he'd let Agosto stay on at the same rent for as long as he wanted, which turned out to be around six months. The old man died up there, and the only reason anyone found out was because the downstairs people were being driven crazy by his scratchy Enrico Caruso record, which kept skipping endlessly.

It was a nice apartment, and it actually got a lot more light than the downstairs. The kitchen seemed to be in pretty good shape, as did the bathroom, and I checked all the ceilings—no leaks.

The walls were a dreary faded green. Like the downstairs, it all needed a good coat of paint. I set up my bed in my old room overlooking the cemented-over backyard, even though it was smaller than the other bedrooms. I stretched out on the bed, stared at the ceiling. I fought an urge to cry, then an urge to laugh. What the fuck had I gone and done? Then I remembered something. I went to the window, got down on my knees and looked up at the overhang of the windowsill.

And there it was, printed in faded but bold blue letters on the bare wooden underside that had never tasted paint: *JOEY WAS HERE*. Oh yes. And now, he was back. I flopped on the bed as if I'd been cold-cocked from behind and slept for ten hours.

Like a man possessed, I got to work fixing up the house. Number one on my list was a paint job, top to bottom. I hired Eddie Everything to drive me to the nearest Home Depot to load up on supplies. He couldn't believe my choice of color. "Whoa, whoa, bro. White paint, for everything?"

"That's right."

"You gonna have to go two, maybe three coats in the bedrooms."

"I don't mind."

We loaded up on paint, rollers, brushes and drop cloths. On the ride back Eddie tried to get in on the job.

"Lotta work."

"I've got the time to do it."

"You want me to help, just say so."

"I got another job for you, Eddie. I want you to remove the bars from my windows."

We were on Atlantic Avenue by this time, just a few blocks from home. Eddie pulled over to the side and braked the car. "Hey, Mr. A. That ain't such a good idea."

"Can you do it?"

"Yeah, man, I can *do* it, but you're gonna be sorry." He put his hand over his heart. "You understand, I'm losin' money with this advice I'm givin' you, but hey, money ain't everything."

"I'm deeply moved, Eddie, but I can't stand looking out through those bars. Makes me feel like I'm in prison."

Eddie chuckled. "The people you gonna get tryin' to come in through those windows, *they* belong in prison."

"I'll take my chances. Can you do the job, without damaging anything?"

Eddie chuckled knowingly, a craftsman having patience with a knucklehead. "Gotta break the cement when I pull out the bars. I'll do a good patch job, don't worry."

"All right, Eddie, you're hired."

"You sure you wanna do this?"

"Absolutely. Think how much easier it'll be to wash those windows with the bars gone."

He put the car in gear. "I'm workin' for a crazy man," he muttered to the windshield as we rolled along.

When I got home I called Taylor's cell phone. She answered with a cheery hello, which told me she did not have caller ID.

"Taylor, it's . . . your father."

Maybe I was exaggerating by calling myself her father, but what else was I?

A long, chilly silence. She'd refused to take the name Ambrosio, but she was one of us, all right, with an ability to nurse a grudge into the next millennium. In a left-handed way I was proud of her for the way she was making me grovel.

"I moved to Brooklyn," I continued. "Thought you should know, in case you were looking for me."

She chuckled, or maybe it was a snorting sound. Looking for me? That's the last thing she'd ever be doing!

"I'm surprised you're not banned from Brooklyn," she replied at last.

"Huh? Oh, you mean because of the Brooklyn Bridge thing!"

"Yeah. I'm sorry about your father. Hell of a way to find out my grandfather was dead."

"I'm sorry, Taylor."

"It's okay. It's not like I really knew him."

"Well, I kind of flipped when he died."

"Evidently."

"But I'm okay now."

"Glad to hear it."

Would it have killed her to say, "Glad to hear it, *Dad?*" She never called me "Dad," or "Pop," or even "Joe." I would have settled for "shithead." She never called me anything. She just gave minimal answers to any questions I had, as if she were on the witness stand going toe-to-toe with a prosecutor bent on tripping her up.

I struggled to keep the conversation, such as it was, alive.

"How are you, Taylor?"

"Fine."

"Care to add a detail or two to that reply?"

"Look, I'm kind of busy right now."

"I'm sorry. Could we meet for coffee? I could come to you, if you don't feel like going to Brooklyn."

"I've got your number. I'll call you."

"All right. The sooner the better. Thanks, Taylor," I said, but I'm pretty sure she hung up before I thanked her.

I started work on the upstairs apartment, intending to paint my way down to the basement. There was no rush. I had no deadlines to meet, no new book in the works. I spent a lot of time on the prep work, sanding the woodwork and patching the walls. The radio was good company—WCBS FM, playin' all the oldies. There were no ties to cut, either. I had no close friends and I hadn't bothered with a girlfriend for more than a year. I could do whatever I wanted with my time. The only obligations I faced were my meetings with the shrink—every other Wednesday, two p.m., at his office on West Seventy-First Street.

I decided to be punctual about that. I was actually early for our first appointment, twelve days after I'd climbed to the top of the bridge.

It was a small office, cluttered with books and a plant with dusty leaves. The lone window looked out on a sooty brick wall. Dr. Rosensohn gave me a friendly greeting but again, he didn't offer to shake my hand. He sat at his desk and I sat across from him in the room's only other chair.

"So," he began, "what's new?"

"Nothing much."

"Did you enjoy being in the headlines?"

"I could have done without it."

"Bet you sold some books, though."

"A few."

An ambulance wailed, not far away. We were both New York enough to ignore it. Rosensohn folded his hands on the desk.

"What have you been up to since we last met?"

"I bought a house."

He chuckled. "I ask you what's new, you say nothing much. I'd say buying a house qualifies as *much!*"

"Guess you're right."

"So tell me about this house."

"It's in Brooklyn. The East New York section."

Rosensohn's eyes widened and he let out a long, low whistle. "Not the safest neighborhood in the world."

"You know it?"

"Lived there when I was a baby, until my parents moved to Manhattan. *Fled,* actually. I take it the neighborhood is still..." He couldn't bring himself to come up with an adjective, so I helped him.

"Dangerous?"

"Well, for want of a better word...may I ask why you moved there?"

I told him all about the summer of '61, and the way I'd ridden out to Shepherd Avenue on that crazy impulse for the first time in half a century and banged on the door and offered to buy the house from a stranger, and how my crazy plan had actually worked.

"So I figure it was meant to be," I concluded.

All Rosensohn could do was stare at me. At last he said, "Believing in fate is tricky. Sometimes things happen for no reason."

"What are you saying here, Doc?"

He unfolded his hands and blew out his cheeks with a long sigh. "I'll be straight with you. I didn't believe you when you told me you didn't have suicidal impulses, up on that bridge."

"Really."

"So now, you come to me and tell me you've bought a house where you're bound to be the only white person on the block...do you see where I'm going, here?"

"Spell it out for me and don't spare my feelings."

This was awkward for him. He was Jewish, certainly raised to be a Democrat with liberal leanings, and he didn't like saying what he had to say. So he leaned forward and all but whispered, "Moving to a dangerous neighborhood could be viewed as a kind of a gaslight suicide attempt. You don't do it by your own hand, but you get yourself killed, which is the objective." He hesitated before asking, "Is that your objective?"

I couldn't help laughing out loud. "Doc, you're so far off, it isn't funny."

"You sure about that?"

"Absolutely."

That pretty much did it for our first session, and I think he believed me. However, I did not tell him about hiring Eddie Everything to remove the safety bars from my windows.

Didn't want him to think I was nuts.

Chapter Seven

On Shepherd Avenue people didn't greet a new neighbor with casseroles and cakes, especially one who appeared to be insane enough to take the protective bars off his windows.

I had my morning coffee by those windows and watched people go past on their way to the elevated train, some dressed for office jobs, some in jeans and construction shoes with protective helmets and lunch pails in their hands. Working people, just trying to get by.

But it seemed that everybody who passed my house took a moment to stare at the windows, and the newly patched holes where the bars had been.

Eddie Everything also removed the bars from the basement windows. He did a good job and I paid him fifty bucks on top of the price he'd quoted. I knew I was going to need him for more work and wanted to keep him sweet.

I told him to take the bars and keep whatever he could get for the scrap metal, but he refused, instead stashing them in my garage.

"You'll pay me again when you beg me to put 'em back," he said with a smile.

"Are the neighbors making fun of me, Eddie?"

He waved away my question. "Man, they got problems o' their own. You can paint your house pink and let an elephant shit on your front porch, and they won't give a fuck."

The paint job was working muscles I hadn't used in years. My arms and back were sore and I fell asleep at night as if I'd been drugged, to the hum of traffic on Atlantic Avenue and the inevitable wailing of police and ambulance sirens.

I'd been a runner for most of my life, two or three miles a day, and intended to keep up the tradition in East New York. I had a lot of manual labor ahead of me and needed to stay strong, or so I convinced myself.

Highland Park was nearby, a beautiful oasis of more than a hundred acres of trees and fields on the Brooklyn-Queens border, and that's where I headed for my daily runs. I forced my body to take a lap or two around its obsolete reservoir before heading back to Shepherd Avenue and the day's work.

Things were working out. The house was shaping up and I was dropping a few pounds I didn't need, which was nice.

And in the midst of all this I met my first Shepherd Avenue neighbor, not counting Eddie Everything.

It happened when I was taking a pre-run stretch, about a week after moving in. I stood facing my front stoop and put my right foot on the top step before easing my chin to my knee to get the muscles stretched. I shut my eyes as I did this, and when I opened them he was standing next to me as if we'd had an appointment to meet.

A tall, coffee-colored kid in athletic shorts and a T-shirt, gently shifting his weight from foot to foot. Bulging biceps and thighs, and a muscular neck leading to a clean-shaven head. If an oak tree could suddenly morph into a human being, it would have looked like this guy.

The greenest eyes I'd ever seen regarded me calmly from a smooth brown face.

"Seen you runnin' in the morning," he said softly. This could have been an observation or an accusation. He put his hands behind his back, as if to show he meant no harm.

I hesitated. "Yeah," I finally said, "I run in the morning."

"How far?"

"Coupla miles."

He nodded. "Okay if I join you?"

I noticed his feet. They were clad in a good pair of brand-new Nike running shoes, not the basketball sneakers I'd stereotypically expected him to be wearing.

I liked to run alone. It was the one precious part of my day when nobody could bother me.

But I was the new guy on the block, and the last thing I needed was to develop a rep as the snobby white guy.

"You stretched yet?" I asked. He nodded. "So let's go."

I let the kid set the pace—long, loping, silent steps. He was like a big cat, ridiculously strong and fit. I was going to have to work hard to keep up with him.

Up Shepherd Avenue we trotted, in the middle of the street. The elevated train rumbled over our heads as we made our way toward Highland Park. We were like two strangers in the prison yard, checking each other out with our peripheral visions.

"Reservoir?" he asked, without loss of breath.

"Yeah," I gasped. "That's what I've been doing."

"Okay."

We headed for the reservoir, which was surrounded by a rough dirt path. Suddenly he stuck his hand out in front of my chest, as if to stop me, but he didn't break stride. He was introducing himself.

"I'm Justin."

"Joe."

We shook hands without stopping. It was the firmest grip I'd ever experienced, a hand thick with calluses.

"You're in some shape, Justin."

"Pretty good, I guess."

"One of us is breathing hard, and it ain't you."

"We can take it down a notch."

"No, no, it's good for me to get pushed a little. Let's go."

He chuckled. "Two laps?"

"Hey, why not?"

We completed two laps around the reservoir, ending it where we started, me collapsing with my hands on my knees, Justin remaining upright and actually running in place, just to show me how much he had left.

"Hey, man, you okay?"

"Mild coronary. Nothing serious. Easy trot back, okay?"

"I'm good with that."

I felt great. A hard run breaks out a deep sweat you don't get from a lazy run, and the cool-down run that follows is almost like a vacation. We were moving at an easy conversational pace. I could run and talk at the same time.

"You on a track team, Justin?"

He shook his head. "Baseball."

"No kidding? What position?"

"Short."

I stopped running and grabbed his elbow. He was startled and jerked himself out of my grip, then squared off, ready to fight.

"What the *fuck*, man?"

I held my hands out, palms up, to show I meant no harm.

"I'm sorry! It's just—are you Justin *Wilson?*"

"Yeah."

I've been a baseball fan all my life, and I followed the game in the pages of the *Post*. Justin Wilson of Franklin K. Lane High School was being touted as the greatest Brooklyn high school player since Shawon Dunston, who'd gone number one in the 1982 draft and went on to play eighteen years in the majors.

And here he was, eyes wide, fists clenched, ready to pound the shit out of this crazy Caucasian who'd grabbed his arm.

"Easy, guy," I said, making placating motions with my hands. "I've been reading about you. You're some ballplayer."

He lowered his fists, seeming embarrassed. "Don't go grabbin' people 'round here," he said. It was friendly advice, not a lecture.

"You're right. I'm sorry."

"Cool."

We walked the remaining two blocks. I dared to speak again.

"Do you live on Shepherd Avenue?"

"Uh-huh. Across the street from you. You just got here, right?"

"Well, I lived here when I was a kid."

"No shit?"

"No shit. Same house I just bought."

"Oh, man," he chuckled. "Never heard of nobody movin' *back* here!"

"Well, I always liked the house."

"You gonna regret takin' them bars down."

"Hope not . . . want to hear something funny? My uncle, who grew up in my house, was a baseball star. Got signed by the Pittsburgh Pirates, back in '61."

Justin stopped walking. "No shit?"

"Swear to God. He played shortstop for Lane. Had good power, just like you. It was unusual in those days for a shortstop to have power."

Justin hesitated before asking, "He make it?"

I shook my head. "Washed out in his first year in the minors. Couldn't hit the curve."

Justin squared his shoulders. "Huh. Curveballs don't bother me none."

"That's what I hear."

It was incredible. This kid without a line on his face was about to get the better part of a million dollars to sign with whatever team drafted him, according to the New York sportswriters.

Unless he accepted an offer from one of the dozen or so colleges offering him a free ride. It was a tough choice and it was coming up soon, yet somehow he seemed as calm as the Dalai Lama.

We reached Shepherd Avenue, and now came an awkward moment. Was Justin going to join me every morning for a run? Would I be expected to wait for him before taking off? I liked the kid but didn't want to get hemmed into a schedule.

He made it easy for me, patting my back and saying, "Thanks for the run, man. If I see you, I see you."

With those words the greatest baseball prospect in America was gone, trotting across the street and into a little clapboard house that looked as if the hard slam of a door would send it crumbling to the ground.

Chapter Eight

In the afternoons, with the day's painting done, I took leisurely walks in the neighborhood. But not *too* leisurely. It was wise to look as if you had a destination while walking in East New York.

I went past the house where my tough little friend, Mel DiGiovanna, had lived with her aunt, until she was banished to another relative on Long Island after we were caught playing "doctor" in my grandfather's garage. Past the house where Johnny Gallo lived, the auto mechanic and resident heartthrob who'd knocked up his girlfriend at age eighteen. And past the tiny brick house that was home to Zip Aiello, the strange old odd-job man who'd taught me how to collect and redeem deposit bottles, a scheme that was going to finance my escape from Shepherd Avenue—an escape that was thwarted when I tripped and fell on a midnight run to the elevated train, with my 200-pound grandmother hot on my heels.

Ten years old, making a break from those mean streets—only to return fifty years later.

I crossed Atlantic Avenue and made my way to St. Rita's church, where my grandmother dropped her skepticism for an hour each week to worship God, just in case He did exist. This was where I'd come to know Deacon David Sullivan, the man who caught me and Mel in the garage and ratted us out to our families.

I dared to enter the church in my paint-spattered clothes. The church is always the best-maintained building in a poor neighborhood, and St. Rita's was no exception. The floors gleamed and an old Hispanic woman with her hair tied up in a bright red bandanna was busily digging wax out of the candleholders, whistling softly as she worked. She didn't hear me approach and clutched a hand to her chest at my sudden appearance.

"Jesus, you scared me!"

"I'm sorry. I used to come here when I was a kid. Just wanted to see the old place."

She gestured at me with her wax-digging tool. "Shouldn't go sneakin' up on people like that."

"I really am sorry . . . Listen, this is a long shot, I know, but would you happen to know a priest named David Sullivan?"

"Who?"

"Actually, he was a deacon at the time. We called him Deacon Dave. I realize it's a crazy question. I mean, this was back in 1961."

A jolt of awareness came to her face. "Oh, that guy!" she said, quickly crossing herself. "I heard about him! Yeah, he died. Been dead a long time."

"Really?"

The old lady looked left and right before whispering, "He had the AIDS." She shuddered, crossing herself. "That's what they say."

"Whoa."

"Yeah, well, maybe you wanna say a prayer for him, got a feelin' he can use it."

She shrugged and turned back to her work, whistling away.

I went outside and resumed my walk up Atlantic Avenue, numb over the news of Deacon Dave. My grandmother used to feed him Sunday dinners to get brownie points toward heaven, and after he left she'd say: "He's a nice man, but he seems . . . delicate."

I was approaching the building where I'd redeemed all those deposit bottles I collected in '61. Back then a gray-haired guy known in the neighborhood as "Nat the Jew" paid a nickel per bottle. The place was still standing but now it was a garage, with tire recapping a specialty.

A skinny man with snow-white hair sat in front of the garage in a folding aluminum chair, the kind you'd take on a picnic. His skin was pale and the lobes of his ears hung down almost as low as his chin, the way they always do on very old people. Everything he wore seemed too big for him, including his shoes—an old man's shoes, with Velcro tabs instead of laces. The collar of his windbreaker was turned up, though the day was far from cold. He was facing the Atlantic Avenue traffic but seemed to be looking beyond it, like a man on a beach staring at the horizon.

It was the pattern of his hair that jolted me. It was as wavy as corrugated iron, and I'd only ever known one other person with hair like that. It seemed impossible but I had to ask him, as soon as my heart stopped pounding.

"Excuse me, sir, are you . . . Nat the bottle man?"

He blinked at me with cloudy blue eyes. I wondered if he'd heard me. Then those eyes got watery, and I knew he'd heard every word.

"I used to be," he said, startling me with a strong, confident, non-trembling voice. "Who are you?"

"A guy who used to bring you bottles."

"Don't shout! I'm goin' blind, not *deaf.*" He leaned forward and studied my face. "Which guy?"

"You're asking me my name?"

"You catch on quick. Come closer, my eyes are all shot to hell."

I was already directly in front of him, but I squatted so we'd be face-to-face. He squinted as he studied my face, scowling like an archaeologist peering into the past.

"It was a long time ago, Nat. I was just a kid."

"Yeah, yeah, yeah, give me a second . . ."

Minutes passed. It was as if he were in a trance, until he jolted me with the words: "All right, I give up."

"I'm *Jo*-seph Am-*bro*-si-o," I said, punctuating each syllable with a bob of my head, as if to drive the words into the deepest recesses of his memory.

He didn't respond for a few seconds. Then the corner of his mouth corkscrewed in recognition.

"Joseph, Schmoseph," he growled. "We called you Joey. When'd you get so fancy-schmancy?"

"You remember me?"

"Connie and Angie's kid."

"Grandson."

"Whatever. Sal's son. Am I right? Tell me I'm right."

"You're right!"

He pointed at me with a bony finger. "You tried to run away one night. Am I right? Tell me I'm right."

"Right again! And I was carrying all the money you paid me for bottles—my getaway stash!"

"What the hell are you doin' here?"

I spread my hands. "I'm back in the old house, Nat. We're neighbors again."

He stared at me for a few seconds, then shook his head in wonder. He lifted his arm and I thought he wanted to shake hands, but instead he jerked a thumb over his shoulder, toward the garage.

"There's another chair like this one in there. Get it, bring it out here, we'll talk."

I already knew that Nat Grossman was a young man when he was liberated from the concentration camp at Auschwitz, where both his parents had died. Kids in the neighborhood used to point at him and whisper things like, "See that guy? He escaped from Hitler, but he don't like to talk about it!" Nat had lived in the neighborhood for more than sixty years, refusing to move away when his bottle business went belly-up. Instead, he sold his house on Norwood Avenue, moved into a nearby retirement home, and now—at age ninety-eight!—he spent his days seated in that aluminum chair in front of the garage, where the boss allowed him bathroom privileges.

The city's Meals on Wheels program delivered breakfast and lunch to Nat each day, right there in front of the garage. He had his dinner at the retirement home, three blocks away. It was a walk Nat made each morning at dawn and each night at sundown.

I was surprised by that.

"Kind of dangerous after dark, isn't it?"

He spread his hands and shrugged. "Who would mug me? What have I got? What would it *prove?*"

"It's just that you're so . . . vulnerable."

"You mean old."

"All right, old. Damn right you're old! You shouldn't be out on the streets all day!"

"Bullshit! These streets?" He stamped his foot three times, like a horse who can count. "They're mine. This is what I know. This is where I'll stay, until . . ."

He didn't have to finish the sentence. I sighed and said, "I just don't want you to get hurt, Nat."

He chuckled. "I ain't worried about that." He looked left and right, then whispered: "Funny thing about these colored kids, Joey. They look at me like I'm a ghost, and they're *afraid* of ghosts."

He laughed out loud in a way I can only describe as ghostly. "So finally, it's safe for me to be out on the streets, 'cause these kids are superstitious. Lucky me, huh?"

Who the hell was I to challenge the way this man was living his life? I'd forgotten the unspoken neighborhood code, which hadn't changed since '61: Mind your own damn business, and leave everyone the hell alone.

"Good for you, Nat," I said. "Goddamn it, this is a miracle, seeing you again!"

"No, Joey. The miracle is you moving back. All I did was stay alive. No miracle in that."

"It is these days."

"Oh, you think it was safer here, back then? This was always a rough neighborhood. And no offense, but your people were some of the roughest. Those Italian hoodlums with their guns, they did some real damage!"

He cocked his head, narrowed his eyes. "Ever hear of Happy Maione? He was with Murder Incorporated. Ever hear of *that?*"

I started to worry, because he was getting worked up. Of all the things I didn't want to do, I mostly didn't want to be responsible for Nat Grossman's coronary.

"I've heard of it," I said softly, hoping to calm him down. "It was a Jewish organization, wasn't it?"

"That's right. And the Jews hired that Italian Maione gangster to kill people. And where do you think he spent his free time?"

"This neighborhood, I'm guessing."

Nat grinned, his teeth long and golden. He pointed upward, as if to indicate heaven.

"Upstairs from you," he chuckled. "He was dating your grandmother's tenant, a pretty girl. Can't remember her name. But Happy? Him I remember! Sharp dresser. Always tipped his hat to the ladies. Your grandmother, she loved him. Thought he was a real gentleman."

I swallowed. "Did he marry the girl?"

"No, sir. Happy died in the electric chair. Put a little crimp in his romantic life, know what I mean?"

I shook his hand, oh-so delicately. "Gotta go, Nat. I'll see you soon."

"Yeah, well, I'm easy to find. My address is Right Here—capital R, capital H."

I said good-bye, went home and Googled Harold "Happy" Maione. Sure enough, the bottle man's story held up. Happy had gotten his nickname from the constant grin on his face—a structural thing, like the grin on a dolphin. And according to newspaper accounts of his execution, that grin never left his face, even as all that voltage coursed through his body.

A legendary crime figure, and he'd made love in one of the rooms I'd just finished painting in my grandfather's house.

My house, now. Mine.

And I would never have known about it unless I'd come across an Auschwitz survivor going strong as he approached the century mark, far outliving Happy Maione and a priest who'd died from AIDS.

Life is strange. I'd always known that, but Shepherd Avenue was driving that point home, day by day.

Chapter Nine

With the upstairs painted, I got going on the first floor—a much tougher job, as Eddie Everything had predicted, with those wild colors needing three coats of white for full coverage.

I was in the middle of the second coat on my bedroom walls when I was jangled by the doorbell, the first time it had rung since I'd moved in. There on my front stoop stood a short, slight woman in blue jeans and a black T-shirt, with skin the color of a penny you find in the back of a drawer you haven't opened for a long time.

Her brown hair was pulled back in a ponytail, revealing small ears and the highest, widest cheekbones I had ever seen. Stunningly attractive, but also a little bit scary, as if she were a werewolf just starting to turn from human being to beast at the rising of the full moon.

But this was a sunny morning on Shepherd Avenue, not midnight in Transylvania, and the woman glaring at me with raisin-dark eyes was clearly not happy as she stood there with squared shoulders, shifting her weight from foot to foot like a boxer eager for the bell.

"May I help you?"

She rested her fists on her hips. "What the hell you doin' with my boy?"

A dangerously deep voice, not at all shrill or whiny. I wasn't expecting that. I cleared my throat.

"I'm sorry?"

She folded her arms and shook her head, making the ponytail flick from shoulder to shoulder.

"Don't bullshit me. You're the one goes runnin' with my Justin, right?"

"Oh, you're Justin's mother!" I extended my hand, which she ignored. "I'm Joe Ambrosio. Would you like to come in?"

She hesitated, then strode into my house like a parole officer, arms still folded across her chest.

"I just made coffee," I said, following her to the kitchen. When she got there she whirled to face me.

"Look, I gotta know right now—you a chicken hawk?"

"A *what?*"

"You one of those old guys likes young boys? 'Cause my Justin, he ain't no fag. Just shy with the girls, is all."

I wanted to laugh but stifled the impulse. This was a fiercely loyal mother, barging into a stranger's house to protect her son. If I'd laughed she might have socked me.

"I'm no chicken hawk," I said. "I run in the morning and once in a while Justin goes with me."

"That's it?"

"That's it."

She uncrossed her arms, let out a long sigh and sank into a chair at the kitchen table, breathing hard, as if the two of us had just gone running. Then she scowled at me again.

"You gonna pour the coffee or what?"

She asked for it light, with one sugar. I passed her the mug and watched her take a slow, thoughtful sip.

"It's good," she said, closing her eyes for a moment as she let the caffeine take her on a ride to a saner world, where gray-haired white guys didn't go running with young Puerto Rican baseball stars.

When she opened her eyes I was still there, a problem to deal with, but at least I could make good coffee.

"I'm Rose," she said. "What am I smellin' here, paint?"

"I'm painting the house, yeah."

I showed her my spattered hands and arms. She chuckled.

"You gettin' any on the walls?"

"Now and then."

She couldn't help smiling. I wasn't exactly winning her over, but the chances of her killing me were dropping by the moment.

We clinked coffee cups, a gesture of peace.

"Sorry I was such a bitch."

"You're not. You're a good mother."

"Justin don't think so."

"He's a good kid. You've done a good job."

"It ain't over yet. Luckily his father ain't around."

I proceeded with caution. "Divorced?" I ventured.

"Dead."

"Oh."

"Best thing he ever done for us. Fell off a bridge he was paintin' when Justin was two. Probably hungover, or maybe still drunk."

"I'm sorry."

"Yeah? I'm not. You didn't know him. Handsome black dude, but a real prick." She shrugged. "Hey, his life insurance pays the rent, so everything works out in the end, right?"

"If you say so."

"Yeah, I say so."

"Which bridge was he painting?"

"The Williamsburg. Not the one you climbed."

I felt my face flush as Rose winked at me, chuckling in a friendly way.

"So you know about me."

"Saw you on the news when you done that crazy thing. Hey, no big deal, we all go nuts sometimes. Just as long as you ain't harmin' my boy."

I had to admire her. It was rough enough to be a single mother in East New York, and unimaginably tougher to be a single mom whose son was on the verge of being chosen number one in the Major League Baseball draft. Such a success story could not have happened without a mother possessing the vigilance of a lioness guarding her cub against the perils of the street. Justin had undoubtedly been raised in the midst of a hailstorm of troubles, and Rose had shielded him from every one.

He was a mama's boy who could hit a baseball five hundred feet, but I'm guessing he couldn't walk ten feet without his mother asking him where he was going.

I topped off her cup while she looked around the kitchen.

"Hey, Joe. Can I ask you a personal question?"

"Shoot."

"Did you really pay half a million for this house?"

"I certainly did."

"Damn. I thought Rico was bullshittin' about that. Always talkin' big, that guy. I'm glad he's gone." She took another sip of coffee and pointed at the ceiling. "And is it true you ain't rentin' the upstairs, even though you're all by yourself?"

"That's right."

It was kind of exciting to find out I was being gossiped about on the block. Thank you, Eddie Everything!

Rose wouldn't let it go. "I don't get it. Why do you need that whole upstairs, a bachelor like you?"

It was funny to hear the word *bachelor*, a term long gone out of style, but not to Rose. Men who lived alone were bachelors, and probably gay. She'd established to her satisfaction that I was not a chicken hawk, but I could still be a homosexual, and this was knowledge worth having. It was time to put her mind at ease.

"Thing is, I have a daughter," I said. "I want her to have a place to stay overnight when she visits."

That was true, but it was also bullshit. The chances of Taylor ever setting foot on Shepherd Avenue were remote, and the chances of her staying the night were nil.

But I'd given Rose what she needed to hear. Her face brightened with relief. I was a father, no menace to her son in any way.

"That's right," she said. "Your daughter comes to see you, you don't want her goin' home after dark. Not around here, that's for damn sure." She drained her coffee cup, put it on the table. "Gotta go to work."

She jumped to her feet and hurried to the front door.

"It was nice meeting you," I said to her back.

"Yeah, you too," she said over her shoulder, and then she was gone, out the door and down my front steps.

But she did look back at me just once as she crossed the street. A little peek, that's all, but there it was.

"So," Dr. Rosensohn began at our second session, "how goes it?"

"Not bad."

"How are you spending your time? Working on a new book?"

I hadn't published a children's book in three years, and had nothing in the works. "No," I said. "Been busy painting my house."

"You're doing it yourself?"

"Yeah. I'm enjoying the process."

"What is it you enjoy about it?"

Was this a trick question? I gave it a moment before saying, "Clean surfaces. A fresh start. You know. Nothing too mysterious about that, is there?"

"What else?"

"What else what?"

"I don't know . . . any strange dreams?"

"Jesus, Doc, is that the best you've got?"

"Hey, it's what they tell us to ask in shrink school. Sometimes a new environment can generate some interesting dreams."

"It's not a new environment. It's an old environment. I used to live there, remember?"

He sighed, like a father struggling to be patient with a precocious child.

"I'm just trying to get a sense of things, Mr. Ambrosio."

"Tell you the truth, Doc, they're not much like dreams. More like home movies from my life, playing while I sleep."

I was telling him the truth. Shepherd Avenue had become a silver screen for memories that hadn't visited me in decades.

Rosensohn leaned back and folded his hands behind his head.

"Take me to the movies," he said.

I shrugged. "Okay. I'll tell you about Casablanca and Milan. Two memories that made for a hell of a double feature."

My father decided he wanted to live in Italy for a while, and booked passage for the two of us on the SS *Constitution*. A twelve-day trip across the Atlantic.

I liked the voyage best when we were in the middle of the ocean, with no land in sight. Somehow that made me feel safe. The only thing that existed was our ship, and the rest of the world was water. That should have freaked me out, but it didn't.

Every few days we'd stop somewhere on the way to Genoa. The ship docked in Casablanca, and that's when it happened. I was walking the crowded streets with my father, clinging to his hand as tightly as I could. I'd never seen anything like the horrors of Casablanca.

The stench of raw sewage filled the air. Beggars were every-where—blind beggars, beggars with milky eyes, beggars with missing eyes, beggars whose outstretched palms ended in blunt knuckles. Leprosy. It was like walking down a corridor of hell.

And suddenly I was out of my father's grasp. I looked around wildly and he wasn't there. I was eleven years old, alone on the fetid streets of this foreign land, with no idea of how to find him, or how to get back to the dock and the safety of the ocean liner.

So I stood there and screamed to the sky. The blind beggars turned their faces toward the noise and chattered at me like a cluster of enraged monkeys. A man with a long beard and a tasseled cap grabbed me by the shoulders, staring at me with eyes that looked as if they were about to burst into flame. I twisted out of his grasp and ran ten steps before slamming blindly into somebody's belly. My father's.

"Why are you trying to get rid of me?" I roared.

He was frightened. "For Christ's sake, Joey, I've been here all the time!"

"The hell you have!"

He smacked my face to quell my hysteria but I kept screaming. A man with an official-looking cap entered the fray, blowing his whistle.

"He's my son, he's my son!" my father told the apparent cop.

"Take me back to the boat!" I roared. "I wanna go back to the fucking boat!"

Here the film in my head snapped and another reel began playing, this one in the city of Milan, where my father and I had settled when we reached Italy. It was a gloomy city, gray and smoggy. We had an apartment near the Duomo, and I was enrolled in an international school filled with kids from the United States, England and Australia. All the kids seemed to be in a state of mild to severe sadness because they were so far from home, for reasons only their parents could explain.

The playground was a dusty field without a single blade of grass. The only game to play was soccer and I was no good at it, having been raised in America, where hands and arms play such crucial roles in sports.

While I was at school my dad went to museums and cafés all day with his notebooks, trying to write another book. At least, that's what I think he was doing. I had a feeling he was trying to write about my mother, but somehow that book never came together.

He was overly cheerful about the great adventure he said we were having in Milan, and when the cheer wore off—it takes a lot of steam to sustain cheer, and my father was not a naturally cheerful man—he'd fall into a funk that put him at the bottom of the ocean.

That's when I'd try to cheer him up, with my own false cheer. We lived like a pair of human pistons: one up, one down. Never up or down together.

One day not long after we'd moved to Milan he sent me on a solo mission to buy bread at the bakery around the corner. We'd been there together a few times and I knew the drill: Walk to the window display, point at a long loaf of Italian bread and say, "*Uno di questi*"—"one of these." He gave me the exact amount of lire I'd need for the bread, so there'd be no fussing over change. Pay and go.

But when I got to the bakery the long loaves were all gone. I looked in panic at the bottle blonde behind the counter, a scary sixty-ish woman with a wart near her lower lip that an American woman would have had removed. Her eyes were kind but her voice was fierce.

"*Cosa voglia?*"—"What do you want?"—she boomed.

I wanted to run but I was too scared to move. I squeezed the coins in my hand so tightly that I later found ridge marks on my palm. The woman came out from behind the counter and squatted in front of me, talking even louder, as if sheer volume would help me understand.

Then her husband the baker joined the fray, attracted by the noise. He stood there waving his fat, hairy arms, the hairs whitened by flour. Then a customer joined the scrum, a bent-over crone all in black. The three of them jabbered away, and all I could do was point to the empty place where the long loaves used to be.

"*Non ce anchora!*"—"There aren't any more!"—the bottle blonde roared, and that's when I snapped.

"*Why'd my fucking mother have to die?*" I shrieked, and the three of them fell into a stunned silence. They didn't know what I'd said, but they clearly thought I was a crazy American, and while they murmured among themselves I gathered my wits, pointed at another bin with smaller loaves and held up two fingers.

"*Due,*" I managed to say, remembering the word for "two" from the elementary one-to-ten count my dad had drilled into me. The blonde put two small loaves in a paper bag. I gave her my coins, tucked that bag under my arm and ran home, ignoring the shouts behind me.

I was out of breath when I burst into the apartment and broke down sobbing. My father asked me what was wrong and I told him.

"Why are you crying?" he asked in wonder. "You did great. It was a new situation, and you handled it like a man."

"I didn't like it," I replied. "And anyway, I'm *not* a man!"

A funny smile crossed his face, the kind of smile I'd see whenever he was privately amused, usually by something bittersweet.

"You're not supposed to like it, buddy," he said softly. "You're just supposed to be able to handle it."

"Why?"

"Good practice for the future, when things really go wrong. Situations always change. You'll see. Today it was bread. Tomorrow, it'll be something else."

He was right, of course. Situations change all the time.

But it's not the kind of thing you want to hear when you're eleven years old, and motherless, and thousands of miles from home.

Dr. Rosensohn didn't say anything at first. Then he said, "Sounds like your father had some unconventional parenting skills."

"To say the least."

"But you hit the nail on the head, with that tantrum in the bakery. If your mother hadn't died you wouldn't have been in Casablanca, or Milan, or Brooklyn. Her death really spun your world off its axis."

"You can't blame a person for dying."

"No, but feelings are feelings, and the worst thing we can do is ignore them."

"I'm not ignoring my feelings, Doc. I'm just telling you what's been going on in my head since I moved back to Shepherd Avenue."

He pursed his lips. "All in all, would you say you're happy with the move?"

"Well, I wish my daughter would call me, but other than that . . ."

"You haven't called her since you were arrested?"

"I *have* called her. She told me to wait for her to call me."

"So you're obeying that command."

"I wouldn't call it a *command*. More of a request, which I'm respecting, if that's okay with you."

"The main thing is that it's okay with *you.*"

"It is, okay?"

"What caused this rift between you and your daughter?"

I was the one who brought it up, so I must have wanted to talk about it. I took a deep breath and said, "I didn't go to her mother's funeral."

Dr. Rosensohn just stared at me.

"Big mistake, right?"

"Were you on bad terms with this woman?"

"We weren't on *any* terms. She lived three thousand miles away. She never came to New York. I hadn't seen Moonchild in years."

"Moonchild?"

"Yeah, and she really fit that name. Good-natured, but a total space cadet. I knocked her up, she had the kid, she left town. I did the long-distance-dad thing, but Moonchild and I hardly ever spoke. She had a husband by the time she died, so what the hell was so important about me being at the funeral?"

Dr. Rosensohn hesitated before saying, "Have you ever heard the expression that funerals are for the sake of the living?"

"Yes I have. It's bullshit, Doc, and if there's one thing I'm really grateful about regarding my father's death, it's the fact that I didn't have to stand in a room with him in a box, and his dead hands holding a rosary while all the fucking mourners stood around, talking old times."

"Calm down, Mr. Ambrosio."

"See, I don't do death very well, probably because I got my first taste of it when my mother died, and then my grandfather died right next to me on a Ferris wheel, and then my grandmother died, and then I turned eleven."

His eyes widened. "Your grandfather died on a *Ferris wheel?*"

"Yes, he did. A fatal heart attack, with me sitting right next to him. We were at the top of the ride when it happened, and that's when they started unloading the passengers, so I had to sit there for like twenty minutes with the corpse while the wheel went down, a notch at a time. Took two guys to pry his dead hands off the bar. He had some grip, my grandfather."

Rosensohn shook his head. "Wow."

"Is that dramatic enough for you, Doc?"

He nodded. "Almost as dramatic as climbing the Brooklyn Bridge to scatter your father's ashes."

"Are we back to that?"

"Back to it? It's the reason you're here."

"I don't know *why* I'm here."

"I think you do."

"Enlighten me."

"You thought about jumping, didn't you?"

"Oh, Jesus—"

"Didn't you?"

"Fucking-A right I did!"

The words burst out of me as if I'd been Heimliched, and the sudden silence that filled Rosensohn's office wasn't really silence. It was more like a high-pitched scream no human could hear. But we were both aware of it and sat quietly for its duration.

"Can't believe I just said that," I said at last, more to myself than to him.

Not that I ever would have done it, but let's just say it *had* flashed through my head like a bad movie—a running jump off that tower to follow my father's ashes into the sky, and then into the water. From that height, it would have been like landing on a highway. Instant death. Painless. Or so I told myself.

But I didn't do it. That was the main thing. Wasn't it?

"I thought about what it would be like to jump," I said, trying to make myself clear. "That's not the same as intending to jump, right, Doc?"

Rosensohn sighed and jotted something in his notebook. I had a feeling I was making things worse for myself, like a man struggling in quicksand.

"Okay," he said. "Now I think maybe we're getting somewhere."

"Shit, what's next? Going to have me put on suicide watch?"

"Of course not. The fact that you're painting your house is a good thing. Life-affirming. Optimistic. I believe you've turned a corner." He looked at his watch. "Time's up. Go home, keep painting. By the way, judging from the splotches on your elbows, I must say that's not a very practical color for Brooklyn. Brilliant white? Jeez, I'd have gone with cream, or even beige."

Chapter Ten

I was wired when I left Rosensohn's office. I needed someone to talk to, but I had no real friends and just two relatives, one of whom wasn't talking to me.

So I took the subway out to Queens to see the other one.

I hadn't spoken with Vic since the day he'd come to get me at the police station. He wasn't home, but I knew where to find him.

He stood behind the rusted backstop at a dirt baseball field near his house, arms folded above his substantial belly. A baseball cap was tilted low over his brow as he yelled advice to the kid at bat, who couldn't have been more than twelve years old.

"Eye on the ball, Dermot!" he called out. "I ain't gonna say it again!"

The pitch came in, and the kid fouled it back.

"All right, you made contact!" Vic yelled. "Hallelujah! Now let's see if you can hit it *forward* for a change!"

Then he yelled to the pitcher: "Lay it in, Brian, it's only practice!"

The pitcher did as he was told. Dermot hit the ball up the middle, a clean single. Vic applauded.

"Good boy, Dermot! But remember: In a real game, the pitcher ain't your ally!"

I joined Vic at the backstop, folded my arms over my belly just like him and stood beside him, waiting to be noticed. A few pitches later he turned his head, saw me, did a double take, took off his hat and swatted me with it. This was a "hello" in the Ambrosio family.

"What the hell are you doin' here?"

"I was in the neighborhood."

"You in trouble again?"

"No, no, no. Can't I visit my uncle without setting off alarms?"

He shrugged, put his cap back on over his thick, bristly hair. "Practice ends in ten minutes. There's a diner across the street, if you feel like gettin' us coffee."

"Still take it light, two sugars?"

"Yeah. Christ, that's some memory you got."

I had to laugh. "Believe me, Vic, it's an affliction."

We sat in the bleachers with our coffee, watching the kids take their mandatory lap around the field.

"Look how they cut the corners," Vic said. "One lousy lap and they can't hack it." He got to his feet and bellowed: *"Around* the field, not *across* it!"

He sat back down. "See how lazy they are? They live maybe three blocks away, and their mothers drive them here. I got one or two can play a little, but they won't stick with it. They'd rather play video games."

"So why do you coach them?"

He smiled. "I love this game. Also, I got nothin' else to do."

He gulped half his coffee down, gave his throat a second to settle and then finished off the rest the same way.

He crushed the cup in his fist. "The suspense is killin' me. Gonna tell me why you're here, or what?"

I put a hand on his shoulder, the way you do when you're about to break shocking news.

"Thing is, I wanted you to know that I did something a little crazy."

"Yeah? Crazier than the bridge thing?"

"You tell me." I swallowed, hesitated. "I bought the old house on Shepherd Avenue."

He made a snorting sound, then laughed. "Bullshit!"

"Swear on my life."

Vic's face went pale. All he could do was stare at me in wonder before gasping: "What the *hell?*"

"Yeah. It's mine. I own it."

"Don't fuck with me, Joey."

"No, it's true. I'm all moved in. I'm living at two-oh-seven Shepherd. Gettin' it in shape. It's going good."

He folded his hands in mock prayer. "Joey. Please, *please* tell me you didn't do this thing."

"It's done, Vic. I thought you should know."

He threw his crumpled coffee cup toward a wire garbage basket, twenty feet away. It went right in, without even touching the sides.

I clapped my hands. "Three-pointer! You've still got it, Vic."

He startled me by grabbing my shoulders. "Why would you do a fucked-up thing like that?"

I shrugged myself out of his grip, squared my shoulders. "It's where I was happiest."

He laughed out loud. "Are you kiddin' me? You were happy with my mother and the way she treated you? Please tell me what was so great about *that!*"

It was a good point. Connie was never affectionate with me. She never hugged me or kissed me or told me I could grow up to be whatever I wanted to be. She wasn't a dreamer. Her horizons reached only as far as the back burners on her trusty stove, which still stood in the kitchen I now called home.

"Think back, man," Vic said. "She was brutal to you, absolutely brutal."

"She could be, yeah."

"So why were you happiest under my mother's roof?"

"Well, I could count on her, Vic. Haven't had a lot of people I could count on, and she was one of them. Consistency, you know? Not many consistent people around, when you think about it."

He let that sink in. I plunged ahead.

"And your father was the best man I ever knew. Who was better than Angie?"

Vic's eyes went bright with tears. "Nobody." A grin split his face. "I ever tell you about the time I went with him on a plumbing job in the neighborhood? This was probably before you were born. Some poor young widow had a busted pipe under her kitchen sink. Water everywhere, her little kids runnin' around, splashin' all over the place. A real mess. I went with him to help out. Took a few hours to install a new pipe, him workin' under the sink, me holdin' the flashlight, and when we were done—we even mopped up the water!—the widow says, 'What do I owe you, Anj?' 'Forget it,' my father says, and off we go. His time, his materials—no charge. On the way home I say to him, 'Why didn't you charge her, Pop?' He shrugs and says, 'Ahhh, she needs the money more than me.'"

Vic wiped his eyes at the end of the story. "And that's not the only time something like that happened. It's not like he was rollin' in dough, either."

"Well, maybe now you understand why I bought his old house."

"No, I *don't* understand. I'd understand if you went to their graves once in a while—*that* I could understand. Let me break it to you gently, nephew: They're gone. Doin' what you did ain't bringin' 'em back."

"I don't want to bring them back."

"Then what do you want?"

I had to think about that for a moment. "Peace, I guess."

He snorted. "Peace, on Shepherd Avenue. Good luck with that."

We were both quiet, watching Vic's ballplayers gather their equipment and walk away.

"So . . . what's the old neighborhood like these days, anyway?"

I turned my face so he wouldn't see me grinning. I knew curiosity would get the better of him.

"Looks pretty much the same. Lot of bars on the windows, things like that, but the houses haven't changed much."

"Lotta blacks?"

"Yeah, and Puerto Ricans . . . Hey, you won't believe who lives across the street. Justin Wilson."

Vic sat up straight. "Holy shit."

"I run with him some mornings in Highland Park. Nice enough kid."

"He's about to go first in the draft!"

"That's what everybody says. And get this: Remember Nat the bottle man?"

"Nat the Jew?"

"Right. Still alive, still around."

"Come on. He must be a hundred!"

"Ninety-eight. Looks pretty good, too."

"Jesus H. Christ!"

"Come see the old house, Vic. I really want you to see it."

Vic buried his face in his hands. I thought he'd be smiling when he took his hands away, but he wasn't. He looked about as happy as a headstone.

And he stared straight ahead at the empty ball field through eyes brimming with tears when he spoke again, so softly I could barely hear him.

"I wish you a lotta luck, Joey," he said, "but I am never, *ever* goin' back there again."

Chapter Eleven

There was something wrong with Justin. We were trotting around the Highland Park reservoir at an unusually slow pace when suddenly he came to a halt, as if he couldn't run another step. He looked a little pale.

"You okay?"

He shook his head. "I'm freakin' out, man."

"Why?"

"Gotta get on a plane today."

"No kidding! Where are you going?"

"I don't know ... Arizona? Gotta look at this college that wants me to go there."

"Arizona State? That's a top baseball college! Lot of great players went there."

"That's what I hear."

"I think they offered a scholarship to my uncle."

"The guy who washed out?"

"Yeah. Maybe he should have gone to Arizona ... So what's the deal? You're not turning pro?"

"I don't know what the fuck I'm doin', man."

He sat down on a bench and let his hands hang between his knees as if they were too heavy to hold up. I sat beside him. He was actually quivering.

"What's wrong, Justin?"

"Ain't never been on a plane before."

"You scared?"

"Little bit."

"There's nothing to it."

He looked at me. "You been?"

"Many times."

A plane crossed over our heads. Justin watched it go and shook his head in wonder.

"How the fuck do they *do* it? Big heavy thing like that, way up in the sky."

"That's nothing for you to worry about. All you have to do is sit back and relax."

"Maybe I won't go."

I dared to put an arm across his shoulders. "Buddy, if you're going to be a ballplayer, college or pro, you're going to ride in planes. That's the deal. Might as well get started."

He forced a brave smile. We got up off the bench and trotted back to Shepherd Avenue.

Things were moving along. I couldn't stand my white metal front door, so I hired Eddie Everything to replace it with a brown wooden door with a big, heavy knocker. I also hated the sound of that damn doorbell, so I had Eddie disconnect it.

I got to work painting the window frames and sills in the bedrooms. The woodwork was always the toughest, most time-consuming part of any paint job, but it was also the most gratifying. I used semi-gloss paint that left a sheen even after it dried, and in the waning afternoon light I was happy to see how much brighter my home seemed. It was almost like I was resurrecting the place, and with that happy thought I showered, flopped on my bed and fell into a deep sleep, from which I was jolted by the very first knocking at my front door.

The pounding continued as I tugged on my jeans and a T-shirt. I tripped on a drop cloth on my way to the door and when I opened it Rose was standing there, breathing hard and looking annoyed, as if I'd stood her up.

"What are you, deaf?"

"What's wrong?"

"It's my son, my Justin."

"Come in."

She hesitated. "Is this a new door?"

"Yeah. I hated the other one."

"How can anybody hate a door?"

"Are you coming in or what, Rose?"

I led her to the newly painted kitchen. She sat at the table and I offered her coffee. She rolled her eyes.

"You don't got a beer?"

I cracked open two cold ones and sat with her. She took a long swallow and shut her eyes, as if that would help speed the alcohol to its destination. The suspense was killing me.

"What's wrong with Justin?"

"He left. That's what's wrong."

"Yeah, he told me. He's on his way to visit Arizona State."

"Uh-huh. Thanks to you."

She said it accusingly.

"Wait a second. You didn't want him to go?"

"You catch on quick, don't you?"

"Whoa, whoa, Rose—all I said was that it's no big deal to fly!"

"Yeah? What if the plane crashes?"

"It won't."

"Who are you, God? You know everything?"

"I know that Justin will be fine."

She took another long slug of beer, closed her eyes again.

"He's gonna be gone three days." She held up a dramatic forefinger. "And this is the first time he's ever been away from me. You believe that? Shoulda seen him pullin' away in that car the college sent for him, lookin' back at me like a puppy."

"This experience will be good for him."

She cocked her head. "You think?"

"Rose, you've done your job. He's a good kid. Have faith."

"I'm thinkin' I shoulda gone with him, but I couldn't get the days."

"Days?"

"My job. I manage the Laundromat on Fulton."

"I didn't know that."

"Well, why the hell would you? You, with your own washer and dryer!"

"You're pissed off at me because I have a washer and a dryer and a new door?"

She saw the absurdity of her anger, sighed, let her shoulders sag.

"Ahhh, I ain't mad at you." She wiggled her empty bottle. "We're gonna need more beer, Jo-Jo."

Nobody had ever called me "Jo-Jo" before, and I'm not crazy about nicknames, but instead of protesting, I did the only thing that seemed appropriate, under the circumstances.

I got two more beers. And that's how it started.

Rose told me about her life: marriage at sixteen, motherhood at seventeen. I quickly did the arithmetic and realized she was thirty-six years old—which is to say, twenty-four years younger than me.

I'd been around the world, seen so much of it with my restless father. Rose had seen Brooklyn. And only the roughest parts of it.

She was young. I was old. We had absolutely nothing in common, except for maybe one thing:

I'd managed to alienate myself from the only two people on the planet connected to me, and Rose's lone link to the human race was in a plane bound for Arizona.

So for the moment, we were both alone in the world.

When it comes to bonding, loneliness has everything else beat. Especially when you've each had four beers, and night is falling, and the idea of spending the night by yourself is too much to bear.

"You know," she said, gesturing at me with her nearly empty beer bottle, "you're a good listener."

I shrugged. "It's easy when the other person is a good talker."

"You sayin' I talk too much?"

"I'd really have to know you better."

"Is that what you want?"

My blood tingled. Rose finished her beer, got up from her chair and came to my side of the table. She startled me by gripping my shoulders and going nose to nose with me, like a basketball coach giving advice to a player he's sending into the game.

Even with all that beer in me, I knew this was going to be nothing but trouble, and the last thing I needed was trouble while trying to settle into my new life. But at least when you're in trouble you feel alive, and that was a sensation I'd been lacking.

She nuzzled my nose with hers. "You gonna kiss me, Jo-Jo?"

"Rose. You don't know me."

"My boy likes you. That's all I gotta know."

"It's getting dark, so maybe you can't tell that I'm old enough to be your father."

"I didn't ask for your birth certificate. I asked if you were gonna kiss me."

"I'm thinking about it."

"If you think too much, it won't happen."

"So you're saying I should just do it."

"Ahh, never mind, I'll do it."

And she did, with an amazing blend of passion and gentleness. That first kiss went on and on, through the approach, passing and fading of a wailing fire engine that roared down Shepherd Avenue.

At last Rose drew back. She took my hand, pulled me to my feet and said, "Which room?"

I had to chuckle. "Any one you want. They're all mine. But the one with the bed in it is straight down the hall, facing the backyard."

She smiled, the first time I'd ever seen her do that. Her teeth were beautifully white in the moonlight.

"That's the one we want," she said, leading the way.

Luckily I'd packed a box of condoms when I moved to Brooklyn, never really expecting to use them, the way you buy a fire extinguisher with that same attitude.

But once we got going I realized it was a good thing I'd brought the condoms, and a shame I'd procrastinated about getting a fire extinguisher.

Hot, hot, hot. In the midst of it Rose actually gasped an apology.

"I'm outta practice, man," she said. "If it ain't right, say so."

"It's right. Jesus, is it ever right! I think I'm the one who's been wrong all these years."

"No, no, you're doin' good."

"Yeah, well, nothing like the smell of fresh paint to get a man going."

She laughed, a wonderful sound, somehow rich with both glee and regret.

"You are one crazy white guy . . ."

I conked out as if I'd been hit with a baseball bat, and when I awoke Rose was sitting on the edge of the bed, fully dressed and tying her shoes. The bed creaked when I sat up and she turned to me, startled.

"Shit! Didn't wanna wake you."

"You're leaving?"

"Yeah, I gotta go. Justin's gonna call me in ten minutes."

She showed me the face of her cell phone. It was ten minutes to ten.

"So take the call here."

"Are you *crazy?*"

"Why not? I'll be quiet."

"Can't take that chance, Jo-Jo."

Her shoes tied, she jumped to her feet. "I'm outta here." She kissed my forehead. "Go back to sleep, you earned it."

"I'll walk you home."

"No way!"

"I'll walk you to the door."

She couldn't object to that. So I followed her to my front door, which she opened a crack to peek out on the street.

"So what's the deal?" I asked. "Am I going to see you again?"

She turned and looked at me as if I were insane. "Whachoo think, man? I'm right across the street!"

She held up an instructive finger. "But I come to you. You don't come to me. We got a deal?"

I nodded, or maybe it was a shrug.

Whatever it was, it was what she needed to bolt down my stoop, across the street and into her house, slamming the door as if it owed her money.

Chapter Twelve

The next morning I did a risky thing. I took a walk down Fulton Street to the Laundromat where Rose worked.

It was a long, narrow place, like a tunnel, between a fried-chicken joint and a check-cashing place. A row of washers lined one wall, facing a row of dryers against the other. The only natural light came from the front window. It was one of those places where fluorescent bulbs burned all day.

People could do their own laundry or leave it for Rose, whose ponytail flicked back and forth as she struggled with mountains of laundry. I watched her tug a huge load of sheets from a washing machine into a wire cart. Then she rolled the cart to the other side, loaded the sheets into a dryer, fed a few coins into the machine and got it going.

Heavy work, all-day work. A customer at the front desk needed change, and before Rose could catch sight of me out there on the sidewalk behind the *LAST WASH AT 6 P.M.* sign, I ducked my head and hurried home.

I was restless. There was plenty more work to do on the house, but I couldn't get down to it. I craved contact. My daughter had frozen me out, my uncle refused to come near the place and Rose had made it clear that whatever was to be with us, she would be calling the shots.

So I went to my laptop and did a crazy thing. I started searching for people from the old days on Shepherd Avenue.

Johnny Gallo used to live down the block with his parents. He was my Uncle Vic's age, the local Romeo who was either working on his car or humping girls on its back seat. When he was eighteen

Johnny got a girl pregnant, and they got married. My grandparents threw him an engagement party in our basement, and that was one sad party.

I always liked Johnny, and we even committed a crime together. Late one night, when the White Castle hamburger joint at Shepherd and Atlantic was under construction, Johnny and I busted a few of its plate-glass windows.

Gallo, Gallo. . . . it wasn't a name like Smith or Jones, but it was a fairly common Italian name, especially in Brooklyn. There were J. Gallos galore in the residential listings, so I figured maybe Johnny had stuck with his abilities as a mechanic and found a listing for *J. Gallo Auto Repair* in Bay Ridge.

Could it be the same one? With a trembling hand I dialed the number. It rang just once.

"Gallo repairs," said a voice I hadn't heard in fifty years. Unmistakably Johnny's. Holy shit.

"You probably don't remember me," I began, "but a long time ago I lived down the block from you on Shepherd Avenue, and—"

"Holy shit! Long Island, is that *you?* "

He'd always called me Long Island because I'd grown up there, and because certain Italian-Americans feel obliged to tag you with a nickname within minutes of being introduced, which is what Johnny Gallo did to me in 1961.

"Yeah, it's me, Johnny. Can't believe you recognized my voice!"

"You kiddin' me? You still talk like a prince! Ain't heard many voices like yours in my life, Long Island . . . Hey. Who died? Vic?"

"Nobody died. Well, my father died, but that was a while ago. You probably knew about it."

"Yeah, I read the papers. You, up on the bridge with his ashes! Christ, Long Island, are you okay?"

"I'm great. I just wanted to get in touch with you."

"Yeah? Why?" His voice darkened with suspicion. "Somethin's up, don't bullshit me."

"Well, I wanted to tell you that I'm back in the old neighborhood. I moved into two-oh-seven Shepherd Avenue."

A long, dead silence, save for the whine of power tools in the background. Then: "Get the fuck outta here."

"Block's looking pretty good, actually. I'm doing a lot of work on the house."

"Long Island, Jesus! Why didn't you just buy a house in Afghanistan? Be a lot cheaper, and probably a lot safer."

"It's not as bad as you think, Johnny. Lot of working people, trying to get by."

"I'll bet."

"I was wondering if I could see you."

"Sure! I wanna hear all about this. Come over tonight for supper, Nancy won't believe it. Oh, excuse me—I meant to say *for dinner*. Isn't that what they call it on Long Island?"

"You're still with Nancy?"

"Of course I'm with Nancy. Be fifty years in September. Take down my address. Supper *and* dinner at six. You comin' alone?"

"Yeah."

He chuckled. "Now, why doesn't that surprise me? Six o'clock, Long Island. Try not to get mugged on the way."

Johnny Gallo's house in Bay Ridge was part of a once all-Italian enclave that was now getting as Yuppified as Greenwich Village. Kids on the rise who couldn't afford Manhattan rents had "discovered" neighborhoods like this, and they were willing to hack the long subway ride in exchange for a few decent rooms and direct sunlight, the kind that didn't have to struggle down an air shaft.

Johnny had a green-shingled house on a corner, under the shade of a big oak tree. It had a screened-in porch, a front yard the size of a ping-pong table and a low white-picket fence in need of paint. I climbed the steps and rang the bell, clutching a bottle of Johnnie Walker Black Label scotch.

The door opened, and there he stood.

"Holy shit. Long Island himself, on my front stoop."

Then he grabbed me in an embrace that was long and steady enough to soften the five decades since we'd last seen each other.

"Jesus, man, it's good to see you," he said into my shoulder.

Johnny was still Johnny. A potbelly marred his once-lean physique and his hair had thinned, but in an even way, all over his head. He combed what was left of his silvery locks straight back, as he did in the old days. It was like a corn field with alternate rows missing.

Those sky-blue eyes were the same, though, alive with mischief.

They glistened with happy tears as he pulled back from the hug, regarding me from head to toe.

"Guess you turned out all right."

"You too, Johnny."

"I hope you're hungry."

I handed him the bottle. "I hope you're thirsty."

"Oh, Long Island, you've got class."

There were seven of us at the table, and we sat down immediately and really hit that meal: rigatoni with red meat sauce, broccoli rabe, and plenty of Italian bread. Everybody served themselves from bowls in the middle. It was a happy table.

Johnny's wife, Nancy, sat to his left. I hadn't seen her since that awkward engagement party all those years ago. She was surprisingly slim and pretty and told me she was a firm believer in daily Pilates exercises, which made Johnny roll his eyes behind her back. Next to them sat their son Nicky and his wife Christina. Nicky was just an embryo on the night of that engagement party, and now he was a fireman on the verge of his fiftieth birthday who vowed to get rid of his "love handles" before hitting the half-century mark, but that didn't seem likely, the way he was chowing down on his mother's meatballs.

And across from them sat their twentysomething son Marco, a Wall Street go-getter, whose wife Megan, a violet-eyed, dimpled Irish beauty, was unashamedly eating for two during the sixth month of her pregnancy.

"I grew up reading the Sammy Suitcase stories!" Megan said. She patted her belly. "This one's going to be reading them, too."

Sammy Suitcase was the hero of my most successful books, a little boy who traveled the world with his footloose father after the death of his mother. Sammy was always the new kid in school, the outsider, the last one chosen for games in the playground, and yet he always found a way to come out on top.

Yes, it was a lot like my own life, except for the part about coming out on top.

And after what Megan said, it suddenly hit me like a lightning bolt: Johnny Gallo, the onetime heartthrob of Shepherd Avenue, was soon to become a great-grandfather.

I watched them in action, fascinated. They swiped food from each other's plates and laughed at each other's bad jokes. They kidded each other and knew just how far they could go with the kidding, and ultimately there was no such thing as going too far, because they really knew each other, and liked each other. A grudge in this family wouldn't simmer for years. It would evaporate like mist in the morning sun.

Nicky was teasing his son about how seriously he took his golf game up there in Westchester, and Marco fired back with a line about how he grew up thinking the smell of smoke was his father's cologne, because that's how he always smelled, and just about then I started feeling dizzy.

"Hey, Long Island, you okay?"

I snapped out of my daze and stared at Johnny down that long table, the way a sailor might gaze at a distant lighthouse.

"I'm fine, Johnny," I assured him. "I was just thinking, this is a great family you've got here. Just . . . amazing."

It was a thought that I'd somehow spoken out loud, as if I'd been talking in my sleep. Everybody stared at me. I'm guessing the Gallos had been called many things over the years, but never "amazing." At last Christina spoke.

"You never got married, huh?"

"No. But I have a daughter. Haven't seen much of her lately."

"You've got to bring her next time," Nancy said. I noticed that she and Johnny were holding hands under the table, like two kids on a first date.

Suddenly Nicky let out a gasp. "Holy shit, it just hit me," he said, wide-eyed. "You're the guy on the *bridge!*"

The rest of them looked down at their plates. Johnny leaned across to tap Nicky on the back of his head, as if he were a five-year-old who'd just spilled his milk.

"You hadda bring that up?"

"Pop, I'm sorry, but . . ." He turned to me. "That was you, wasn't it?"

I nodded, feeling my face grow hot. "The human fly, in the flesh."

"Thing is, I know the guy who brought you down! An emergency-service cop, Billy Debowski! Right?"

I hoisted my wineglass in a toast to the absent Billy. "He treated me well."

"Yeah, he's a friend of mine! I was with him last night, and tonight I'm with *you!* That's really—what's the word I'm lookin' for?"

"Ironic?" I suggested.

"Yeah. Really ironic."

"How is Billy?"

Nicky chuckled. "When the bullets are flyin', he knows just what to do. He'll disarm a wacko with an automatic weapon, no sweat, but he has a panic attack when he can't figure out what to get his girlfriend for her birthday. Which is why he's always breaking up with his girlfriends on their birthdays. He's famous for that. They call him Birthday Billy. Not to his face, of course."

"Please give him my best."

"Will do."

He reached over to bump fists with me. Everybody at the table relaxed, and I saw that Johnny and Nancy, those lifelong lovebirds, were once again holding hands.

An hour later it was just Johnny and me outside in his screened-in porch, sipping Johnnie Walker over ice. Nancy had gone to bed and everyone else had gone home. In the distance the lights of the Verrazano-Narrows Bridge twinkled, and I could smell the sea.

"Sorry about Nicky," Johnny said. "Sometimes I think he's inhaled a little too much smoke, with the things he says."

"No harm done. He's a nice guy."

"Yeah, I guess. We wanted more kids, but it didn't work out that way."

"But you and Nancy—looks like that worked out pretty well."

He seemed surprised. "Why wouldn't it?"

"Well, it's just . . . the circumstances . . ."

Johnny's eyebrows went up. "You knew about that?"

"Everybody on Shepherd Avenue knew, Johnny."

He sighed, shrugged, sipped his whiskey. "No complaints. I got lucky. She's a good girl, better than I deserved. What am I gonna kick about?"

We clinked glasses and drank. Johnny topped off both drinks, enjoying himself and these stolen moments away from his clan. I could tell he wanted me to linger a little bit to talk over old times.

"What's it like back there?" he asked. "Is anybody left?"

"Remember Nat the bottle man?"

"Sure."

"Would you believe he's still around?"

"Get the fuck outta here!"

"Swear to God. Hangs out on Atlantic Avenue all day."

"Christ, he's gotta be ninety-five!"

"Ninety-eight."

"Jesus, what keeps him goin'?"

"The neighborhood, Johnny."

"Yeah? That's what shoulda *killed* him! What about Vic? He ever get married, or what?"

"No. He's a peculiar guy, my uncle."

"No kids?"

"Not that I know of."

"Shame the baseball didn't work out for him. Jesus, he could give the ball a ride, couldn't he?"

"Oh yeah."

I was going to tell him about Justin Wilson, but didn't feel like going into it. This was precious time for me and Johnny, maybe the last time we'd ever see each other, and I didn't want to waste it on current events. I suspect Johnny felt the same way. He yawned, and I knew he had to get up early to be at his garage, but when I rose to leave he urged me to sit back down, have another drink.

"Hey, Johnny. Remember the time we busted those windows at the White Castle?"

He rolled his eyes, shook his head. "Glad you didn't bring that up at the table. My family thinks I'm a model citizen."

"You were upset. Your father had just died."

"Yeah, and your mother had just died, and your father was on the road. Funny time for all of us, Long Island."

"Would you believe the White Castle's still there? Got a drive-through window now."

Johnny laughed. "Window's probably bulletproof glass."

"I wouldn't be surprised."

"Remember the night you ran away and fell down on the sidewalk? I was the first one there."

"I remember, Johnny."

"Madonna, how you screamed."

A foghorn sounded out on the water. Our glasses were empty, and Johnny made no move to fill them.

"I'd better get going," I said, but when I rose to my feet he reached for my elbow, as if to steady me.

"Long Island. Why'd you move back there? You chasin' ghosts?"

"I don't believe in ghosts."

"What, then?"

I couldn't do anything but shrug.

He held up a thick forefinger. "Can I give you one piece of advice?"

"Shoot."

"This daughter of yours—"

"I really don't want to talk about her."

"We won't. All's I'm sayin' is, don't let her disappear on you. Do not let that happen."

We shook hands.

"You're happy, aren't you, Johnny?"

He seemed surprised by the question. "Why wouldn't I be?"

"Didn't you ever feel . . . trapped?"

He smiled, and it was the smile of the boy that made all those East New York girls swoon back in the day.

"Thought I'd feel that way, at first," he said softly. "But we got married, and Nicky came along, and then a funny thing happened: I got to know Nancy." He chuckled. "We hadn't been dating long, you know. Just a few weeks . . . all of a sudden, we're man and wife. Sleepin' in the same bed, eatin' off the same dishes." He shrugged. "Turned out, I liked her. Still do."

We embraced. "You're a lucky man, Johnny Gallo."

"Aaay, I knew that before you did."

"Wish I could have made it work with a woman. But I always felt trapped."

He chuckled. "You Ambrosios. Somebody's always runnin' away.'"

"Not anymore, buddy. If you're looking for me, I'm at two-oh-seven Shepherd."

"I'll remember that, Long Island."

I went out and closed the screen door behind me. I heard Johnny latch it, and before I could reach the sidewalk he called to me.

"Joseph."

It was the first time he'd ever used my name. I turned and looked at him, his forehead pressed to the screen like a kid at a train window, those big blue eyes of his fascinated by the scenery, which was me.

"Thing is, it's only a trap if you're tryin' to get out."

Chapter Thirteen

The next day I woke up, looked out the bedroom window at my green-painted, cemented-over backyard and decided I couldn't stand it any longer. I gave Eddie Everything a shout, told him what I wanted and half an hour later he arrived with a pick, a sledgehammer and a wheelbarrow.

"We're working together on this one," I told him, grabbing the sledge and taking a hard, spiteful swing at the middle of the pavement.

I was shocked at how easily the surface broke. With the tip of the pick I was able to pry up a chunk of cement the size of an apple pie, and no more than two inches thick.

Eddie laughed. "A real Puerto Rican pavement," he said. "Just thick enough to dance on." He rubbed the underside of the chunk with his finger and it crumbled like a stale cake.

"Look at this! Mostly sand, not enough concrete. The Italians, when they poured cement—now, *that* was a floor. They buried a body under a bocce court, wasn't nobody ever gonna find it."

"Ah, yes, Eddie, the good old days."

I swung the sledge and Eddie worked the pick. In three hours we had the whole yard broken up and cleared. The newly exposed soil was nearly as hard as the cement had been, but a rainstorm or two would change that.

We loaded the cement chunks into the wheelbarrow and rolled them to Eddie's car, where he spread a ragged blanket over the bottom of the trunk before we piled them in there. He had to make two trips to the dump and charged me a hundred bucks for that service, plus another hundred for the work on the yard.

I paid him on the spot, cash as always, four crisp fifties. He smiled at the money, sniffing the bills as if they were a bouquet of roses.

"You're goin' to a lot of trouble to plant a few flowers, man."

"I don't want flowers."

"Vegetables?"

"No. Well, maybe a few tomato plants, but that's not the main thing."

"The main thing. Oh boy. Let's hear it."

"Well, we had chickens here when I was a kid."

"Here we go."

"They laid eggs and everything."

"Eggs are cheap, Mr. A. You hear what I'm sayin'? Don't need no damn barnyard if you want a few eggs."

"I'll bet you know where to get live chickens."

"Yeah, and I'll bet you know it's against the law in Brooklyn."

"Eddie, I'm going to do this thing. I'm not worried about getting a ticket. The question is, are you going to help me?"

He clapped cement dust off his hands, slowly and dramatically. I was getting to know him pretty well, and suspected I was in for a screwing.

"It's gonna cost you," he said in a singsong voice. "The risk goes up, the price goes up."

"I want half-a-dozen hens, no roosters. Last thing I need is neighbors bitching about the crowing."

"I hear you."

"Can you handle it?"

He pursed his lips. "Do I get to build the coop and the fence?"

Stupidly, I hadn't thought of that. "Have you ever built a chicken coop?"

"No, but what's the big deal? It's a condo for chickens. They ain't fussy, long as they're out o' the rain. The fence is more important. Don't want no chickens runnin' down Atlantic Avenue. Four feet high, all the way around the yard. That oughta do it. Fuckers can't fly, right?"

"How much, Eddie?"

A deep, long sigh. Eddie liked you to believe that your expense was as painful to him as it was to you.

"Fence and the coop? Let's say two-fifty, not including materials. That'll be another hundred and fifty, probably."

Four hundred bucks. I nodded. "And the birds?"

Now he inhaled through clenched teeth, the way a man does when he cuts himself shaving. "Another two hundred."

I laughed out loud. "Eddie. Come on!"

"Hey, I'm breakin' the law doin' this! You wasn't listenin' to my little speech about risk? I get caught, it's my ass!"

"Six chickens for two hundred bucks? Know what that comes to per pound?"

"Yeah, well, it's different when they're alive. You want six Perdue oven-stuffer roasters, gimme fifty bucks."

He smiled. He knew he had me. I reached into my pocket, took out a wad of bills and peeled off six Benjamin Franklins. Eddie's eyes were as big as baseballs.

"Jesus, man, you always walk around with that kinda money?"

"I do when I'm dealing with you." I slapped the bills in his hand. "That covers everything, right?"

"You are a trusting soul, you know that, Mr. A?"

"How soon can you get going on this?"

"I'm already on it, man. Gonna get what I need for the coop and the fence right now."

"I want this done soon, Eddie. And don't tell anybody what we've got going on."

He pocketed the bills and saluted me. "Name, rank and serial number. That's all they ever get outta me."

Eddie took off. I went to the backyard and used the pick to loosen the soil, plowing away like a farmer. I liked the way the yard looked with the soil loosened, as if awaiting seed. A few hours later Eddie returned with lumber and chicken wire, which I helped him carry to the yard.

"How'd you find chicken wire in Brooklyn?"

"Wasn't easy."

It was late, too late for Eddie to start building. He promised to return first thing in the morning. I went inside, tired and sore. A long, hot bath left me even more tired, and I collapsed on my bed for an early-evening nap, from which I was jolted by a knock on the door.

It was dark. I'd been asleep for hours. I went to answer the door, stupid with sleep, and there stood Rose, carrying a six-pack of Budweiser.

"You want company, Jo-Jo?"

I let her in and she quickly closed the door behind her, as if to elude anyone who might have been following.

"I woke you, huh?"

"What time is it?"

"Little after ten. Justin's back from Arizona. He fell asleep five minutes ago. Come on, let's go, I can't stay long."

And before I could respond her mouth was on mine, and she was pushing me backwards to the bedroom with one hand while clutching that six-pack of Bud with the other.

An hour later she rested naked in my arms, but did not sleep, sipping slowly on her third beer.

"Why you got all that wood out there in your yard?"

"Special project."

"You ain't gonna tell me what it is?"

"Not just yet."

"I saw you outside the Laundromat, you know."

That shocked me. "Oh."

"What was you doin,' spyin' on me?"

I hoped it was too dark for her to see my red face. "Just wanted to . . . see where you work."

"Oh yeah. 'Cause it's just so *interesting* to work in a Laundromat, huh?"

She giggled and playfully punched my chest. Suddenly, like a fireman at the sound of the alarm, she jumped out of bed and began pulling on her clothes.

"What's going on, Rose?"

"It's late, I gotta go."

"Why?"

"In case he gets up."

"Rose. It's one in the morning!"

"Yeah, well, he might get thirsty, get up for a glass o' water, and what if I ain't there?"

"He gets up for a glass of water?"

She pointed at me. "Hey, that's your fault. All that runnin' you make him do, he gets thirsty!"

"What's the deal with Arizona State? Is he going there?"

"He ain't sure yet. That's another thing. Colleges, agents, sportswriters, they call the house all the time, don't matter what time it is. Phone could wake him up."

She finished tying her sneakers and was ready to go, kissing my forehead before bounding out of my bedroom. I hopped along after her, nearly tripping as I struggled to get my underpants on.

"I'll walk you home, Rose."

"No, you will not."

"Don't worry, I don't want to come inside."

A sly smile. "Didn't you just do that, coupla times?"

"Oh, man . . ."

She giggled, nuzzled my neck and kissed me. "Be a good boy, Jo-Jo. I'll see you soon."

She reached for the doorknob but I leaned my weight against the door, keeping it closed. She didn't like that.

"Come on, Jo-Jo," she said in a grave voice, "I ain't gonna be nobody's prisoner."

I took my weight off the door. "Just please talk to me, Rose."

"About what?"

"About this. What we're doing, here."

She shrugged. "We're havin' some fun, that's all. No strings, all right? You cool with that?"

I shook my head. "Those have been my lines for forty years. Funny to hear somebody else saying them."

"Well, good. Means we understand each other, right?"

"I guess."

"Don't be lookin' at me like a little boy just dropped his ice cream!" She took my face in her hands. "You're havin' a good time, right?"

"Yes, if it doesn't kill me."

"You don't wanna get married again, do you?"

"I've never been married."

She seemed surprised. "Ain't you got a daughter?"

"Daughter, yes. Ex-wife, no."

"Okay, so it ain't like you wanna walk down the aisle, an old man like you, right?"

"Watch yourself, I'll hit you with my cane."

She laughed out loud. "I like you, Jo-Jo. Let's not go nuts over this, all right?"

"Okay."

She turned the doorknob. I caught her by the elbow, ever so gently.

"Thing is, every time you go, I feel like it might be the last time I'll ever see you."

She eeled her way out of my grasp, pinched my cheek and opened the door.

"Makes it more exciting, right?"

Before I could answer she was out the door and down my stoop, walking briskly as she crossed the street on silent feet, as if she'd just pulled a bank heist and didn't want to attract attention by running. I watched the last few steps of her journey, up the steps to her house and through the door, which she was careful not to slam.

She was so close: the distance of one of her son's throws from deep in the hole at shortstop to first base, that close. But really, she was a million miles away.

It bothered me. It bothered me that we were carrying on like a couple of thieves in the night. It bothered me that I was old enough to be her father. It bothered me that she was calling the shots in whatever it was we were doing.

It bothered me that I was falling for her.

Chapter Fourteen

"So," said Nat, *"nu?"*

I loved that economical Yiddish way of asking a person what was happening, without using a verb. Sitting beside him on Atlantic Avenue, I told him about Justin Wilson and his baseball future, to which Nat could only shrug. He didn't care about sports. I wasn't ready to tell him about Justin's mother and me—that was a dangerous bit of gossip, something I could barely admit to myself.

Nat raised his eyebrows at my plan to raise chickens in the yard, and when I told him I'd seen Johnny Gallo he all but cackled with glee.

"I remember that kid! Good-lookin'! Had a lotta trouble keeping it in his pants, didn't he?"

I had to laugh, hoping I'd sound something like this if I ever got to be ninety-eight years old. "He was a swordsman, all right."

"Got some girl pregnant, didn't he?"

"She's his wife."

"Still?"

"Amazing, isn't it?"

Nat sighed and watched the traffic for a silent minute. Then he hesitated before saying, "Wasn't your mother pregnant with you when your father married her?"

"That's the rumor. Never confirmed. Caused a big rift in the family between my mother and my grandmother, though."

"Ahhh, it doesn't matter." He waved a bony hand. "Your mother loved your father. He loved her. They were happy. That's what matters. Not like that grandmother of yours. A bitter, bitter woman."

"Well, she didn't have it easy. Trying to raise a family during the Great Depression—"

"Wrong, *wrong!* That's not why she was like that! It's because she was second choice!"

I was baffled as well as startled by Nat's outburst. "Whose second choice?"

"Angie's! You didn't know that? Your grandfather was keepin' company with Connie's sister, Josephine. Josephine met another guy and dumped him, so he turned around and went for Connie."

I swallowed. "Just to spite Josephine?"

Nat shrugged. "Who knows? Angie was a nice guy. But even nice guys get mad once in a while."

"I never even knew Connie had a sister."

"She died young. But she was Angie's first choice and Connie knew it. That'll stay with a woman, know what I mean, Joey? They all wanna be the queen."

"You know a lot about women for a guy who never got married, Nat."

"I never got married because I know too much." He sighed and stared at the sky, as if in search of the key to an unsolvable mystery. "Sometimes I think I woulda been a lot happier if I were a little stupider. Know what I mean? I think too much, Joey."

"So stop thinking, find yourself the wrong woman and settle down, already."

"Yeah, you wish. We'll have my funeral right after the wedding. You can be my best man and my undertaker."

"I'll write a toast and bring a shovel."

Nat cackled. "You're all right, you know that, kid? You weren't here long, but these streets sure rubbed off on you."

I sank back in the folding chair. "My grandmother had a sister. Who knew?"

"Funny thing is, Connie was a lot prettier than Josephine. Nicer, too."

I had to chuckle. "Never heard anyone use the word *nice* to describe my grandmother."

Nat blinked watery eyes and blew his nose with a trembling hand. "She wasn't very nice to your chickens, was she?"

My scalp tingled. "No, Nat, she wasn't."

The chickens. Oh boy. I was surprised Nat knew about it, but then again, what happened to my chickens in 1961 was the stuff of neighborhood legends, and legends die hard.

* * *

It was the most horrifying thing I'd ever witnessed. My grandfather had bought a bunch of chickens to keep in the backyard, young pullets that quickly grew into full-grown egg-layers. I fed the birds and collected the eggs, tasks I was happy to perform, but it all came to an end one sunny afternoon when my grandmother caught and strangled the birds, one by one, claiming they were sick.

That was bullshit. She'd had a meltdown because my father was AWOL and so was Vic, hitting the road after his baseball career crashed without even saying good-bye to her. That crazy summer had worn the old lady down, and she lashed out against the chickens.

In the midst of the slaughter I ran to the house to get my grandfather, but by the time we returned Connie was twisting the neck of the last bird, which evacuated horribly all over the front of her dress before she dropped it.

And of course this was the story that dominated my next session with Dr. Rosensohn, after telling him that I was going to raise chickens in my backyard.

"Wow."

"You can say that again, Doc."

"What was it like for you, seeing your grandmother kill those chickens?"

"Unpleasant."

"I'm going to need more than that, Mr. Ambrosio."

"Come on, man! I'm ten years old, feeding my birds, and the old lady suddenly picks one up and twists its fucking neck! It shits all over her, and she doesn't even seem to notice! I think it's fair to say I was traumatized!"

"What were the other birds doing?"

"Jesus, *I* don't know. They were running around. I remember a lot of squawking. Then Connie caught another one and did the exact same thing."

"So she killed two birds in front of you, and then you ran to get your grandfather."

"Right."

He scrawled something on his notepad, or maybe it was just a doodle. "I'm just wondering . . ."

"Stop wondering and ask me."

"Well, by the time your grandfather got there, all the birds were dead, is that right?"

"Actually, she was just killing the last one. That bird let out some shriek, I can tell you that."

Rosensohn hesitated before asking: "Instead of running to get your grandfather, why didn't you try to stop her yourself?"

I laughed out loud, for the first time ever in his office. "Doc, please. This was not a woman to be stopped, especially not by a little kid. Even if Angie had gotten there, I'm not sure he could have stopped her. Connie was a hurricane. You got out of her way, or you got flattened."

Rosensohn was looking right into my eyes, with *breakthrough* written all over his chubby face.

"You've never been married, have you, Mr. Ambrosio?"

"Oh, are we done with the chickens, now?"

"Because it occurs to me that after your mother died, Connie became your major model for what a woman is."

"Hmm."

"And it sounds to me like she was one fearsome model."

"Are you married, Doc?"

The question jolted him. "I am," he said after a moment.

"How's it going?"

"We aren't here to discuss my marriage."

"If a guy's going to say that my fucked-up history with women is all because of my chicken-murdering grandmother, I'm going to want to know a little about that guy."

He took off his glasses and slowly wiped the lenses with his handkerchief.

"My wife and I are well-suited."

"What the hell does that mean? It sounds like you both go to the same tailor."

"It's a strong, vital marriage."

"Well, good. Obviously nobody in your family had homicidal tendencies toward poultry."

"Mr. Ambrosio—"

"Why'd you take your glasses off when I asked you about your marriage?"

His face flushed. He looked at his watch and said, "Time's up."

"Ooh, and just when I was getting in a few good shots."

I got up, went to the door and turned to face him. "You know, I think you're right about the lasting effects of what my grandmother did."

"You do?"

"Oh, yeah. When it came to marriage, or any kind of serious commitment, I always . . . chickened out."

He rolled his eyes. "See you next time. By the way, it's illegal to raise chickens within city limits."

"Are you going to report me?"

He shook his head. "I'll leave that to your neighbors."

Once again, I laughed out loud.

"My neighbors are probably staging cockfights in their cellars," I said. "I doubt they'll be calling the cops over my chickens."

Chapter Fifteen

A rhythm of life: I was actually falling into a rhythm of life on Shepherd Avenue. A morning run, shower and a shave, and then a stroll on the streets—these were my stations of the cross, performed with pleasure. I waved to my wary neighbors if they happened to be sitting on their porches, and eventually one or two actually waved back.

Then on to Atlantic Avenue—always at least a nod or a quick conversation with Nat—and then shopping along Fulton Street, under the elevated tracks. I wanted to support the local shops as much as I could. I bought meat from an eternally smiling butcher who was wildly proud of his products, always saying the same thing before wrapping up my purchase: "Is that a chicken, *or is that a chicken?* Is that a pork chop, *or is that a pork chop?*"

Fruits and vegetables came from an open-air stall that spilled out onto the sidewalk, probably in violation of the law, but who was going to complain? The vendor was an unshaven guy who wore a black wool cap and fingerless gloves in all weathers and always looked left and right as he made change from the dirt-streaked apron around his waist. He sold the best tomatoes I'd ever tasted, and when I asked him where they came from he glared at me as if I'd asked if I could sleep with his wife.

"They come from the ground," he deadpanned. A true East New York response.

And you got the truest sense of the neighborhood from the liquor store. Only the cheapest of wines were out on display, and everything else was behind a floor-to-ceiling Plexiglas barrier with a sliding window. On the other side stood the owner, a nervous, narrow-eyed guy in a black shirt who always took the money first before passing the bottles and the change through the window. I made half-a-dozen visits to the store before I earned my first nod of recognition from the man. At that point I was going to introduce myself, but the window slid shut before I could open my mouth.

I was careful to steer clear of the Laundromat where Rose worked. The last thing I needed was to get caught lurking again.

I even ventured into the White Castle for an occasional lunch, for old times' sake—something my grandmother would have forbidden in the old days. The Italians on the block shunned the place when it went up in '61. Fast food was a sign that the neighborhood was changing, and it was time for them to pack up and get out, while the gettin' was good.

They were still making the same square little hamburgers, fried in diced onions and slapped onto the world's softest buns. You could eat half a dozen and still have room for french fries and a chocolate malted.

The girl behind the counter was a sad-eyed creature with a flawless cappuccino complexion. Even with her hair up in a sanitary net she was pretty, and I suspected she'd be even prettier if she smiled, which she didn't.

I ordered three burgers, fries and a chocolate malted, aware that I was the only white customer in the place.

"Eatin' it here?"

"I'll take it with me."

She brought my food in a bag and I paid up, stuffing a buck into the tip jar.

"I remember when they built this place fifty years ago," I told the girl, hoping she'd respond with surprise or curiosity, but her face remained blank until I added: "Me and this other kid smashed the windows while it was under construction."

Still no smile, but at least her eyebrows went up. "You get caught?"

"No."

At last, a smile. "This job sucks," she whispered. "I'd like to smash some windows here."

"I'd advise against it. Surveillance cameras everywhere nowadays."

"Yeah, that's true." She sighed. "You were lucky in your day, man. The shit you didn't have to worry about."

"True dat," I replied, and went home to enjoy my cholesterol festival.

Eddie Everything was jerking me around, as I'd feared he might when I paid him in advance. I'd hear him hammering in the backyard, then suddenly he'd be gone after an hour or two of work, claiming he had other jobs he couldn't ignore.

"Eddie. I really want this coop finished and full of chickens before the snow falls, you know?"

"Boss, you gonna have it before the Fourth of July, or your money back."

"Could I have that in writing?"

"My word is my bond, man."

"Eddie . . ."

Justin Wilson was big news as he was selected in the first round of the Major League draft by the Seattle Mariners. He was the third pick overall, the first two picks being pitchers, which made sense, as most clubs believed in building their teams around superior pitching.

Justin turned down the college scholarships and decided to go straight to the pros, signing with the Mariners for a sum the newspapers were calling "the better part of a million dollars," according to his newly acquired agent, a big-name guy with a shaved head, a diamond earring and a capped-teeth smile.

Everything was happening fast. First stop for Justin as a professional baseball player would be Rookie Ball in Arizona. For the second time in less than a week he'd be getting on a plane, and this time he wasn't coming back, unless he washed out.

On our final morning run together Justin admitted he was a little disappointed he wasn't chosen first overall.

"Pitchers are wusses. Play every fourth, fifth day, always complainin' 'bout their arms hurtin'. I'm out there every day, man, bustin' my ass."

"Come on, you did great. You're a first-round draft choice!"

"Coulda got more money, if they'd picked me first overall."

I was dying to know exactly how much he'd signed for, but didn't dare ask. "I'm sure you did all right."

"Yeah, I ain't complainin'. Want to move my mother to a nice neighborhood, but she won't go."

I felt my scalp tingle. "Really?"

"She's stubborn."

We ran hard the last few blocks of the way home, and Justin waited for the cool-down walk on Liberty Avenue to break it to me.

"I know what's goin' on, man."

I froze. We stopped walking. Justin's head was bowed and a drop of sweat hung from the tip of his nose. When would it fall? It quivered, quivered . . .

"What's going on?" I dared to ask.

"Come on. You and my mom. Don't treat me like a jerk. Saw her comin' outta your house the other night, late."

Jesus. He'd gotten up for a glass of water after all.

He wiped the dancing sweat drop away with the back of his wrist and looked at me, *through* me, breathing as hard as a bull preparing to charge.

"Okay, yeah," I said at last. "Yeah, it's . . . going on."

Justin let me suffer for five excruciating seconds before putting a hand on my shoulder.

"It's cool," he said calmly, the faintest of smiles on his lips.

I swallowed. "It is?"

"Yeah. I'm glad she has a . . . friend. Just don't hurt her."

Oh boy. "I'd never do that."

It seemed like the right time for a handshake but neither of us moved to do that. Instead, the hand on my shoulder clamped into a vise and he held up a forefinger with his other hand.

"One thing. She don't know that I know about you. Wanna keep it that way."

"So how come you want me to know you know?"

"'Cause I like you. I think you're a good guy. A little weird, but good."

He released my throbbing shoulder. We started walking again, side by side. I took a deep breath and felt my eyes moisten. "You realize I'm a lot older than her, Justin."

His eyes flared. "You backin' out?"

"No! Not at all! Just stating a fact. I'm no kid."

"She ain't either."

"Yeah, but I'll bet she doesn't get AARP mail."

We were half a block from home. Justin turned and held me by both shoulders this time, a blend of strength and affection.

"She's happy. I see that. Ain't seen her happy in a long time, and I'm goin' away, and I don't wanna be worryin' 'bout her. Gotta focus on my fuckin' game."

He dared to hug me, and when he pulled back from the hug his eyes were moist.

"Ain't askin' you to marry her, or nothin' like that. Just be good to her. And don't be givin' me a lotta bullshit about how old you are, Joe. You still got a coupla good innings left, far as I can tell."

He ran the rest of the way at a pace I could never keep up with, and that was his good-bye to me.

Chapter Sixteen

I thought for sure that Rose would be banging on my door the day Justin left for Arizona, but she didn't. Maybe she didn't consider me a shoulder to cry on. She must have had other people in her life for that, or maybe she chose to suffer alone.

Or maybe I'd never see her again. At that point, I really didn't know, and the suspense was killing me.

So I focused on my house, figuring I could move the chicken-coop process along if I offered to help Eddie Everything. But he insisted upon working alone, however sporadically.

"Eddie. How soon before this is done?"

"Boss, I don't wanna rush it."

"I don't need the Sistine chicken coop, here. Just something that shelters the damn birds!"

"Who's Sis-teen?"

"Never mind."

Against Eddie's advice, I embarked upon another project: the restoration of the floor in my front room, which my grandmother had always referred to as "the parlor." It was a beautiful parquet floor gone dark with years of varnish and stains and footsteps, and I knew the room would be a lot brighter if I sanded it down and coated it with clear shellac.

So I rented a belt sander from the hardware store around the corner (one of the few tools Eddie Everything did not have), donned a dust mask and got down to it.

It was a loud machine, and you had to keep moving it evenly to avoid gouging the wood. I had about a third of the floor done when I was jolted by a hand on my shoulder.

I shut off the sander, pulled off my mask. "Jesus, Eddie!"

"Sorry, Mr. A., but there's a cop bangin' on the front door!"

"A *cop?*"

He nodded. "Big guy in a uniform. Looks mean."

More banging.

"What the hell could he want?"

Eddie hesitated. "Maybe he heard you were gettin' chickens."

"How the hell would he know that?"

"Hey, somebody sees me buildin' a coop, they make a phone call . . . it ain't complicated, man!"

"Go out the back way. I'll deal with the cop."

Eddie hurried away. A heavy fist continued to bang on the door until I opened it, and there indeed stood a cop almost as wide as the doorway, and half a head taller than me. He would have been a terrifying sight if his face hadn't broken out in a friendly smile that was oddly familiar.

"Hey, Mr. Ambrosio, how ya doin' ? Remember me?"

He pointed to his name tag, *DEBOWSKI*, and I burst out laughing. I was pleased, amused and relieved to be reunited with the man who'd escorted me down from the top of the Brooklyn Bridge.

"Billy!" I said, extending my hand for a shake, "what the hell are you doing here?"

"I could ask you the same thing," he replied, and then we were both laughing as I urged him to come inside for a cup of coffee.

He'd found out where I lived from his friend Nicky Gallo, Johnny's son, and wondered if I could do him a favor.

"Name it," I said, and from his backpack he took out one of my books. It happened to be one of my personal favorites: *Sammy Suitcase and the Big Bully*, in which our hero, the new kid in school, teaches a lesson to the class bully.

This bully steals one of his classmate's lunches every day—literally victimizing the kids in alphabetical order. So Sammy knows exactly which day his lunch is going to be stolen, and that morning he stirs a load of pepper into the peanut butter in his sandwich—and begs the bully not to steal it. When the bully bites into the sandwich and feels that his mouth is on fire, he's stunned to find that his thermos has been emptied of its nice, cold lemonade by—who else?— Sammy Suitcase!

Fourteen ninety-five at Barnes & Noble. I waved the book in Billy's face.

"You're a little old for this kind of literature, aren't you?"

"Yeah, well, the thing is, I'm datin' this woman and she's got a seven-year-old son, and he gets picked on, so this kid loves your books, 'cause Sammy always knows what to do in a bad situation. Next week is his birthday . . . would you mind signin' this one for him?"

I took pen in hand. "What's the boy's name?"

"Hector. Jesus, he's not gonna believe this!"

"Should I write him a little note?"

"Aw, that'd be fuckin' great."

I wrote: *Hector, I wish you a happy birthday and I hope you enjoy this story. Best wishes, Joseph Ambrosio.*

Billy read the inscription. "He'll go wild! Thanks, Joe."

"You're a brave man, dating a woman with a young child."

Billy's eyes widened and his smile evaporated. "Think I should stop seein' her?"

He was serious. Just like that, he was ready to dump her, if I gave the word. Unbelievable!

"No, no! I'm just saying, when there's a kid involved it can get . . . complicated."

"You're right. Maybe I should break it off."

"I'm not right! I don't even know these people!"

He was actually starting to sweat. He rubbed his damp face with trembling hands. "Jesus Christ, what the hell am I *doin'?* All the single women in New York, I gotta go and find one with a kid!"

"You're doing a nice thing for Hector, that's what you're doing. Take it easy, Billy, everything's fine."

I thought I'd show him the work I was doing on the parlor floor to calm him down, or at least distract him. He regarded the half-sanded surface and said, "Jeez, they don't make 'em like that anymore, do they? What's that, oak?"

"I think so."

"Nothin' but linoleum on my floors."

The panic returned to his face. "That's another thing. She's hintin' about movin' into my house with Hector. You believe that? Two months we're dating, and already she's movin' in with her son! Instant family! Whadda you think about that?"

I shrugged. "Seems a little soon to me."

"Fuckin'-A right it's too soon! Who the fuck does she think she is? Christ Almighty, I gotta end this mess!"

Through the parlor window we saw a police car pull up, a cherry-red light flashing on its roof.

"That's my partner," Billy said. "I gotta go. Great seein' you, Joe." He shook my hand and raced for the door. I ran after him, down the stoop and all the way to the squad car, which took off as soon as he jumped inside.

"Billy, wait!" I screamed, running after the car. His partner jammed on the brakes as they reached Atlantic Avenue and Billy rolled down his window.

"You forgot this," I said, handing him my book.

He smacked himself on the forehead. "Oh, shit! Don't know if I'm gonna give it to him now, but thanks, Joe, thanks anyway."

His partner hit the gas, and just like that they were gone.

I went back to work on the floor, sore in my hands and shoulders by the time I got it all sanded down. Eddie Everything was gone for the afternoon, spooked by the sight of a cop. The chicken-coop project would be another day behind schedule.

I vacuumed the floor, then laid down a coat of clear shellac. It looked great in the late-afternoon sunshine, and made a bright room even brighter. Then I took a shower before hitting my laptop computer with another project that had become my obsession:

The search for Carmela "Mel" DiGiovanna, the little girl who'd been my very best friend on Shepherd Avenue, back in the day.

She was a year older than me, an orphan and a tomboy who'd lost her parents in a car crash and lived with an aunt up the block. We did everything together on those hot summer days, including playing a game of doctor in my grandfather's garage that ended suddenly when that deacon from St. Rita's caught us standing there naked.

Mel was shipped out to another aunt on Long Island, and from there to a set of relatives in Arizona, and that's the last I knew of her.

Where to start on a trail gone cold, half a century ago? At least *DiGiovanna* was an unusual name, unlike *Gallo*, but what if she'd gotten married and taken another name?

I checked phone listings in Arizona and on Long Island. No dice. I Googled her name and got nothing.

I was down to Facebook and halfheartedly punched in her name. Up popped CARMELA DIGIOVANNA BOCCABELLA, along with a head shot of a woman with short gray hair and a big smile.

Her nose was now tiny, but the features surrounding the gap where it had stood were unmistakable. The fury in those eyes, the smile that went all the way to her back molars ... this was my very first girlfriend, all right.

Status: single. Residence: Manhattan, New York.

My God. Mel was in the city.

I'd have to join Facebook in order to leave her a message, and I didn't want to do that, so I went to the residential listings in Manhattan and found the only *C. Boccabella* in the book, an address on Central Park West.

The phone rang just once. "Hello?"

She didn't sound happy, as if she were anticipating an annoying sales pitch.

"Is this Mel?" I ventured.

"Who the hell is this?"

It was Mel, all right.

"Uh ... this is Joe Ambrosio. Do you remember me? From Brooklyn? Shepherd Avenue, a long time ago?"

Heavy breathing. "Oh my God. Joey. *Joey!"*

"Hey! How are you, Mel?"

"Oh ... my ... *God!"*

"I finally tracked you down!"

"Joey! Where are you?"

"I'm here, in New York. I know this is out of the blue, but I was wondering if I could see you some time."

"Yeah, sure. Now."

"Excuse me?"

"Now! Get over here, we're having dinner at my place."

It was amazing. Nothing had changed. I was still doing whatever she said we were doing, when she said we were doing it. I had no choice!

It was wonderful.

She gave me her address and insisted that I get my ass over to her apartment immediately.

I laughed out loud. "Jeez, Mel, it's just like the old days. You tell me what to do, and I do it."

"Stop complaining. It's penthouse B. The doorman'll expect you."

A doorman and a penthouse. Looked like my old friend had done all right for herself.

Chapter Seventeen

It was a tall white building in the high seventies on Central Park West, like a giant wedding cake with windows. Freshly showered and shaved, I carried a bottle of good white wine and a cone of small red roses as I entered the immaculate lobby.

It had a black marble floor that undoubtedly got buffed every day, and a doorman with gold braid on his cap and on his shoulders. He called Mel's apartment on the intercom phone, then smiled and spoke those three words everyone who visits a building like this dreams of hearing:

"Go right up."

A quick elevator ride to the penthouse floor, thirty-four stories up—my ears actually popped, and when the doors opened she stood at the end of the hall in a simple black dress and high heels.

And her hands were on her hips just like in the old days, whenever she was bracing for a confrontation. On trembling legs I walked right up to Mel, and despite her high heels I towered over her.

"The ultimate tomboy in heels and a dress," I said. "Never thought I'd see the day."

"Joey." She raised her hands to my face and held my cheeks, as if to make sure I wasn't an illusion. "I can't believe it's you!"

"Hey, didn't you used to be taller than me?"

"Yeah."

"Well, I can't believe I was ever afraid of a shrimp like you."

She cackled, threw herself in my arms and hugged me with the kind of strength women get from obsessive gym workouts.

"I'm little, but I can still beat you up!"

"Don't I know it!" I laughed and the ice, if ever there had been any, was broken.

* * *

Dinner on her roof terrace, overlooking Central Park: Cornish game hens, wild rice, and the best arugula and tomato salad I'd ever tasted, cooked and served by a skinny young man with a shaved head and a white smock who grinned like crazy but never spoke a word.

Mel ate with real gusto, explaining that between treadmill running and something called "soul cycling" she could eat whatever she liked without gaining weight.

Her life since Shepherd Avenue brought new meaning to the word *turbulent*. The last I'd known, she'd been shunted out to relatives in Tucson, Arizona. Turns out she made life so miserable for those sunbaked cousins that she was bounced right back to her Long Island relatives within a few months.

But that didn't bring peace. She ran away from home four times by the time she was seventeen, and on her eighteenth birthday she quit school and headed for San Francisco on money she'd saved working at McDonald's.

In San Francisco she knocked around from job to job, eventually becoming a waitress at a fish restaurant. The owner of the restaurant, ten years older than Mel, fell in love with her. They married when she was twenty, and with Mel's encouragement—or "nagging," she admitted with a giggle—her husband eventually expanded the business to ten restaurants on the West Coast.

They were rich. They had three children and four grandchildren before the husband dropped dead of a heart attack last year, in the bedroom of his latest girlfriend.

"So," said Mel, coming up for air, "I said to myself, What the hell, I'm goin' back to New York. Always wanted to live in Manhattan, so I sold the restaurants and bought this place."

Three bedrooms (for when her kids and grandkids came to visit), a sunken living room and drop-dead views of the city. I gestured toward the park, golden-green in the early-evening sunlight.

"Not bad for your first New York apartment."

"Yeah, until I find something better."

I hesitated before asking, "Your husband died with his girlfriend?"

"Oh yeah. He came and he went." She toasted the sky with her wineglass.

"You don't seem too upset."

"I was upset after the funeral, when his girlfriend tried to claim their little love nest belonged to her. I straightened her out, don't worry about that."

She smiled, and her eyes flashed with the same fury I remembered when I'd strike her out playing stickball. In those days she had fast hands, and I'd never even see the punch to my stomach coming.

"What'd you do?" I dared to ask. "Beat her up?"

"In a manner of speaking."

"Jesus, Mel!"

We both laughed. Then she shrugged and said, "Hey, he wasn't a bad guy, my Mario, but we kinda drifted apart. That'll happen after forty years together. Only guy who ever asked me to marry him."

"Not true, Mel. I asked you."

"No, you didn't. I'm the one who told you we were gonna get married someday, Joey."

I laughed, remembering. "That's right. You always called the shots."

"I was older than you."

"Still are."

"Screw you for reminding me. Sixty-one. Christ. Ever heard of this dating website, Golden Years?"

"I don't do that stuff."

"Oh no? Got a girlfriend?"

"Sort of."

"Lucky you. I just joined this website. Jesus, the losers I'm meeting! Always fatter and balder than the pictures they put up. Not that I'm any prize."

We fell silent. How strange this was! We'd lived a vivid few months together as children before being torn apart, and now here we were, suddenly reuniting as graying geezers.

It was like being in a weird play where nobody knew their lines. We'd shared an overture and were now sharing a finale, with no acts in between. What might those acts have been like if we'd been together through adolescence and young adulthood? We'd never know, and there was no point in wondering. *Too Late* might as well have been tattooed across our foreheads.

Maybe that's why there was no sexual tension between us. We were like two old soldiers, sharing war stories from the battles we'd lived through, and then I remembered one major battle she'd missed.

I leaned close and patted the back of her hand. "Hey. Bet you didn't know I tried running away from Shepherd Avenue to be with you."

Her eyes widened. "Are you shitting me?"

I told her all about the money I'd saved collecting deposit bottles, and how I had a map of the United States so I could find Arizona, and how I'd sneaked out in the dead of night but tripped and fell running for the elevated subway, with my grandmother in hot pursuit. Mel was blown away.

"Holy shit! That's, like, the most romantic thing I've ever heard!"

"Imagine if by some miracle I'd made it?"

She exhaled, long and hard. "Yeah, imagine."

I didn't think mosquitoes could fly that high, but they could, so to avoid being bitten we moved inside, where Mel showed me pictures of her children and grandchildren, living all over the country. I had no pictures of my daughter.

"I take it you're divorced."

"I don't believe in divorce, Mel, which is why I never married."

"Joey, you're such a knucklehead."

Then I told her all about my Brooklyn Bridge fiasco, which she never knew about, because she never read the papers or watched the news. Mel shook her head in wonder over my mad deed, and was astonished by my career as a children's-book author.

"Christ! You must really have talent. I remember those pictures you used to paint."

"That was the start. My father's old art supplies. Connie gave 'em to me."

"Well, she was bound to do one good thing, wasn't she?"

"Ahh, she wasn't so bad."

"Loyalty. I like that in a man."

Mel poured wine from the bottle I'd brought. "You haven't mentioned my nose."

"That's because it isn't there anymore."

She chuckled. "Was that a king-sized honker, or what?"

"It had character."

"I passed it on to one of my sons and two of my grandchildren. Genes, huh? There's no stopping 'em! Your face is the same, Joey. Few lines, that's all. Same big, sad eyes."

"The Ambrosios have the sadness gene. Dominant on both sides."

"Wiseass . . . ever wonder whatever happened to that priest who caught us in the garage?"

"Deacon Sullivan."

"That's the guy!"

"Died of AIDS, about twenty years ago."

"No kiddin'? Can't say I'm too surprised. He had tendencies, you know? My oldest grandson, sixteen years old, he's headin' that way. Loves his show tunes . . . hey, it's no big deal being gay anymore, right? They're everywhere. I'm thinkin' it's the hormones they inject in the cattle these days. Boy eats a hamburger, next thing you know, he's tap-dancin' on a tabletop, singing 'What I Did for Love.' What's so funny?"

I was laughing so hard I could barely breathe. "Mel," I said when the fit passed, "it's been wonderful seeing you, and I haven't laughed like that in years, but I do have something shocking to tell you."

"Oh really? More shocking than climbing the Brooklyn Bridge to scatter your father's ashes?"

Suddenly the grinning servant was in front of us, serving coffee and cake before vanishing silently on slippered feet. Mel rolled her eyes at the intrusion.

"I gotta put a bell on him," Mel said when he was gone. "He's great, but I can never hear him comin'. He just appears. Come on, Joey what's so damn shocking?"

I sipped coffee and leaned close to her. "I bought my grandparents' old house on Shepherd Avenue, and that's where I live now."

Silence. Her smile collapsed and her face darkened, as if a shadow had fallen across it.

"You do not!" she cried.

"I do too!"

What were we, kids again?

"Joey, pardon my mouth, but that is a bullshit thing to say."

"It isn't." I held up my right hand, like a witness being sworn in. "It's the truth. I'm living on Shepherd Avenue again."

"Why would you do a crazy thing like that?"

An unanswerable question, so I ignored it.

"I'm fixing it up real nice, and when it's done I'm hoping you'll come over for dinner."

She ignored her coffee and poured herself another glass of wine. "Is your rooftop strong?"

I was puzzled. "What do you mean, strong?"

"Strong enough for a helicopter to land on it? Because that's the only safe way to get to that neighborhood, Joey."

"Come on! It's not that bad."

Mel made a snorting sound. "It was getting bad when I left, and that's a long time ago! Don't tell me East New York is becoming gentrified!"

"Maybe not, but I'm sleeping better than I have in years."

"Oh, Jesus!"

"Aren't you curious, Mel? A big part of our lives happened on Shepherd Avenue. I had dreams about it for fifty years."

"You mean nightmares, don't you?"

"Please come."

Her hand trembled as she lifted her wineglass to her lips.

"I gotta think about it, Joey. I really do." She jerked a thumb over her shoulder to indicate the past. "That part of my life . . ." She actually shivered, though the night was far from chilly. "Not sure I want to stroll down that memory lane."

"You might be surprised."

"We'll see. We'll see."

She spoke those words in a cold, flat voice. This was the Mel I knew: tough and stubborn, a true survivor. I was never going to talk her into coming to Shepherd Avenue. She'd do it or she wouldn't, and that was that.

It was getting late. I told her I had to get going, rose to my feet and gave her a hug.

"Great seeing you, Mel. I'll call you when the house is done."

"Yeah, you do that."

We linked elbows as she walked me to the elevator. She needed to lean on me. My shocking news had sapped her strength.

"Hey," she said softly, "do you remember how we wrote each other those letters after they took me away from Shepherd Avenue?"

"Oh yeah."

"Wish to God I'd saved those letters."

"Me too."

"How come we always save shit, and lose the good stuff?"

"Great question."

She kissed my cheek, embraced me one more time.

"Joey. That time you ran away to be with me . . ."

"Yeah?"

"Well . . . I wish you hadn't tripped."

She blinked back tears, and then the elevator arrived and I was plummeting back to Planet Earth, thirty-four stories below, trying to blink back my own tears so the doorman wouldn't see them on my way out.

Chapter Eighteen

It was past ten when I got back to Shepherd Avenue, and moments after I was in the house there was a knock on my door.

It could only be one person, and that's who it was.

"Hurry up and let me in!" Rose hissed when I opened the door, and as she brushed past me to get inside she stopped and sniffed at me the way a dog might.

"Perfume? Is that *perfume* I'm smellin'?"

I hadn't even noticed it. Mel must have been wearing perfume, which rubbed off when she hugged me.

"I guess it is."

"You had a date?"

"I was visiting an old friend."

"A woman."

"A woman I hadn't seen in fifty years. She used to live on this block."

"You got all dressed up for her, huh?"

"Rose, nothing happened."

"Hey, I don't give a shit what you do."

"I didn't do anything but catch up with an old friend. Come on, let's go to the kitchen."

I tried to guide her by the elbow, but she yanked it away from me. So I walked to the kitchen alone, praying she would follow, which she did, sulking all the way.

We sat at the table. I got us a couple of beers, and after the first sip Rose took a deep breath and suddenly made a scrunched-up face.

"Man, what's that smell?"

"I sanded down the parlor floor today. That's the varnish, probably still drying."

"Whoo! What a stink! I like the perfume better."

"You going to break my balls about that? I told you the truth. I went to see an old friend. She was eleven the last time I saw her."

"Yeah? How's she look now?"

"Old, like me."

"I'll bet."

"Hey. Give me a break here, Rose. For all I knew, you were never coming back. Justin left three days ago, and I haven't seen you in three days."

She finished her beer, setting the bottle down gently on the table.

"I been cryin' for three days, missin' my boy," she said in a broken voice, and then those fresh tears flowing down her cheeks made it a fourth straight day of crying, and all I could do was hold her until it was time to go to bed.

Which we did together, but once again she fled into the night, saying, "I'll see you soon, Jo-Jo," refusing as always to stay until morning, even though her beloved son was playing baseball 2400 miles away, and even though he knew all about us and was cool with it.

I wanted to tell her that, but I'd promised Justin I wouldn't. When a man gives his word as seldom as I do, he likes to keep it.

And if she'd stayed until morning she would have seen an amazing sight outside my bedroom window, which made me cry out with joy.

Project Chicken Coop was complete.

Eddie Everything was proud of himself. "Came back last night and worked until nine o'clock," he said. "Good thing I had a flashlight."

"Eddie, it looks great."

It was true. A four-foot chicken-wire fence surrounded the backyard, and the coop itself was simple but functional, with a slanted rain roof and a series of perches for the birds.

Eddie had scattered a layer of straw across its floor, assuring me the birds would make their own nests.

"How about the birds?" I dared to ask. "Any time soon?"

He clapped a hand on my shoulder and winked dramatically.

"I'm gettin' 'em tonight, after dark. And you gotta come with me."

"What for?"

"Need a lookout, my friend, and that's you."

"Eddie. Is this a dangerous mission?"

"No! Not at all." He laughed, his big white lima-bean teeth shining in the morning sun. "Unless we fuck up," he added.

He told me he'd be back that night and that I should wear dark clothing, which was lucky, because I didn't have any other kind.

In the midst of all this excitement I nearly forgot my appointment with Dr. Rosensohn. Luckily the elevated train to Manhattan arrived as soon as I reached the platform, and I got to his office right on time.

The last thing I needed on my record was a parole violation, especially just before the great chicken caper.

It started off as a fairly sedate session. I filled him in on my Internet searches for Johnny Gallo and Mel DiGiovanna, and the visits that followed.

He ventured a smile. "What made you do such a thing?"

"I'd say I'm just catching up with old friends from Shepherd Avenue."

"How's that working out?"

"Do you know Raymond Chandler, the mystery writer?"

"One of my favorites."

"Chandler said, 'The swans of our childhood were probably just pigeons.' "

He chuckled in appreciation. "What does that mean to you?"

"It means: Be prepared to be shocked when you see someone you haven't seen in half a century. Especially an old girlfriend."

His eyebrows rose. "This Mel person was your girlfriend?"

I rolled my eyes. I didn't feel like going into the whole business of us getting caught playing doctor, so I shrugged and said, "I was ten, she was eleven. She moved away from Shepherd Avenue, and I never saw her again until yesterday."

Rosensohn was wearing his "hmm" expression. "Living in the past is always risky, Mr. Ambrosio."

"That's not what I'm doing."

"But you did look up an old girlfriend. There's so much of that going on these days, with social media—"

"I have a new girlfriend, Doc."

I was instantly pissed off at myself. I hadn't meant to tell him about Rose, but my stupid ego got the better of me. I had to show him I still had what it took, at age sixty. Idiot!

Rosensohn seemed intrigued. "Tell me about her."

"Well, she's younger than me, but who isn't?"

"How much younger?"

I sighed. I was in this deep, so I might as well go all the way. "Young enough to be my daughter, which freaks me out a little."

"Have you seen your daughter yet?"

"No. Let's leave that one alone, please."

"Where'd you meet this new woman?"

"She lives across the street."

"Black?"

"Puerto Rican. I thought you guys were supposed to be blind to race and color."

"We're also supposed to tell you that everything's your mother's fault. Is this a serious relationship?"

"I don't know."

"Yes, you do."

It was time to stun the shrink.

"Basically, she just knocks on my door at night when she wants sex. And she always leaves before morning."

It worked. Rosensohn's mouth literally fell open. "Come on!"

"Swear to God."

"And you're okay with that?"

"I wouldn't mind being allowed to knock on her door once in a while, but that's not the deal."

"So she's the one calling the shots."

"Yeah. And that's a first for me."

He leaned back, making his swivel chair creak. I'm convinced he never oiled that chair because the squeak gave dramatic punctuation to whatever words he was about to speak, which in this case were these:

"Why do you suppose you've become involved with a woman so much younger than you?"

"It just happened."

"Nothing just *happens*, Mr. Ambrosio."

"Aw, why don't we save some time here? Just give me your theory."

"Well, chances are you won't outlive her."

I had to laugh. "That's pretty much a lock."

He leaned forward, making his chair squeak in a different, more ominous tone.

"What I'm saying," he said softly, "is that no matter what happens in this relationship you probably won't have to deal with another death, which as we know you're not very good at."

I hated it when he was right.

"Bull's-eye, Doc! Are we done for the day?"

He glanced at his watch. "We are. Don't be upset by what I said. It's just a perception."

"I'm not upset. You were worth your two bills today. I mean that."

I left without another word, though I was tempted to tell him I had to get back to Brooklyn to serve as a lookout in an after-hours black-market chicken heist.

Chapter Nineteen

Eddie Everything wouldn't tell me where we were going. It was past ten p.m. as we rattled along in his station wagon, the two of us dressed in black, a cigarette dangling from Eddie's lips as he squinted against the smoke and checked the rearview mirror every few blocks.

"Do you think we're being followed?"

"You never know, man."

"This is crazy, Eddie! When I went with my grandfather to get live chickens we did it in broad daylight."

"Different world."

"Yes, but is all this drama really necessary? You look as if you're about to rob a bank!"

He looked at me as if I were a stupid child who just didn't get it.

"We're about to break the law, Mr. A. I like to get serious before I do that."

"Worst-case scenario, we get caught transporting live poultry. What's the penalty for that, a fine? A little community service?"

He snorted. "Me, I'm gone. Kicked outta the fuckin' country."

"What the hell does *that* mean?"

He laughed out loud, the way you do about something that isn't funny. "I ain't no citizen, Mr. A!"

"Oh."

"*Oh*, he says. Nice. We get arrested on this caper, I go to trial, you can be a good character witness for me. Stand up in court and tell the judge, 'Oh.'"

"Eddie, I had no idea!"

"Well, now you know."

As the miles rolled on Eddie filled me in on his history, beginning with a ride on a leaky raft from Cuba all the way to Miami, thirty years earlier, when he was just seventeen. He made his way north, keeping his head low until he got to Brooklyn, where he'd heard of a Cuban community that looked after its own. He worked a variety of odd jobs, all off the books, staying with his newfound friends until he eventually rented an upstairs floor in a house on Shepherd Avenue from someone who knew someone who knew someone . . .

It was a tangled tale, but after all these years it shook out this way: Eddie Everything had a place to live and a garage to keep his car and his tools safe. No wife, no kids, no documentation of any kind to prove his existence.

This blew my mind as we rambled along Atlantic Avenue.

"So you don't have a driver's license."

"Negative."

"Maybe I should be driving."

"No way, Mr. A."

"No Social Security number, no passport?"

"Double-negative."

"So what happens if you get sick and have to go to the hospital?"

"I don't get sick," he replied, taking a last drag from his cigarette and throwing the butt out his window. "No time for that."

"How do you *do* it, Eddie? I'd be freaking out in your shoes!"

He smiled, as if he'd been hoping I'd say that.

"You get here the way I got here, you don't freak out. A leaky raft, middle o' the night, sharks all around, grown men cryin' like babies, no land in sight . . ."

Eddie chuckled, lit another cigarette. "Knew if I made it to shore, I'd never worry again. Stepped on that Florida sand and never asked God for nothin' since. Got all I need, and if I need more, I can get it. Life is good, man. God bless America."

"I guess I get your point."

He jabbed his cigarette in my direction. "You, *you* should be as careful as me, man! Ain't you still on probation for that bridge thing?"

Holy shit. Eddie had a point.

"Jesus, I hadn't thought of that!"

"Well, think about it. Stay on your toes. Do as I say and nothin' bad can happen."

He slipped me a sly wink. "Now let's get these motherfuckin' chickens. My man here wants his fresh eggs, he's gonna get 'em!"

We rode deeper and deeper into the Brooklyn night, at last pulling up into the lot outside an industrial zone of red brick buildings shuttered for the night. In the midst of those buildings was one with a hand-painted sign saying *LIVE POULTRY* over the front door, gated shut for the night, but that wasn't the door we were headed for anyway.

Eddie parked in the darkest part of the lot and led the way around to the back of the poultry building, through a path of waist-high weeds littered with abandoned tires. We reached a rusty metal door and Eddie knocked on it three times.

It opened a crack. He whispered something in Spanish, and the guy on the other side of the door swung it open just long enough for the two of us to plunge inside.

We were in a huge windowless room with cinder-block walls, illuminated by humming overhead lights. Stacked against the walls were sacks of cracked corn and crates of live chickens, all of them clucking like crazy. The stench was enough to make my eyes water. Eddie hugged the man who'd let us in, a short guy in knee-high rubber boots who'd just finished hosing down the floor.

"Nando, say hello to Mr. Ambrosio."

I shook hands with Nando, whose grip made my knuckles tingle. He turned to Eddie.

"This guy cool?"

"Cool enough."

"Awright, I got your birds right here."

He dragged a wooden crate to the middle of the floor, where the light was best. Inside were six white chickens, about half the size of the ones crammed into the rest of the crates.

Eddie turned to me for my approval.

"Hang on," I said. "These are much smaller than the rest of the birds."

Eddie turned to Nando. "Why you givin' us such little chickens?"

Nando rolled his eyes. "'Cause my boss won't notice 'em missin'. Besides, what do you care? Know how fast these suckers grow?"

Great. We were not only buying illegal, undersized chickens, we were buying stolen birds from a thieving employee.

"Come on, guys, we got a deal or what?" Nando asked. "I'm stickin' my neck out here. Nothin's supposed to leave this place alive. And I hadda go through every crate to find these little guys."

"Guys?" I said. "No roosters, Nando, that was the deal!"

Nando arched his back. "Workin' here ten years, you think I don't know the difference between a hen and a rooster? They're all hens! You want 'em, say the word. Otherwise, have a nice night, fellows."

Eddie pulled me to a corner for a private conference.

"Take the deal, Mr. A."

"I feel like I'm getting shafted."

"Nando's all right. The birds will grow. Here." He thrust two fifties into my hand. "You pay him. He'll like that. And let's get the fuck outta here, the stink is killin' me."

I returned to Nando, who stood with one foot up on the bird crate, his brawny arms folded across his chest.

He saw the fifties in my hand and reached for the money, but I pulled it back.

"Throw in a sack of corn and it's a deal."

Eddie couldn't muffle a laugh. Nando shrugged.

"What the fuck, he never counts the sacks."

I slapped the bills into Nando's hand. Eddie carried the crate and I carried a twenty-pound sack of corn. We stopped right outside the door we'd come through, where Eddie instructed me to carry the corn to the car and put it in the back seat. Then I was to look in all directions to make sure no cop cars were in sight, open the tailgate and whistle to let him know the coast was clear.

I looked. I whistled. Walking briskly, but not running, Eddie reached the car, slid the crate into the back, tossed a blanket over it and closed the tailgate.

And we were on our way home, with our clucking cargo.

We didn't speak for a mile or two. Then Eddie said, "You got some balls, gettin' Nando to throw in a sack o' corn. Coulda fucked up the whole deal right there."

"Eddie, correct me if I'm wrong, but didn't you say the price for the birds was two hundred dollars?"

"Sure."

"I paid Nando a hundred."

"The rest is my commission." He braked the car, looking at me wide-eyed. "You want your other hundred back? That's cool, I'll let you and your birds out right here. Bus'll be along in about an hour."

"Forget it, forget it. You're right. I'm just a little wound up."

"You did fine, Mr. A. You got what you wanted."

We continued rolling along and hit a bump, causing a chorus of frantic clucking.

"Shut up, ladies," Eddie said over his shoulder. "You don't know how lucky you are. Ain't nobody broilin' your asses anytime soon."

When we reached Shepherd Avenue I again checked for cops in all directions before Eddie carried our illegal cargo to the backyard. He opened the crate in the middle of the yard and the birds were free, clucking gently as they scurried about in the moonlight.

I filled big metal bowls with water and corn and set them inside the coop. The birds went crazy, shoving each other aside as they fought for food and drink.

I watched in fascination. Eddie put his arm across my shoulders, partners in crime. "You want the crate, boss?"

"Take it."

"You happy now, man?"

"I guess so."

"Can't guess about happiness. You're happy or you ain't."

"Well, I'm not unhappy."

He chuckled. "Man, you're one strange dude, Mr. A."

"I'm just hoping your friend knows his business, and there aren't any roosters in that bunch."

Eddie laughed, hoisting the empty crate. "You'll find out when the sun rises. You hear crowing, you got a problem."

I could barely sleep that night. I was fully awake by dawn, tensed up in anticipation of cock-a-doodle-do-ing.

There wasn't any. Nando knew his stuff, just as the guy who'd sold chickens to my grandfather fifty years earlier had known *his* stuff.

The six little birds running around in my backyard turned out to be hens, every one of them.

I had my chickens. Now it was just a question of when they'd start laying, but that was nothing to stress over. I wasn't going anywhere.

Chapter Twenty

For the next few days I was obsessed with my chickens. I fed them, watered them, watched them, just as I had when I was a kid. There was something comforting about the sight of them strutting around, scratching the ground.

They felt they were home. I was jealous. I wanted to feel as they did.

Eddie Everything dropped by to check them out.

"Man, they got it made."

"You got that right."

"Gonna need more corn soon."

"I think I'll just give them table scraps when I run out."

"Yeah, they'll eat anything."

There was a knock on the door that afternoon and I figured it would be Rose, who generally waited three or four days between visits, but then I realized Rose wouldn't drop by until after dark. I opened the door and a tall, slender young man with intense brown eyes and a wide brow stood there, looking at me as if I owed him money.

An agent with the ASPCA, I told myself, here to slap me with a summons for the chickens! One of my neighbors had dropped a dime on me, but which one? I really didn't need this shit.

"Mr. Ambrosio?" he asked, the way a lawyer asks a question when he already knows the answer.

I nodded, and he seemed relieved. "I'm a friend of Taylor's. May I come in?"

I could feel my heart pounding at the bottom of my throat. "Is my daughter all right?"

"She's fine, she's fine!"

"Come in."

I brought him to the kitchen table, where we sat across from each other like hostage negotiators. He introduced himself as Kevin Caldwell.

"What's going on? Are you a cop?"

"A cop? No, I told you, I'm a friend of your daughter's! I know you two are . . . estranged? Is that the right word?"

"Close enough." I swallowed, waiting for the pounding in my throat to recede. "So now, I'm guessing you're here on behalf of my daughter."

He shook his head. "I just wanted to meet you."

"Why?"

He shrugged. "Maybe so I can understand Taylor better."

That seemed like a weird answer. "How did you find me?"

"From the address on the letter you sent to her."

I'd written to Taylor inviting her to Shepherd Avenue, figuring that words on a page might have greater impact than another chilly phone call.

"You're reading my daughter's mail?"

"She showed me the letter."

"That was nice of her."

He laid his hands flat on the table. "All right, I'm just going to say it." He took a deep breath. "We live together, Mr. Ambrosio."

I sank back in my chair. "You're her boyfriend?" I asked, with my usual gift for grasping the obvious.

He nodded. "Yeah. For about six months, now."

I was so far behind in my daughter's life that it was hard for me to imagine her in a relationship. She was still a child to me, a twenty-seven-year-old child. I actually scratched my head, like a befuddled hillbilly.

"Are you two . . . married?"

He shook his head. "No reason for that. Marriage usually doesn't work, and we have separate health plans, so what's the point?"

"I'm with you on that."

He reached across the table to pat the back of my hand. "I realize this is a lot to absorb, Mr. Ambrosio."

"What is it you want, Kevin?"

"A little healing, I guess." His eyes grew shiny with tears. "This situation between you and Taylor isn't good."

I rose from the table and blinked back tears of my own. "Come with me," I said, leading the way downstairs. "I have to feed my chickens."

"Chickens?"

His mind was blown by the sight of the coop and the birds. I lifted the corn sack and was about to fill the metal bowl when Kevin stopped me.

"Mind if I do this?"

He took the sack from me, grabbed a fistful of corn and scattered it wide around the yard. The birds raced in all directions to feed.

"You don't want to dump the corn into a bowl," he said. "If it's all in one place, the dominant birds get it all and the others starve."

"How would you know a thing like that?"

"Grew up on a farm in Pennsylvania."

"What's a Pennsylvania farm boy doing in the big, bad city?"

He threw more corn. "Came here to make it as an actor. Too tall, too skinny, too whatever."

"So you gave it up."

"Not exactly. I'm a personal trainer. I act as if I can get my fat clients into shape. It's a pretty good performance, most of the time."

He turned to me with a closed-mouth smile, crooked on one side: the smile of a person who could find victory within defeat, and didn't care if anybody else saw it that way.

At that moment, Kevin Caldwell won me over.

Suddenly it started to rain. The birds hurried into their coop, and Kevin and I went inside.

Back in the kitchen I uncorked a bottle of red wine. "My grandfather made wine in the basement of this house," I said. "Rough peasant stuff, from a big wooden barrel. This is a lot smoother."

"None for me, thanks."

"You going to make me drink alone?"

"I don't drink."

"At all?"

He hesitated. "I'm a recovering alcoholic. Sober two and a half years, now."

He wasn't ashamed and he wasn't proud. He was simply stating a fact.

"Good for you," I said at last. I was holding the wine bottle in both hands, like an altar boy who's forgotten his moves. Kevin chuckled.

"Go ahead, have your wine. I can be around it."

I poured myself a glass. "I take it Taylor knows about your . . . alcohol situation."

For the first time, a look of concern crossed Kevin's face. He fought with himself over whether or not to tell me, and suddenly it was out.

"Truth is, we met at a meeting."

It didn't hit me at first, and then it did, like the fucking night train. An Alcoholics Anonymous meeting. My one and only child was an alcoholic who stood up in church basements, drank bad coffee and confessed her problem to strangers.

"Holy shit," I breathed.

Kevin eased me into a chair, like a corner man guiding a dazed boxer between rounds. I took a long swallow of wine.

"Are you all right, sir?"

"I had no idea."

"We all hide it."

"This is a hell of a punch, know what I mean?"

"I know what you mean."

"Mr. Ambrosio—"

"Joe! Call me Joe. We're practically in-laws!"

Kevin laughed. "You got a Coke for me, Joe?"

"Water's all I can offer, besides coffee."

"Water'll do."

I sipped wine while Kevin drank water and told me about Taylor's drinking history. She'd been dry for six months, after a few years of leaning hard on the vodka bottle.

I'd never even imagined my daughter drinking, much less being a fall-down drunk. And Kevin couldn't tell me anything about what Taylor had been like on the bottle, since they'd met at AA after they'd both quit.

"Her mother's death brought the problem to a head," he said.

"And my not going to the funeral didn't help."

"I didn't say that."

"You didn't have to."

"Joe, your daughter's doing well now, and I want you to know that I love her very much."

By this time I'd knocked off half that bottle of wine, so I was a little fuzzy, but that didn't diminish the punch in his words.

"I love her, too."

"You've got to call her."

"I did. She instructed me to wait for her to call."

"I wouldn't obey that particular instruction, if I were you."

"She has my number, Kevin. It's her move."

He rolled his eyes and got to his feet. "You're both so stubborn!"

"It's an Ambrosio specialty."

"Someone has to make a move!"

Now he was shouting at me. What balls! I was both impressed and convinced as I got to my feet.

"Okay, Kevin. You made the move, and I appreciate it, so now *I'll* make the move."

I got up to shake his hand, a gesture that morphed into an embrace. It was like hugging a tin soldier, all hard angles. "I'll call her. And I won't tell her you told me about her . . . problem."

Kevin broke the embrace. "No, that's all right. Go ahead and tell her. I'm going to tell her I came here today, and told you everything."

"Really?"

Now his smile was sad, pitying. "We tell each other everything, Joe. That's what people do when they're in love."

I walked him to the front stoop. The rain had stopped and there was a blissful freshness to the air. I watched Kevin trot up Shepherd Avenue, toward the elevated train. Halfway up the block he suddenly turned and ran back to my house, stopping at the stoop but continuing to run in place. I braced myself for something profound.

"Remember, scatter the food when you feed those chickens!" he said, and then he turned and sprinted away.

I felt wobbly on my feet. The wine had me woozy, so I went in the house to lie down and slept until a familiar knock jolted me awake after dark.

Rose stood there looking puzzled, sniffing the air I was fouling with my sour wine breath.

"What are you, boozin' all alone, Jo-Jo?"

"I just found out my daughter's an alcoholic, so it seemed like the right time to get drunk."

"Jo-Jo, man, I'm so sorry!"

"What are you sorry about? You don't even know her. Shit, *I* don't even know her! Come out back with me, I have to do something."

She followed me down the stairs and out to the backyard, where she let out a gasp at the sight of the chickens, strutting around in the moonlight.

"You crazy, or what?"

"You like it? Eddie Everything built the coop and the fence. They'll be laying eggs pretty soon. Ever had a freshly-laid egg?"

"Jo-Jo, I think maybe you're crackin' up."

I tossed handfuls of cracked corn around the yard, just as Kevin had instructed me.

"You might be right," I said. "But I like looking at my birds."

She took me by the elbow. "Come on, we can watch 'em from your bedroom window."

It was the gentlest lovemaking I'd ever experienced. We lay there afterwards, looking in each other's eyes without looking away. I wondered if Rose might stay the night. This lying-after business was a step in the right direction.

"You gonna see your daughter?"

"I'm going to try."

"That's good. I know how you feel. I miss my Justin."

"This is different. You and Justin are connected, no matter where he is. Me and my daughter . . ."

I let the sentence dangle. Rose stroked my hair. "Hey, guess what? I read those books you gave me."

She was referring to three of my Sammy Suitcase books, which I'd given her the last time she was over.

"Did you like them?"

"Yeah, good stories. That kid's one tough little mother."

I laughed. "Best description of Sammy I ever heard."

"Those pictures you drew, Jo-Jo, I gotta ask: Who taught you to do that?"

"I pretty much taught myself. Funny thing is, I started in this house, fifty years ago. Used to draw and paint in the basement."

"You just, like, *wanted* to do it, so you did it?"

"Guess so."

"Kept on practicin' 'til you got good?"

"Yeah. Kind of like Justin, with his baseball."

Rose shook her head. "No. It's different. Justin, he just does what he does, kinda like an animal. It's his muscles and his speed . . . don't take much brains, and some day he ain't gonna be able to do it. What you can do is special."

"I don't really do it anymore, but thanks."

She sat up. "What do you mean?"

"Well, I haven't done a book in a long time."

"Why not?"

"Guess I'm out of stories."

"Bullshit. Tell another one! You can do it, Jo-Jo. At least one more."

"Why?"

" 'Cause you gotta write a happy one."

I sat up. "A happy one?"

"That's right. This kid Sammy, he has his adventures, he makes friends, then he's gotta move. Always sayin' good-bye to everybody, his father draggin' him off someplace, right?"

"Yeah."

"Well, you gotta settle him someplace. He can't keep movin' forever. Maybe his father meets a woman, buys a house . . . I don't know. You're the writer, it's your problem."

"I wasn't aware I had a problem."

"Jo-Jo. I ain't tryin' to pick a fight with you. Just sayin' you gotta give Sammy Suitcase a break, man, 'cause even when he wins, he's still so damn sad."

A tremor ran through me, so fierce that had I to lie back down. Rose had struck a nerve nobody had ever gone near. What instinct!

I swallowed hard, hoping to keep my voice from trembling. "You're right, Rose. Sammy Suitcase is a sad kid."

"Aw, Jo-Jo, I don't wanna upset you." She cuddled up with me and stroked my cheek. "Childhood is sad, 'cause it don't last."

I wiped my eyes, rolling over so she couldn't see me crying. "No, baby. Childhood is sad because it never ends."

I fell asleep with Rose stroking my shoulders. When I woke up it was still dark, and of course I was alone.

I went to the window. The moon was shining bright and three of my chickens were sleeping in the yard, outside the coop, their heads tucked into their sides in that funny way that chickens do.

It was a comforting sight, the birds swelling slightly with each breath they took. I was eager for the sun to come up so I could feed and water them before heading to Manhattan to see my daughter.

Chapter Twenty-one

The next day I called Taylor. I just did it without thinking about it, the way a timid kid shuts his eyes and forces himself to jump off a high dive, and to my shock she agreed to meet me for coffee in Greenwich Village. I fed the chickens and headed to town to see my estranged, alcoholic daughter.

Never dreamed I'd ever write a sentence like that last one.

Taylor was sitting there waiting for me at a Starbucks on Sheridan Square, and when she saw me the deadpan expression on her face did not brighten, and she didn't get up out of her chair. I might have been a homeless person, about to hit her up for spare change.

It's hard for me to describe my daughter because in my mind, she just *was*. Maybe the easiest way would be to describe her late mother first. Moonchild was long and lanky, with untamed hair, like a cluster of windblown snakes. She had wild hazel eyes and a tiny button nose which, combined with her eternal wackiness, made her seem much younger than her years.

Now take that person and darken her pale complexion, the way a spoonful of cocoa powder darkens a glass of milk. Tame the hair into a tasteful shoulder-length cut, and replace the wildness in the eyes with a cool serenity.

And lastly, take that grinning mouth and tug its corners downward into a seemingly sad expression having nothing to do with her mood of the moment.

As you may have guessed, she got that last trait from the Ambrosio side.

Now you had my daughter Taylor, a combination of two human beings who didn't come together so much as they collided.

But one thing was different from the last time I'd seen her: My once-chubby daughter was now jackrabbit slim, with cheekbones and a swanlike neck. I couldn't think of a way she could have looked more beautiful.

I knew I would have to speak first. "Am I late?"

"No, I'm early," she said in a voice that was flatter than the floor.

"My God, Taylor, you've lost a lot of weight!"

"Yeah, well, that's what happens when you live with a personal trainer."

I gestured toward the counter. "What can I get you?"

She hoisted her latte. "I'm all set."

I got myself a drip coffee from a worker in a green apron who moved like a deeply anaesthetized man. His coworkers existed in the same dreamy state. I guess they stayed away from the product they peddled.

Then I sat down across from her, and as I took my first sip she said, "You're a chicken farmer?"

"Well, I have six hens."

"What in the world possessed you to get chickens?"

"I guess they're sort of pets."

"You couldn't get a cat, or a dog."

"I wanted chickens. I had chickens when I was a kid on Shepherd Avenue."

She shook her head. "Unbelievable."

"Kevin seemed to get a kick out of them."

"Kevin isn't familiar with your bullshit."

"Taylor, please. Get it right. It's *chicken* shit, okay? I don't have room for a bull."

She sighed, shook her head, checked the time on her cell phone. "What do you want?"

"I want to apologize. I should have been there when your mother died, and I'm sorry. I just couldn't do it."

"Apology accepted."

"That didn't sound sincere."

"It's the best I can do." She leaned closer. "What do you really want? Do you want to catch up on my life?"

"Well, yeah, sure. We're both catching up. You find out I'm a chicken farmer, I find out you're an alcoholic."

She was ready for that. As Kevin had told me, they had no secrets from each other. She took a long sip from her cup and offered a bland smile.

"What do you want to know?"

I shrugged. "Whatever you want me to know. I'm here to learn."

"Well, I started boozing pretty hard about two years ago."

"When your mother died."

"Around that time, I guess."

"You guess?"

"That's the thing about drinking. It blurs the lines."

"Yeah, but I'm getting the feeling this is all my fault, for not going to the funeral."

She stared at me in what appeared to be disbelief.

"My God," she said, "your ego knows no bounds!"

"Hey, it's just a theory. You don't hate me?"

"I was disappointed, but it was never hate. I don't have time to waste on hate."

"So you're saving time by not hating me."

"Oh, for God's sake! Get me another latte, would you?"

That was encouraging. It meant she wasn't going to rush off. I did as I was told and returned to the table, and by then her mouth had tightened up again, and it was as if we hadn't broken any ground.

I wanted to reach across the table to take her hand, but I dreaded the certain rejection, so I clasped my hands together and went for it.

"Taylor, I'm sorry you were so unhappy."

A tiny smile tickled her lips, the same smile she wore when she was a two-year-old, noodling around in the sandbox at the Carmine Street playground.

Which was about two blocks from where we now sat at this Starbucks, formerly a diner, formerly a bookstore. A former dad and his former daughter, eyeing each other like a pair of poker players.

"Unhappy?" she echoed. "What makes you think I'm happy now?"

"Aren't you?"

"Reasonably. Are you?"

"I'm getting there. You feel like walking? I feel like walking. Take that latte with you."

If there was anything about the Village I missed it was the aimless walks in any direction that somehow always lifted my soul. We headed down Bleecker Street, crowded as always in the middle of the day. Didn't these people have jobs? (And who was I to ask?)

"Are we going any place special?" Taylor asked.

"No," I lied, "just walking. Sometimes I miss this neighborhood."

"I like the Upper West Side."

"Well, I like Kevin. I think you're well-suited."

She stopped walking. "Don't patronize me."

"I'm not. I'm impressed by him. You're not an easy person, and I'm sure he isn't either, but I've got a feeling you're both worth the trouble."

Her eyes moistened. "Well, *he's* worth the trouble, anyway." She checked the time. "I've got to get back to work."

"Walk with me a little more. Just one more block."

"Okay, but there's something I need to know."

"Shoot."

"You might not want to tell me, so don't promise anything."

"All I said was *shoot*."

"Why'd you and Mom name me Taylor?"

We stopped walking. "Your mother never told you?"

"She refused."

"It's nothing bad."

"So tell me."

We resumed walking. "You sure you want to know?"

"I think I'm entitled to know, and I obviously can't ask her anymore, so don't give me any bullshit about how you liked the way it *sounded.*"

Here goes nothing, I thought. "You were conceived at a loft party in SoHo, on top of a bed covered with coats. And the one under your mother was from Lord and Taylor."

Her eyes widened, but not with rage. She was actually smiling, broadly enough to reveal her teeth, which I was delighted to see were straight and white.

"Is that the truth?"

I crossed my heart, held up my hand. "Could have been worse. We could have called you 'Lord.'"

"My God."

"Taylor, it was the eighties. We were all a little bit crazy and careless, and your mother, I'm sure you noticed, was a bit of a flake."

She actually chuckled, to my great relief. "All this time . . ." she said, letting the sentence trail off.

"All this time what?"

"Well, all this time I had my own idea about it."

"I'm listening."

She hesitated. "I thought maybe I was named after Elizabeth Taylor."

I shrugged. "Stick with that version, if you like it."

"There aren't any versions to the truth!"

"Oh, Taylor. Where did I go wrong with you?"

She laughed out loud, then said she really had to get back to work. I urged her to walk one more block with me.

We crossed Cornelia Street and walked to the front gate at the Carmine Street playground. It was teeming with kids on swings and monkey bars that looked to be newly installed.

"Remember this place? I took you here until you were two years old."

Taylor peered between the bars. "Guess it's vaguely familiar."

"There used to be a sandbox in that corner, and you'd play there for hours. Funny, it's in better shape than it used to be, but the old playground had more character."

"Did I ride on a little red train on wheels?"

My heart jumped. "You sure did."

"Yeah. Yeah, I remember."

I dared to hug my daughter.

"This was an extremely manipulative maneuver," she said into my shoulder.

"Yeah, well, I was desperate."

She didn't hug me back but at least she allowed it, and I clung tightly to her as I spoke again.

"You have an open invitation to my house in Brooklyn. You and Kevin can stay the night if you want. I have an upstairs apartment that's waiting for you."

I let her go. Her face looked years younger than it did in Starbucks.

"I'll think about it," she said. She touched my cheek, and then she turned and walked away.

And I began the long journey back to East New York.

"Well, Doc, I found out a stunning thing about my daughter."

I wasn't even seated as I spoke those words to Dr. Rosensohn, who'd just finished watering his sagging plant.

"Sit down and tell me all about it."

"Turns out she's an alcoholic."

He put on his best professional face, the one they wear to show you they've heard it all before.

"May I ask how you arrived at this knowledge?"

"Her boyfriend came to see me. And get this—they met at an A.A. meeting."

"You sound skeptical, but this scenario isn't as unusual as you might think."

"Two alcoholics hooking up in a church basement on the Upper West Side isn't unusual? And maybe even a little bit dangerous?"

"When people go to A.A., they open up. They're being honest. Laying themselves bare, so to speak. Sorry, that didn't come out right."

"You're telling me."

"Many happy unions have resulted from such encounters. The partners give each other strength."

"Or one falls off the wagon, and to keep him from feeling lonely the other one joins him."

"That's a truly negative attitude."

"Don't get me wrong, I *like* my daughter's boyfriend. He convinced me to call her, so I did, and we had coffee yesterday."

"That's wonderful! What's she like?"

"Smart. Stubborn. Sarcastic."

"Sounds like your genes came through."

I pressed hard on my eyeballs with the heels of my hands. "Spending time with Taylor made me realize I don't know who the hell she is."

"You're finding out! Detail by painful detail, you are finding out. Will you see her again?"

"She and her boyfriend have an open invitation to come to Shepherd Avenue."

"Think they'll take you up on it?"

"Well, I told Taylor about my chickens, and I think her curiosity about a Brooklyn barnyard might actually get her on the J train."

"Okay, it's a start. Good for you, Mr. Ambrosio. This is big. You're reconnecting. And even if it doesn't work, it's a noble failure."

"I gotta tell you, Doc, if that's a pep talk, it needs work."

"Look to the future, man! You could be a grandfather before you know it!"

A grandfather. I suddenly felt dizzy. "Jesus, I guess you're right. Never thought that far ahead."

He nodded. "Thinking far ahead isn't exactly one of your strengths, is it, Mr. Ambrosio?"

I had no answer.

Chapter Twenty-two

When the sack of corn ran out I switched the chickens to table scraps. Suddenly I had no more garbage. Stale bread, leftover macaroni, meat loaf—anything old or stale got chopped into bits, thrown into the yard and gobbled up.

The birds were getting bigger by the day. One morning I was feeding them when I noticed that one chicken remained on her nest while the other five fed. She looked as if she might be suffering, but as I approached the coop to see what was wrong she stretched her neck, cackled and leaped up to join the others, leaving behind a dung-streaked egg.

I reached in to get it, still warm from its mother. My first egg. The pleasure it gave me was almost perverse.

The following morning three more eggs appeared in the nests. I upped their food supply.

I brought that first egg to Atlantic Avenue to show it to Nat, who was not impressed.

"Want to hold it?"

"Why would I want to hold it? There's shit on it!"

"Is that all you have to say?"

"I don't eat eggs. Never liked 'em."

"I don't like them much either."

"So what the hell's the deal with all these stupid chickens?"

He had a point. I was about to have a steady stream of eggs with nothing to do but waste them.

Then it hit me: My next-door neighbors, on either side of the coop! I'd been living here all these weeks, and I still hadn't even met them! Maybe it was time to knock on their doors to officially introduce myself, and make a neighborly offer.

Thanks to Rose, I knew a little bit about them. A black family, the Washingtons, lived in the house to the left of mine. The husband was a subway motorman, and the wife was a nurse who worked at Brooklyn Hospital. They had two small sons.

That afternoon I rang the Washington doorbell. A plump, pretty woman in a nurse's uniform answered the door and eyed me as if I were a Jehovah's Witness.

"Good afternoon. I'm your next-door neighbor, Joseph Ambrosio."

She nodded. "Bertha Washington."

"Pleased to meet you, Bertha."

She jerked a thumb behind her back. "Those are your chickens out there."

"Yes. That's what I wanted to talk about. I hope they're not disturbing you in any way?"

She continued to stare at me. "Not yet."

"Anyway, they've begun laying eggs, and I just wanted to say that you're welcome to as many eggs as you like."

She shook her head and chuckled. "Are you kidding?"

"No, ma'am. I can leave them in a basket on your porch."

I suddenly ran out of words. I felt like an idiot. She broke her stare to look at her watch. "I gotta get ready for work."

"Oh, I'm sorry."

"You keep your chickens in your yard, we won't have no problems."

"Thank you."

"But we don't need no eggs."

She closed the door before I could say another word.

Tingling with embarrassment, I went to the house to the right of mine and rang the bell. Rose had told me an old man with a big moustache lived here, and that's all she knew.

I waited and waited, and just as I was about to give up and go home I heard the lock turn and there stood the old man—bleary-eyed, as if I'd just awakened him, and clutching the doorknob as if to keep from falling. He could have been Russian, or Croatian, or Hispanic . . . definitely not American-born, that's all I could tell for sure. He swayed as if he were on the prow of a boat, in a high wind. I smelled beer on his breath. His handlebar moustache drooped over his mouth.

I gave him pretty much the same rap I'd given the nurse. I don't think a word of it got through. He just stood there hunch-shouldered, until a tiny chickadee of a woman appeared and nudged him aside, breaking his grip on the doorknob.

"Whadda you want?"

Another foreigner of indeterminate origins. I put on my best smile.

"Hi. I'm your neighbor."

"You the guy with the chickens?"

"That's right."

"Better not be any roosters! We don't need no crowin' in the morning."

"No, no, they're all grown up now, and they're all hens. I was telling your husband—"

"He can't hear so good."

"Oh. Sorry. Anyway, I was telling him that they've begun laying eggs, and you're welcome to as many as you want."

"We don't eat eggs."

"Oh."

"And you won't get no baby chicks from your eggs, not without a rooster."

The last thing I expected was an impromptu biology lesson, but in the interest of harmony I listened as this little woman laid it out for me.

"See, without the rooster, the eggs are, whaddayacallit."

"Unfertilized?"

"Right. You want babies, you need a male."

"I get it."

She gave her husband's shoulder a shove. He drifted sideways and did not complain.

"This is my male," she said. "Not what he used to be. Good luck with your chickens."

Before I could thank her she slammed the door, and as I walked away I could hear her yelling at the man for boozing in the daytime.

So much for my neighborly efforts. In the end, Eddie Everything agreed to take the eggs off my hands.

I wouldn't have been surprised if he had a little fresh-egg business on the side, but that was okay by me. I still needed Eddie for one more major project.

I wanted to turn my basement back to the way it was.

*   *   *

Eddie whistled at the sight of it, the way a mechanic does when he looks over a car in need of major repairs.

"Boss, ain't nobody done nothin' down here for a long time. It's like a damn bat cave!"

"Well, it was a great eat-in kitchen back in the day, and that's what I want."

Eddie's eyes widened. "You talkin' appliances?"

"Sink, stove, refrigerator—"

"I can't do the stove, man, that's gas."

"Plus, I want you to build a long table with built-in benches on both sides."

His eyes got even wider. "You talkin', like, a picnic table?"

"Exactly. I also want a new floor. We should do the floor first, right?"

Eddie's smile couldn't have been wider as he silently added up the payments to come in his head.

"Tell you the truth, boss, this room needs paint bad. That's job number one. Wanna do that before we lay the floor, so we don't be drippin' on it."

"That's all yours, Eddie, I'm all painted out."

He clenched his teeth in mock concern over the impending expense, pointing a callused finger toward the network of paint-flaking pipes in the ceiling.

"Lotta prep work, lotta nooks and crannies," he crooned. "You gotta know this ain't gonna be a fast job."

"Time is what I've got, Eddie. Get to it."

While Eddie painted the basement I got down to writing my final book. My agent had given up nagging me to "knock out" another one to take advantage of the publicity generated by my Brooklyn Bridge fiasco. Now she was stunned to hear from me and distressed when I told her it was going to be the last in the Sammy Suitcase series.

"Don't shut the door all the way!" she said. "Leave it open a crack."

"This is it," I insisted. "It's time for little Sammy to be home at last."

"Well, we don't have to play it that way."

"There's no 'we' in this deal," I said, hanging up before she could reply.

I set up a work table in the parlor, looking out on Shepherd Avenue. I always wrote the story first and followed it with the illustrations, but I was having a hard time with it. It's easy to write about someone who's in constant motion. If nothing else, you've got the new scenery to carry you along.

What was I going to do when I had Sammy and his father settled for good in one place, the suitcase stored forever in the attic? And where would this special place be? I spent a lot of time staring out the window, watching people go by, waving when they looked my way. Nobody waved back.

By this time it was late July, hot as hell, and Rose was coming over every other night. Sometimes I wondered if she was in it for the air-conditioning. With Justin away she stayed later each time, but she always left before dawn. It was important for her to wake up in her own bed. Maybe it helped her believe that whatever was happening between us was not really happening.

Meanwhile, Justin was an absolute sensation. He tore up the Rookie Ball league in Arizona and was quickly promoted to the Mariners' Double-A team in Tennessee, where he continued to pound the ball, and after just two months of pro ball the Mariners promoted him to their Triple-A team in Tacoma.

He was eighteen years old and one step from the Major Leagues. True, it was a long step, but it was still just one step.

And during his first two weeks with the Triple-A team, Justin led the team in batting, home runs and runs batted in.

The New York papers reported his progress with an almost hysterical enthusiasm. He was the Natural and the Babe rolled into one.

He was also cooler than Steve McQueen. Nothing seemed to bother him. Somehow Justin remained the same calm, polite kid who'd asked me if I minded him coming along on a morning run when I first moved to Shepherd Avenue.

Eddie Everything, a baseball fanatic, could barely believe how well Justin was doing.

"You believe this freakin' kid?" he asked me. "What are they doin', pitchin' to him underhand? Ain't *nothin'* he can't hit!"

Justin phoned his mother every day, sometimes twice a day. He kept trying to get her to quit the job at the Laundromat and move someplace better, but Rose refused.

I worried that I was keeping her on Shepherd Avenue, but quickly dismissed that idea. Rose put the *I* in *independent*. She wasn't going to take anything from her son, and she was going to keep the only home he'd ever known until he came back.

But was Justin ever coming back? That was the question that nagged at his mother.

"I'm worried about him, Jo-Jo. It's happenin' so fast."

"He's smart. He can handle it."

"You think?"

"He's doing great so far."

"Ain't talkin' about baseball. I'm talkin' about *girls*. They're gonna be all over him, and he don't know *nothin'*. Probably marry the first one who lets him in."

That surprised me. "Are you saying Justin is a virgin?"

"He was when he left. I'm pretty sure. Now?" She sighed, punched the pillow and started putting her clothes on. "I don't know, I don't know. I could be a grandmother before you know it."

"Funny, my shrink just told me I could be a grandfather before I know it."

"That's how life is. *Boom*, here comes a baby, now you gotta worry the rest o' your damn life."

"Want to come to the beach with me, Rose?"

She looked at me as if I'd lost my mind. It was a crazy out-of-the-blue question for me to throw out there, but I knew she had the next day off, so I took a shot. I had a desire to feel sand under my feet and look at that limitless, watery horizon I'd first seen with my grandparents, fifty years earlier.

Of course Rose didn't know any of that. She just saw a crazy white guy with gray hair, making a wild invitation.

"I'm tellin' you 'bout my son gettin' trapped, and you're talkin' 'bout *beaches?*"

"Yeah. You need a break from your worries, and I need some inspiration if I'm ever going to write this new book. Rockaway Beach. Ever been there?"

"No."

"It's great. Used to be, anyway. Hope it still is. What do you say? A little swimming, a few hot dogs—"

"I can't be goin' out with you, Jo-Jo!"

"No problem. We'll leave our houses separately, ten minutes apart. You can meet me at the subway station. I'll wait on the platform."

"The train goes to the beach?"

"Yeah. Isn't that amazing? What do you say?"

She stood there in the dark, buttoning up her shirt. I actually held my breath, awaiting her answer.

"Always wanted to see the ocean," she murmured at last, more to herself than to me.

It was jarring to see her walking toward the ocean in a one-piece blue bathing suit, in full sunshine. She couldn't suddenly take off and run home. Like it or not, we were together on this trip. We were a couple.

It was like having a beautiful, wild creature in captivity, and finally being able to study it as it paced the cage. But Rockaway Beach was no cage. It was without a doubt the biggest, most wide-open space Rose had ever seen, and I knew it was blowing her mind as much as she was blowing mine.

"Stop starin' at me, Jo-Jo."

"Can't help it. You are ridiculously beautiful."

"Get over it."

"I can't."

It was true. I couldn't quite believe that I was in the company of such a glorious creature. Rose's skin was flawless, her belly was flat, and her face! My God, how it came to life in full sunlight and salty breezes!

And here she was at the beach with a graying, thick-around-the-middle man. Anyone looking at us would have pegged me for her father, or an uncle, or a pervert.

"You gonna stare at me all day?"

"Maybe."

"I ain't kiddin', Jo-Jo—cut it out."

I obeyed, turning my gaze toward the water. It was a beautiful day, hot but not humid. We settled down about twenty yards from the surf and sat side by side on towels she'd brought. She let me apply sunblock to her back and shoulders, which were surprisingly muscular—tugging all that laundry out of washers and into dryers, day after day.

"This is nice, Jo-Jo."

"I knew you'd like it."

"You came here when you were a kid?"

"My grandparents took me once. I had this little plastic strainer to shake sand through. Found a bunch of coins. First money I ever made."

"No shit?"

"Yeah, that was a good day. Should we go in the water?"

She laughed, a cackling sound. "You crazy? I ain't goin' in the water!"

"People go to the beach to go swimming, Rose. It's actually the main reason they go."

She wrapped her arms around her knees and seemed to shiver, despite the heat.

"You wanna go in, you go. I'll watch."

"Let's just get our feet wet."

"*No!*"

I was startled by her tone, and then it hit me.

"You can't swim, can you?"

She let her head fall. "No," she said to the sand. "Never learned how."

I held out my hand. "Like I said, we'll just get our feet wet. No big deal."

"Somebody'll steal our stuff."

"If they knew how to steal, they'd be in the Hamptons. Come on."

Like a frightened child, she took my hand as we walked toward the water. With all our antics between the sheets it was odd to realize that this was the first time we'd ever held hands.

"I'm scared, Jo-Jo."

"Relax. We're just going to stick our toes in the water."

"Don't let go!"

"I won't."

Her grip tightened as we waded in, and she let out a cry of excitement as the foam broke around our ankles.

"Hey, it's cool!"

"Feels good, doesn't it?"

"Oh yeah!"

"Want to go a little deeper?"

She stopped walking and tugged on my hand. "No tricks."

"Absolutely not. We'll stop whenever you want."

She studied the surf. "Maybe a little deeper."

We inched our way forward, up to our calves, up to our knees—then a wave rolled in and soaked us to our necks. Rose screamed with delight, still clutching my hand as if she were never going to let go.

"Let's go back, Jo-Jo!"

"Hang on, Rose. Give me your other hand."

Her ponytail dripped seawater and her eyes narrowed. "Why?"

"Just do it."

We were up to our waists at this point, and the ocean was in that calm state between waves. I held out my free hand, but Rose ignored it. She looked like a frightened child who was trying to be brave. I'd never seen her so vulnerable. She believed her life was in my hands.

"Whachoo gonna do?"

"Just trust me. Do you trust me?"

She shook her head. "Trustin' people ain't worked out too good for me."

"Just this once, trust me."

She took my hand. Now we were facing each other, clasping hands. I sidestepped to the depth of our chests, forcing her to come along.

"Hey, where we goin'?"

"We're there. Just let your feet go back."

"Huh?"

"Never mind, I'll do it."

I walked backwards, forcing Rose to float on her belly. She let out a shriek.

"Jesus, Jo-Jo!"

"Easy, you're doing great."

I continued walking backwards, keeping her chin above water as I pulled her along. The look on her face was pure rapture.

"Oh my God, oh my God, it's like *flying!*"

"Great, isn't it?"

"Don't let me go, Jo-Jo!"

"I won't!"

"Hang onto me!"

"I've got you!"

"Shit, this is amazing! Come on, you can go faster than that!"

"You're going to give an old man a heart attack!"

"Don't go dyin' on me, I want a hot dog and a beer!"

"You shall have it!" I shouted, running backwards as fast as I could.

On the subway home Rose was quiet. She was reliving her first-ever time in the ocean, but I knew it was more than just that.

I'd done a wonderful and a terrible thing, taking her to the beach. I'd given her a great adventure along with a glimpse of the many pleasures she'd missed out on, with the lousy hand she'd been dealt.

"Jo-Jo?"

"Yeah?"

"It was a nice day. Thank you."

"Glad you liked it."

"Listen, I gotta be by myself tonight, okay?"

I was expecting that, the way you expect the rumble of thunder after a flash of lightning.

"I understand."

"You ain't mad?"

"I'm a little sunburned, but I'm not mad."

"You shoulda let me rub the lotion on your back."

"I hate those chemicals."

"*Estupido.* Stubborn." She looked around the subway car before daring to rest her head on my shoulder. "Wanna know somethin'? You're too nice."

"Never been accused of that before."

"You sure you ain't mad?"

"Swear on my life. It's been a big day. I'm going to feed my chickens, and then I'm going to collapse."

"Me, too. I just gotta . . . think about things, you know?"

"I know."

I also knew it was the beginning of the end for us. I stroked her head, feeling the sweet sorrow that comes whenever you realize that something good can't possibly last.

We got off at the Cleveland Street station. I gave Rose a five-minute head start in case anybody on Shepherd Avenue was watching, and then I went home and fed my chickens.

At least they weren't going anywhere.

Chapter Twenty-three

Eddie Everything took three days to paint the basement. There was a lot of prep work, the scraping and sanding of old paint on the walls and the pipes, and then every surface needed two coats of semi-gloss white paint. When he was done the place was practically gleaming.

Next up was the floor, a cheap layer of scuffed green linoleum worn through to the black. I told Eddie I wanted a checkerboard pattern of tiles, red and yellow, which was the floor I remembered from my grandparents' days. Eddie measured the floor and we drove to a tile shop on Atlantic Avenue, where I spent $900 on the best tiles they made.

We had to make two trips in Eddie's station wagon to bring all those tiles home, along with big cans of adhesive and trowels with serrated edges to apply the stuff.

"Floor's pretty flat," Eddie remarked on the second trip home. "We're lucky with that, at least."

"I'll be your helper on this job, Eddie."

He seemed surprised. "Ain't you got a book to write?"

"Yeah, but right now I'm blocked."

"What's that mean? Like, constipated?"

"Exactly. Can't find the words, so I might as well help you. Sometimes physical labor loosens up the words."

"Gonna stink pretty bad downstairs for a while, Mr. A., I gotta warn you. This adhesive we're usin' is nasty stuff."

"We'll open the windows."

"Won't help much."

We rolled on in silence for a few blocks, and then Eddie, almost casually, asked: "How was the beach?"

I looked at him. He was grinning, the kind of grin people grin when they've got the drop on you.

"Pretty good," I said.

"Yeah? You go with anybody special?"

"What the hell are you up to, Eddie?"

He shrugged his shoulders, a little too dramatically. "Hey, I don't mean no harm, man. I just noticed that you got a tan, and Rosie Suds, she's got a tan, so I gotta wonder if maybe youse bumped into each other at Rockaway."

Rosie Suds. I never knew she had a nickname. Rosie Suds, because she worked at a Laundromat. I wondered if she knew she had a nickname. I wondered if I had acquired a Shepherd Avenue nickname. (Crazy Joey No-Bars?)

I felt myself sweat. "Eddie, I'd really appreciate it if you kept this to yourself."

"What am I, WINS news? You give me twenty-two minutes, I'll give you the world?"

"I'm serious, Eddie. I'd like to keep this private."

"Hey, your life is your life, man. I mean, I know you're givin' me all this work, and I appreciate that, but it ain't just business here, is it? We're friends, too, right?"

"I'd like to think so."

"Well, let me tell you something, friend. That is a beautiful woman and a good mother, and you must be a pretty good man to get her, 'cause I asked her out many times and always got shut down."

Holy shit. Where was this going? Proceed with caution.

"I wouldn't say I've *got* her, Eddie. I really don't know what we've got going. It could end any time."

"She's callin' the shots, am I right?"

"You are right."

He chuckled. "Jesus, man, they're all crazy! Women, I mean. My advice to you is, enjoy yourself while it lasts. Justin's gonna be a millionaire any minute now, and he's gonna take her away. Buy her a mansion somewhere. Won't see Rosie Suds no more."

He spoke those final words just as we pulled up to park in front of my house. I didn't bother telling Eddie how Justin had already tried to get his mother to move away, and she'd refused.

He knew too much already.

* * *

The basement floor was worse than Eddie thought. We pulled up the old linoleum and the surface beneath was full of rough patches that had to be smoothed, and that took time. We started at eleven in the morning and didn't wrap it up until six p.m., with no break for lunch.

And Eddie was right: The stink from the adhesive was awful, enough to make me dizzy. I wanted to bail out an hour into the job, but I'd already declared my intention to help lay the floor and quitting would have been unmanly, to say the least.

So I hung in there, spreading adhesive and carefully laying the tiles in a checkerboard pattern. Whenever I reached a wall or a corner Eddie took over to trim the tiles to fit.

"You're doin' good, boss."

"I'm getting a nice buzz from this adhesive."

"Yeah, but the good thing is, it's like you're in a dream, you know? You go to bed tonight, you forget all about it. Then tomorrow morning, you come down here and see you got a brand-new floor, and it's like . . . how the fuck did *that* happen?"

I had to laugh. "Eddie, you're a poet."

"Bullshit, man, I didn't say nothin' that rhymed!"

Eddie had done an excellent job measuring the floor—we had just three tiles left over when the job was complete. I paid him and tipped him an extra fifty bucks.

Neither of us mentioned Rose. I knew she wouldn't be knocking on my door that night, and even if she did, I probably wouldn't have heard her. I simply collapsed with exhaustion on top of my bed, without even showering.

And the next morning, sore in the back and the knees, I staggered down to the basement, and it was just as Eddie Everything said it would be.

I had a brand-new floor of yellow and red tiles, brilliant in the morning sunshine, and how the hell did *that* happen?

I didn't have time to dwell on it, because somebody was knocking on my front door. I'd ordered a sink, a stove and a refrigerator to be delivered that week, and figured one of those items had arrived.

But when I opened the front door it was my Uncle Victor standing there, a baseball cap on his head and a bulging brown paper bag in his hands.

"Jesus, Vic!"

"My father always brought bagels and cream cheese on Sunday morning. Remember?"

I remembered. "It's Saturday, Vic."

"Sue me." He shoved the bag into my hands. "Here's your house-warming gift. You gonna invite me inside, or what? I could get mugged out here. That'd be some headline, right? *Mugged For His Bagels?*"

I embraced him. He didn't hug back. He brushed past me and stepped into the house, breathing hard, like a child alone in a haunted house. He took a moment to gather himself and then walked bravely to the kitchen, stopping dead in his tracks at the stove.

"Don't tell me this is the same one."

"Yeah. The only relic in the whole house that survived from the old days."

"Holy shit."

"They knew how to build 'em back then, huh?"

He ran his hand over the surface of the stove, and I knew he was thinking what I was thinking the day Rico Valdez let me into the kitchen. The countless meals it had cooked, the oceans of coffee that had percolated on its surface . . .

Suddenly the strength drained from Vic's legs. He caught himself on the back of a chair and sat down. He took off his baseball cap, pushed back his hair and looked at me for a long moment before sobbing silently into his hands.

I stood behind him and squeezed his shoulders, as if he were a fighter who'd just finished a tough round.

"Goddamn, Joey," he said, over and over. *"Goddamn."*

I made a pot of coffee and served it up the way he liked it, light and sweet. We each had two bagels with cream cheese, and I remembered how much my uncle liked to eat. The optimism of his appetite always made me wonder about the pessimism of his words.

"The times we had in this house," he said softly. It was a statement that required no response, a you-hadda-be-there-to-know-what-I-mean statement.

He pointed at the stove. "My father tried to make coffee the morning I left to play baseball in Charleston, and he spilled it all over the stove. Couldn't do shit in the kitchen, my old man."

"He never had to."

"He did that morning, because my mother wouldn't say goodbye to me. Remember? Stayed in her bedroom, because she didn't want me to play ball. Wanted me to go to college. That was a lousy way to start my professional baseball career, don't you think?"

"She wanted you to play it safe."

"Yeah, safe. I played it safe, all right. Lost my college scholarship offers after I turned pro, so I drove a city bus for thirty years. They gave me a plaque, a sheet cake and a bottle of Champale for my years of dedicated service. Pension check comes right on the first of every month. Lot to be proud of, huh?"

With a shaky hand he lifted his coffee cup to his mouth, and as he drank I noticed how chubby he'd become, his jowls covered with white beard stubble he hadn't bothered shaving for at least three days.

And that reminded me of the jet-black beard he'd grown when he washed out as a ballplayer and came home to Shepherd Avenue, lean as a cat and mad at the world, until he met a beautiful Greenwich Village painter named Jenny Sutherland and ran off to move into her studio apartment on Sullivan Street, to the horror of his parents.

I'd always wondered about that girl. I had a wild crush on Jenny and even begged her to let me move in with her and Vic, but of course that couldn't happen, especially after Vic woke up alone on Sullivan Street one morning to find that Jenny had taken off in the middle of the night, God knows where.

Did I dare to ask him about the girl who'd broken his heart, half a century ago?

Well, shit, if not now, when?

"Hey, Vic. Whatever happened to that Village girlfriend of yours?"

"Who?"

"Who. The one you moved in with when you came back home, after—"

"After my baseball career went in the toilet?" he said, falsely chirpy. "Good old Jenny Sutherland! Haven't thought about her in about fifty years."

Bullshit, I thought, as I watched the blood flush into his face, red as a rose behind his whiskers.

Vic poured more coffee for himself. "She was a nut job, Joey, plain and simple. A true bohemian."

"I had a wild crush on her."

"Of course you did! *Everybody* did! She was pretty, she was full of life, she was crazy. And bad luck followed her around. Remember the day we were supposed to be taking care of you, and you got hit by a car?"

I remembered. I was spending a day in the Village with them and we were on Sixth Avenue, across the street from the Waverly Theater when I spotted my father—who'd been gone all summer—heading down the subway steps. I ran after him without looking, got winged by a car and wound up at St. Vincent's Hospital, where I was treated for minor injuries and told repeatedly how lucky I was to be alive.

"That wasn't Jenny's fault," I said. "I saw my father and I ran after him."

"What are you, defending her?"

"Take it easy, Vic! We're two old farts, talking about something that happened in 1961! I just wondered if you ever heard from her again."

"Never. Never looked for her, either. Got any more questions about Jenny Sutherland?"

I had a hundred questions about Jenny Sutherland, but the tremble in my uncle's voice quelled them all.

"No, sir."

"Good." He got to his feet and squared his shoulders. "All right, I'm ready to see what the hell you've done to this goddamn house."

We started the tour in the front parlor, which contained my desk and my drafting board, but Vic's gaze was fixed on the gleaming parquet floor.

"Christ, that's a beautiful floor!"

"Yeah. Sanded it down and gave it a coat of shellac."

He shook his head. "Who knew it was under there, huh? And new paint everywhere. You've been bustin' your ass, Joey."

"Just taking it a step at a time."

He pointed toward the ceiling. "You got a tenant?"

I shook my head. "Keeping it empty, in case Taylor ever wants to spend the night."

"Yeah? Not a bad idea. You don't want her goin' home from here after dark."

"I think she'd survive."

"Seen her lately?"

"Yeah. She's got a boyfriend."

"You like him?"

I hesitated. "He's a recovering alcoholic. So's Taylor."

Vic's shoulders sagged. "Jesus, nothin's ever easy in our family, you notice that, Joey?"

"I noticed."

"Hard to imagine little Taylor on the booze!"

"She's not little anymore, and she's been dry six months. Got a feeling this guy's good for her."

"Hope you're right. Hey, I'm sorry I reacted like that, Joey. Just when I figure the Ambrosios are all through with the dramatics, God thinks up another one for us. Come on, let me see our old room."

But he seemed reluctant to enter that room. Back in the day we'd slept on two narrow beds, mine by the window, his against the wall, and now my king-sized bed pretty much gobbled up most of the room.

Vic chuckled. "The other bedrooms are bigger."

"I wanted this one."

"Nostalgic, huh?"

"I guess."

A clucking sound reached us from the backyard, luring Vic all the way into the room. He looked out the window at the chickens and turned to me wide-eyed.

"Oh, gimme a break, Joey. Are you *serious?*"

All I could do was shrug. "Just like the good old days."

"I think you've lost your mind."

"They're good layers, Vic. I get fresh eggs every day. Want to go outside and see them?"

"I can see 'em from here. Don't need chicken shit on my shoes. So what's the deal, here, your neighbors don't complain?"

"What are they going to complain about? No roosters, so there's no crowing."

Vic stared at the chickens, as if he were in a trance. Then he turned to me and said, "Remember when my mother killed all your birds?"

My back stiffened. "That won't happen this time."

I joined Vic at the window. We both watched the chickens strut and preen. It was an oddly calming sight.

"Funny, ain't it, Joey?"

"What's that?"

"How much more peaceful your life becomes when the people you really love are gone. In this family, anyway."

I did not disagree.

We left the bedroom and headed for the steps down to the basement. "Got a woman, huh?" Vic casually asked.

"I'm sorry?"

"Someone left a silver bracelet on your windowsill. You don't wear bracelets, do you?"

Rose sometimes forgot her silver Tiffany bracelet, which Justin had given her after he signed with the Mariners. I felt myself blush. Sixty years old, and blushing over a woman!

"I see someone occasionally," I said.

"Neighborhood girl?"

"Yeah."

"Of course. Who else would come here? Christ, what the hell is that stink?"

"We just put in a new floor down here."

At the sight of the red and yellow tiles Vic turned to me wide-eyed.

"Okay, Joey, now you're scaring me."

"It's like the floor we had down here, remember?"

"Yeah, it's *exactly* like the floor we had down here. Let me guess. You're gonna put in a long wooden table with benches, right?"

I nodded. "Sink and a stove, too."

"Jesus Christ, what are you buildin' here, a museum?"

"I just want it to be like it was."

"Why?"

"Why not?"

Vic shook his head. "So I'm guessing you took the bars off your windows because that's how it was in '61."

"We didn't even lock the doors then, Vic, remember?"

"Sure. I also remember that the world was a very different place back then, nephew!"

I waved his words away. "Not that different. Anyway, I need to fix up the basement so I can entertain."

He chuckled. "What, you're gonna have a party down here?"

"I'm thinking about it. A housewarming party, when it's all done. You'll come, won't you?"

"Oh yeah. I'll have my tuxedo cleaned and pressed. Walk me to the front door, I gotta get goin'."

He climbed the stairs slowly. "Friggin' legs are shot," he murmured. "Might need a knee replacement."

"I'm sorry, Vic."

"*Ayyy*, eventually everything disintegrates."

"My uncle. Always looking on the bright side."

Vic and I walked out the front door and stood on the sidewalk, seeking a goodbye.

"It's good you patched things up with Taylor," he said.

"Well, they're not exactly patched, but I'm working on it."

He hesitated before asking: "You never heard from her, did you?"

I was puzzled. "Who?"

He rolled his eyes and blushed for the second time that day. "Jenny Sutherland, who do you think?"

"No, Vic, why would I?"

"Yeah, that's right, why would you? All right, let me go."

And for the first time ever my uncle voluntarily took me in an embrace, resting his chin on my shoulder. His eyes were shiny when he pulled back, and he gestured dramatically at the houses down the street, their locks, bars and cages giving off a metallic shine in the morning light.

"How 'bout that, Joey? At long last, Shepherd Avenue is a gated community. Who'da thunk it?"

Then he was gone, limping slowly toward the elevated train station without so much as a backwards glance, undoubtedly thinking about the girl who got away.

Chapter Twenty-four

Iwas all fired up to get started on a new mission, but first I had to get things straight with Eddie Everything and my next project.

I made a sketch of the table and benches I wanted him to build, explaining how I wanted everything anchored to the basement floor. I had no idea of how good a carpenter he might be but took a chance and left him to it, stuffing a wad of cash in his hand to pay for the lumber.

I'd barely counted the money. I was obsessed with something else.

I was determined to find Jenny Sutherland.

This wasn't going to be as easy as tracking down Johnny Gallo and Mel DiGiovanna. I couldn't find Jenny on Facebook or LinkedIn or any other type of social media. Of course she might have gotten married and taken her husband's name, but that didn't seem like something the Jenny I remembered would do—get married, or take a man's name. I Googled and I Googled—Jenny Sutherland, Jennifer Sutherland, J. Sutherland . . . lots of names popped up, but the accompanying images from all over the country clearly weren't her.

Forget the country! With a spirit like hers, Jenny could have been anywhere in the *world!* Or was she even alive? The thought of it all made my shoulders sag, and then I looked at it another way.

From the time I'd lived in Greenwich Village I remembered how my bohemian neighbors would impulsively move to cities all over the world, for reasons that were never quite clear. You'd figure they were gone for good but eventually they popped up again like graying homing pigeons. You'd see them waiting on line to buy sausages at Faicco's on Bleecker Street, greeting you with a grumble and complaining about rude waiters in Paris, or how tiny the ice cubes were in London pubs.

Was Jenny one of those eternal Villagers? I Googled *Jennifer Sutherland Greenwich Village* and got nothing. Then I Googled *Jenny Sutherland Greenwich Village* and up popped a weird little ad for JENNY'S CATS. *Leave your cat in our capable hands and enjoy your vacation in peace,* it said. *No term of stay too short or too long. J. Sutherland, Proprietor, 625 East 10th Street.*

I didn't want to phone first, which was stupid, but I had this wild inkling that if I went there in person, I could *will* J. Sutherland into being the Jenny I'd known. Or maybe I just wanted to keep an illusion alive for as long as I could, the way you wish you could have slept a little longer to catch the end of that dream that ended so suddenly when you woke up.

I wrote down the address, told Eddie Everything to let the delivery guys in if they showed up with my new appliances and headed for Manhattan.

I'd always hated the East Village. As far as I was concerned there was an oily grime all over it that no gentrification process was ever going to wipe clean.

I walked east on Tenth Street into Alphabet City, past trendy coffee shops with outdoor tables and heavily tattooed waitresses. A sagging ailanthus tree stood in front of my destination, a brick building that looked as if it had taken a few too many punches over the decades. It needed painting and pity, two things it clearly was not going to get.

I pushed open the dented front door and entered the vestibule, illuminated by the feeble light of a round landlord's-halo bulb overhead. A tag saying *JENNY'S CATS* was taped above a ground-floor buzzer. I took a deep breath and pushed the button, triggering an ugly buzzing sound that seemed to shake the building.

Nothing for a few seconds, and then, from the speaker: "Yes?" A female voice, strained and frantic. "Who's there?"

"Hello, I . . . uh . . . I'm looking for Jenny Sutherland."

"Are you dropping off a cat?"

"No." Wrong answer! "I mean, not just now. I wanted to talk about it."

"Hold on. Second door on your left, ground floor."

A bolder, louder buzzing sound unlocked the dividing door. I pushed it open and walked down a dim hallway reeking of pesticide before stopping at the second door and tapping on it.

The door opened a crack, just a crack, and a woman with hair like corn silk gone gray was looking at me with the unmistakably bright blue eyes that made my boyhood heart swell with desire. They were a pair of sunbeams, cutting through the years like twin lasers, and all I could do was stand there and stare at them.

Nobody else could have had those eyes. It was Jenny.

"Would you like to come inside?" she asked. "Be quick, don't let any of them out!"

She pulled the door open and I stepped inside. She pushed it shut behind me, and when my eyes adjusted to the dim light I saw them all over the place: cats of all shapes and sizes, darting toward corners and swirling around Jenny's ankles. I swear, there must have been a dozen cats in that studio apartment, and the only natural light in that place came from a window looking out on a fire escape and, a few feet beyond that, a brick wall.

In the midst of the madness there was a bed, just a mattress on the floor with a tangle of blankets and sheets. It was the same hippie-ish decor I remembered from the day my grandparents and I barged into her Greenwich Village love nest to find Vic living there "in sin," as my grandmother put it.

No doubt about it: Jenny Sutherland was now an aging hippie, the kind who still had the mojo to march in protest rallies.

I was reluctant to move, disgusted by the crunch of kitty litter under my feet. Jenny seemed shorter than I remembered her but still jackrabbit lean in a pair of blue-jean bib overalls and a loose gray T-shirt—undoubtedly, no bra underneath. Those ripe-apple cheeks of her youth had receded like an outgoing tide, revealing the stony beach that was her true face.

But her eyes! They were still younger than springtime, alive with mischief and magic.

"So," she said, "it's ten dollars a day, including food, unless your cat has special dietary needs."

"I don't have a cat."

"Oh!" She cocked her head. "I don't understand."

My lips had gone papery. I had to lick them before saying, "My name's Joseph Ambrosio. Do you remember me? You knew my uncle. He lived with you for a little while, a long time ago."

She just stared at me, the blue in her eyes seeming to roil around like waters in a riptide.

"His name is Vic. Victor Ambrosio. You had a place on Sullivan Street. I came to visit you once, when I was ten years old."

She seemed puzzled, and then those eyes widened to an impossible size and she covered her mouth with both hands, as if to muffle a scream.

"Oh my *God!* You got hit by a car!"

"That's right. That was me. *Is* me."

And then she literally leaped into my arms, both feet off the floor. It was like catching a butterfly.

"Looks like I found you," I said.

Herbal tea and seaweed cookies. Incredibly, that's what Jenny Sutherland and I shared in her kitchenette, at a tiny wooden table with two battered chairs. She'd brought those same goodies to Shepherd Avenue the one time she visited the house in 1961.

She was eager to talk, and what a life it had been for Jenny, a bit like my father's. When she left Vic she fled to a kibbutz in Israel, harvesting melons in the scalding midday sun. Then she moved all across Europe, backpacking some of the time, living in hostels when she could afford it. She was passionate about her painting, working as a street artist in Paris. Once in a while she would sell one of her works, but it was a struggle, one she eventually gave up.

"My passion," she admitted, "was bigger than my talent."

Then she tried to be a singer. Thanks to her looks a few bands let her shake a tambourine in the background, but her voice wasn't up to scratch, so there was another dream dashed.

Of course there were guys all along the way. As I'd predicted, she'd never married, never borne a child. And here she was now, pushing seventy and minding cats to keep body and soul together.

I told her about my career in children's books. She'd never heard of me because she'd never had kids, but seemed delighted by my success. I told her I had a grown daughter, and then I told her I'd bought the old house on Shepherd Avenue, to which she could only say: "That is *wild!*" The sort of response I'd expect to get from a kid.

Incredibly, Jenny wasn't asking me anything about Vic. I took a deep breath before broaching the subject.

"I have to ask you," I began. "Why'd you run out on my uncle?"

Jenny shut her eyes, the way a squeamish patient does to avoid watching blood being drawn. "It wasn't his fault."

"He was hurt pretty badly."

She opened her eyes. "He would have been hurt worse if I'd stayed."

"Did you just stop liking him?"

"No, no! Victor was sweet. Probably the nicest guy I ever knew." She smiled at some private memory of him. "Like a little boy lost."

"He still is, and he'll be seventy soon."

"Oh Lord. He never married?"

"Not even close. He lives alone in Queens, draws a pension. Drove a bus for thirty years."

"I never take the bus. Too slow."

"Well, no wonder you never crossed paths."

"Please don't be sarcastic, Joey."

"I think you were the one for him, Jenny."

She suddenly jumped to her feet, grabbing a bag of cat food and pouring it into a big metal bowl in the middle of the room. At the tinny sound of the food pellets striking metal, cats appeared from all over, surrounding the bowl jowl to jowl, their tails twitching. A dozen cats at ten dollars a day apiece came to $120 a day, $840 a week, probably tax-free. Certainly more than enough to cover Jenny's existence—feeding cats, scooping their shit, doing it all again tomorrow in this dim, crummy building.

"I still don't get it," I said, tearing my gaze from the hypnotic motions of those cat tails. "If you were happy with Vic, why'd you run off?"

"I was afraid."

"Of what?"

She forced a sad smile. "Same thing we're all afraid of, Joey. Love."

She had me there. I sighed, got to my feet and opened my arms to her. She set the cat food down and hugged me.

"Thing is, Vic was asking about you just yesterday."

"Come on!"

"That's what inspired me to track you down. Would you like to see him?"

She pulled back from the embrace and squared her bony shoulders. "Joey, I don't like looking back. I always try and look forward in life, you know?"

"Yeah, well, as far as I can tell forward's not looking any too promising for you. More cats, more cat shit. Am I wrong?"

I'd struck a nerve. Her eyes blurred with tears.

"Why are you doing this?" she asked, in the voice of a frightened child.

"I don't know. I set myself on a mission to find you, and I got lucky. I won't tell Vic about it, if you don't want that. But I want you to be able to get in touch with me, in case you change your mind."

I wrote my name, phone number and e-mail address on a piece of paper and handed it to her. The note trembled in her hand as she slid it into the bib pocket of her overalls. For all I knew she'd discard it the moment I left—but what the hell, I had to take a shot.

"You're raking things up that should stay buried."

"Sue me."

"You were a sweet boy. Life has made you kinda mean."

"Sweetness is overrated. These days I settle for decency."

I went to the door and had my hand on the knob when Jenny cried out: "Joey, wait!"

A change in heart? Had Jenny Sutherland decided to see Vic, after all? No. She pulled my hand off the knob and opened the door herself, just a crack, just enough for me to squeeze my way outside.

"Can't lose any of these cats," she said, and once I was out in the hallway she closed the door in my face.

I was numb on the long subway ride home, then stunned by the job Eddie Everything had done in my basement. The air down there was piney from the smell of freshly-cut lumber, and the table and benches he'd built were almost perfect replicas of those I remembered. It was as if he'd worked from a photograph of the originals.

"Eddie. Wow."

"Wanted to make sure they was right before I coat 'em with varnish."

"Do it, do it."

"See what arrived while you was out?" He gestured at big cardboard boxes against the wall, one containing a stove, the other a sink. A refrigerator was yet to arrive.

"I can install the sink all right," Eddie said, "but you gotta get the Con Ed guy to do the stove."

He picked up a broom and began sweeping up the sawdust.

"Great job, Eddie."

"We're gettin' there, Mr. A, we're gettin' there."

I went outside to feed and water the chickens, wondering if I was ever going to hear from Jenny Sutherland.

Chapter Twenty-five

The days passed, and no sign of Rose. September arrived, and with it a welcome autumnal chill. I longed for the frantic nighttime knock on the door that didn't come, and cursed myself for ever taking her to the beach.

That was the turning point, I explained to Nat during my usual visit that afternoon. He turned to me with raised eyebrows.

"What, she saw you in daylight and got scared?"

"She saw the ocean and realized there's a whole world out there she's never tasted."

At some point that summer I'd changed my mind about keeping Rose a secret from Nat and told him all about her. Dr. Rosensohn got edited highlights, but Nat was up to speed on every step of this crazy, passionate scenario.

"Doomed from the start," he concluded.

"Hey, thanks a lot, pal."

"Ahh, come on, Joey. It ain't just the difference in your ages, it's everything."

"I know, I know."

"Plus, let's keep in mind, she's a woman. Don't try to figure out a woman, it'll make your head hurt."

"Once again, advice from a guy who's never been married."

"To another guy who's never been married." Nat chuckled. "We're doing our part to keep the divorce rate down, eh?"

I sighed and looked down Atlantic Avenue. "Maybe I'll drop in on her at the Laundromat."

"Maybe you shouldn't do that. Call her on the phone."

"Would you believe I don't have her number? We've never spoken on the phone. Not once."

I was realizing it as I was saying this incredible thing. Nat sighed, grumbled and pulled his baseball cap down low to shield his eyes from the sun. This conversation was making him cranky.

"What do you expect from the woman? She's got a lot on her mind, what with her boy and everything."

I was stunned by that remark. "Justin? What's wrong with Justin?"

Nat laughed out loud. "Nothing's *wrong*. What, you don't read the papers? They called him up, that team he's with, that Seattle team."

I literally gulped. "Justin's been called up to the Major Leagues?"

"Yeah. So maybe she's in Seattle." He chuckled, a rumbly sound. "You, you're so busy walkin' around feelin' sorry for yourself, you're missin' the big picture."

It was true. Justin Wilson had been called up to play for the Seattle Mariners when the team roster expanded from twenty-five to forty players on September 1. Triple-A baseball had proven as easy to him as all the other professional levels of the game. He was hitting .478 for the Tacoma Rainiers when "the Show" came calling.

And just as I was reading all about it online I looked out the window and saw a local TV news crew pull up in front of Rose's house. Moments later a reporter was banging on the door, as a cameraman and a soundman waited on the sidewalk.

They waited and waited. Rose was probably at the Laundromat, and if she wasn't, she was hiding in the house. Or maybe she was in Seattle. Wherever she was, she was laying low.

After half an hour the TV crew went away. I was thinking about disregarding Nat's advice and dropping in on the Laundromat, and then I remembered with a jolt that I was due at the shrink's and had to rush to get there on time.

The last thing I needed now was a parole violation.

I was ten minutes late and Dr. Rosensohn wasn't happy about that.

"You've got to take these meetings seriously, or you're wasting both our times."

"I'm really sorry. I've been upset lately because I think it's over between me and Rose."

I told him about our trip to the beach, and how she'd been avoiding me since. I told him about Justin being called up to the Mariners, and how Vic had come to see me, and how I'd tracked down Jenny Sutherland. He seemed preoccupied or uninterested in anything I was saying, until I told him I was trying to write a Sammy Suitcase book.

"That's encouraging news," he said. "What prompted this?"

"Actually, it was Rose's idea. She read my last three books and said I couldn't just end it where I did, with Sammy and his father hitting the road again. Sammy has to settle down somewhere, so I'll do one more book and be done with him."

Dr. Rosensohn's eyebrows knotted. "What do you mean, one more book?"

"Just what I said. This'll be my last book. *Sammy Suitcase Settles Down*. The title's about as far as I've gotten, to tell you the truth."

"This is a bit disturbing to me, Mr. Ambrosio."

"Why?"

"Well, do you intend to write books in some other genre when you finish this one?"

"I doubt it. I've pretty much told all the stories I want to tell."

"So you're putting a ribbon on this part of your life, and proclaiming it finished."

"I don't know *what* the fuck I'm doing. What the hell are you getting at?"

He spread his hands. "Any time a man says he's doing something for the last time . . ."

"Oh, Jesus, do you still think I'm going to kill myself?"

"I just want to make sure you're not heading down that path. You seem especially vulnerable now because of your situation with Rose."

I stood up. "Doc, I'm spending all my time fixing up my house. Would I do that if I was going to ace myself? Plus, I've got a yard full of chickens who depend on me. Do you think I'd do anything to endanger their welfare?"

"As I say, I just want to be sure you're not heading for a dark area."

"Are you kidding? Life's just starting to get interesting. By the way, am I allowed to give you a present?"

He seemed stunned. "It's viewed as unprofessional."

I had to laugh. This from a guy who took two hundred bucks from me every time we had a conversation.

"Let's not call it a present, then," I said. "Let's call it a good luck charm."

I reached into my shirt pocket, carefully removed the egg I'd been carrying there and gave it to him.

"From one of my birds, laid this morning. Freshest egg you'll ever taste, you have my word."

I left him staring in open-mouthed wonder at the egg in the palm of his pudgy hand.

I didn't go straight home. I went to a bar a few blocks from Dr. Rosensohn's and had a beer to calm myself down. It was a sports bar, with a giant TV screen tuned to one of those shows where a panel of loudmouth sportswriters and gone-to-fat retired ballplayers sit and scream conflicting opinions at each other.

Suddenly a photo of Justin Wilson's face filled the screen, serious beneath a Seattle Mariners baseball cap.

"The kid from Brooklyn makes it to the big leagues!" one of the commentators shouted. "Just three months ago Justin Wilson was a baseball star at Franklin K. Lane High School. Since then he's roared through the minor leagues like a house on fire, and now the question is: At age nineteen, can he make it in the big leagues?"

Nineteen? Justin must have had a birthday since he left home. A year older, a few million richer . . .

"It's the Cinderella story of the baseball season!" another commentator chimed in. "The soft-spoken shortstop is certainly making it look easy. In his first two Major League games Wilson is four for seven with a home run!"

Holy shit. There he was on the TV screen, smashing the ball into the stands and casually trotting around the bases.

"And he'll be coming home this Saturday," the almost-hysterical commentator continued, "when the Yankees host the Mariners at the stadium!"

I pointed at the screen. "See this guy?" I asked the bartender. "I *know* him! He lives across the street from me!"

"Yeah? Good for you, pal."

"I'm serious!"

"I'm sure you are."

I finished my beer and ordered another. Then another. Then a shot of whiskey to break things up a little, and another beer to wash the whiskey down, and another whiskey to wash that beer down, and after that the bartender expressed a reluctance to serve me any more.

Rather than argue with him I staggered outside and headed home. I hadn't gotten blind drunk in a long time and I actually had to ask directions to the subway. Then I fell asleep on the train and overshot my stop, and by the time I reached the Cleveland Street station the moon was shining bright and I knew from the sounds of sirens and radios booming from passing cars that another wild night in East New York was well under way.

My poor chickens! I'd neglected them all day! I hurried home, tore a loaf of bread to pieces and scattered it all over the backyard.

"Sorry I'm late, girls, Daddy was stuck in town."

I watched them tear into the bread, realizing that I hadn't eaten all day, either. But I wasn't hungry. The emptiness I felt wasn't going to be filled by food.

I was soul-hollow, and I went to bed that way, dizzy and confused and lost. I passed out when my head hit the pillow and wondered if I was dreaming when a familiar pounding on my front door roused me.

But it was no dream.

Chapter Twenty-six

Iopened the door and she practically jumped inside, as if she was being chased.

"Thank God you're here, Jo-Jo!"

"I'm always here. You're the one who disappears."

"Don't start with me, not tonight. Just hold me."

She fell into my arms and clung to me tighter than she'd ever held me before. It was out of desperation, but I didn't mind.

"Everything's happenin' so fast!"

"You mean with Justin?"

"What the hell you think I'm talkin' about?"

I pulled away from her. "Hey. Do you realize I don't even have your phone number?"

"Why you wanna phone me when I'm standin' right here?"

"Rose, I got drunk today, and I'm not feeling great, and I can't even tell you how much I've missed you."

"Why'd you get drunk?"

"Because, like I said, I miss you."

"I miss you too, Jo-Jo." She buried her face in my chest. "I hadda hide in my own house all day, 'cause o' those damn reporters."

"What do you expect? Your son's in the Major Leagues now. He's a phenom. They want to know all about the woman who brought him up."

She sighed. "Opened my door this morning, some asshole from the Today Show is standin' there sayin' they'll send a limo to pick me up, and I can stay at the Plaza if I want."

"They're trying to dazzle you."

"Yeah, like a Puerto Rican's never been to a fancy hotel before, 'cept to clean the damn toilets."

"Justin's a big story, Rose. You can understand that."

"Yeah, I understand. Know what else I understand? How much they love that raised-by-a-single-mother bullshit. Look at me real sincere, get me to tell 'em how tough it was bringin' up my boy with no father around, in a *bad* neighborhood . . ."

She held up a finger, as if to warn me and anyone else who might be listening. "I'm no damn hero. I'm just a mom with a kid who plays baseball."

"You're a lot more than that. They want to hear from you."

"Yeah? What I got to say, they don't want to hear."

"What's that?"

She lowered her finger, ventured a crooked smile. "How it got *easier* after his father died. No more fights, no more bullshit. Just me and my boy, lookin' after each other. We gonna stand here in the hallway all night, Jo-Jo, or are you gonna take me to bed and hold me?"

We went to the bedroom and I did hold her, without her usual dash to dress after we'd made love, and it was wonderful, wrapping myself around her as if I meant to shield her from shrapnel.

"He's comin' to town tomorrow to play the Yankees."

"I know. It's unbelievable."

"He ain't comin' to Shepherd Avenue, he's stayin' with the team in a hotel. Sent me tickets for the game."

"That's great."

"Will you take me?"

I pulled her even closer. "You sure you want me to go?"

"I'm scared to go by myself."

That wasn't exactly the answer I wanted, but under the circumstances, I could handle it.

And the sweet circumstances were these: Rose actually fell asleep in my arms and stayed with me until the dawn's early light before fleeing, whispering as she dressed that I should meet her on the subway platform at seven that night.

Rose had never been to Yankee Stadium and I hadn't been there since I was a kid, before the new ballpark was built. The seats were good, ten rows back on the third-base side. I'm not sure the truth of what was happening had actually sunk in until we took our seats—Justin was a Major League baseball player, and if we didn't believe it . . . well, there he was on the field in his Seattle Mariners road uniform, casually chatting with his teammates around the batting cage.

Rose sat absolutely still and seemed to be holding her breath. "Don't wave to him," she said.

"I'm not."

"I don't wanna distract him, even though he knows we're here."

"He knows I'm here, too?"

"Yeah, I told him you were comin'. Oh Jesus, look, it's his turn to hit."

Chuckling over a teammate's joke, Justin stepped in to take his cuts. Line drive after line drive jumped from his bat, and on the fourth pitch he crashed the ball into the right-field seats, to scattered cheers from the cheap seats.

Rose sighed and there were tears in her eyes. "I feel like I'm dreamin,' Jo-Jo."

"Me, too."

"I mean . . ." She gestured toward Justin, the way a child would point at the moon upon seeing it for the first time. "That's my boy on that beautiful field. My *boy.*"

"It sure is."

Justin knocked another ball into the seats, this one even deeper than the last.

"Don't use it all up!" Rose said in an urgent whisper. "Gotta save some for the game!"

When he took his position at shortstop in the first inning Justin looked as if he'd been born on that swatch of dirt between second and third bases, serene as a guru and confident as a cop. With a Yankee runner at first base he made a diving catch of a scorching line drive and almost casually threw the ball to the first baseman, a flawless double play that drew cheers from the crowd.

In the second inning he came to bat with two men on base. The public-address announcer sounded as solemn as a high priest: "Now batting for the Mariners, number thirty-two, the shortstop, *Jussss-tin Willllll-son.*"

The crowd roared. Rose shut her eyes and mumbled a quick prayer while Justin dug in. He disregarded two pitches, the first a ball, the second a called strike, and then he got hold of that third pitch, lashing it down the right-field line for a certain double that he stretched into a triple.

Two-nothing, Mariners. Justin called for time as he dusted himself off, while the crowd screamed for the local boy who'd made good here in the world's most famous ballpark.

It was as if Justin had gotten us seats on the third-base side because he knew he'd be hitting a triple. He looked right at Rose, giving her a slight smile and a tip of his helmet. Through flowing tears she lifted her hand to wave to Justin, the timid wave a mother would venture to her grade-school child struggling through his lines in the school play.

"Look at my boy. Damn, he's tryin' to grow a moustache."

The next batter hit a fly ball deep to left. Justin tagged up and raced for home, sliding in ahead of the catcher's tag and then springing up and trotting to the dugout, where his teammates lined up for high fives. Rose sank back in her seat as if relieved to see him in the safety of the dugout.

"He made it, Jo-Jo."

"He sure did. Great slide."

"No, not that. I mean, *he made it*. He's a real ballplayer."

"You didn't think so before?"

She shrugged, hugging herself at the elbows. "Guess I had to see it with my own eyes. Now I know."

"What do you know?"

She hesitated, smiling bravely through her tears. "He ain't never comin' home."

She got to her feet. "Come on, Jo-Jo, we're leavin'."

"Rose. The game just started!"

"Yeah, but it can't get no better than this. You comin'? Stay if you want, I'm outta here."

We spoke very little on the subway back to Brooklyn, as if we were returning from a funeral. Rose went straight to her house from the Cleveland Street station, while I waited five minutes on the platform to sustain the illusion that we had nothing to do with each other.

Rose made it clear she had to be alone that night, but one major thing did happen before she said good night. She actually gave me her phone number.

I was up early the next morning to read the *Daily News* sports pages online. The Mariners won the game and Justin hit another double in the seventh inning, but there was another story in the sports section that grabbed my attention and nearly caused me to spit coffee on my laptop.

THE BROOKLYN BOY WHO *DIDN'T* MAKE IT, screamed the headline over two photographs of my Uncle Vic—one from back in the day, swinging a bat for Franklin K. Lane, next to a recent candid shot of him unshaven and paunchy, a baseball cap on his head.

The phenomenal Justin Wilson is walking in the footsteps of another top Brooklyn baseball prospect from half a century ago, the story began. *Victor Ambrosio was also a shortstop at Brooklyn's Franklin K. Lane High School, and he even grew up on the same street as Justin—Shepherd Avenue, in the East New York section.*

Like Wilson, Ambrosio, now 69, signed a professional contract right out of high school. His deal was with the Pittsburgh Pirates organization. Like Wilson, Ambrosio was also tagged "can't miss" by everyone who ever saw him play.

But fate had other plans for Ambrosio . . .

The sportswriter laid it on with a trowel: Vic's failure to hit in the minors, his return in defeat to the old neighborhood and his thirty-year career as a city bus driver. His only connection to the game he once dominated? Volunteer coaching at the Little League level.

I caught up with Ambrosio at one of those games, the sportswriter wrote. *He refused to discuss his failed baseball career.*

"I wish him luck" was all he had to say about Justin Wilson, the young star with the bright future that didn't pan out for Victor Ambrosio in the game of baseball.

I immediately called my uncle.

"I just saw the story. You okay, Vic?"

"Oh yeah. I'm a celebrity all over again. Got the kids askin' all kinds of questions about my career."

"Jesus."

"What I can't figure is, how the hell did that writer find out about me?"

"They have archives at the paper," I said, and then it hit me—it could have been *my* fault! The beat reporter who wrote the main story about the ball game also wrote the sidebar about Vic. Justin himself could have told the writer about the ballplayer who used to live across the street! Oh boy . . .

"Archives," Vic grumbled. "Yeah, I guess so. But how the hell did he find me out here in Queens? I'm not on that freakin' Facebook or anything!"

"Vic, these guys are good. They go through real-estate records, phone books ... everything's online these days, whether you like it or not."

"Christ, there's nowhere to hide," Vic grumbled. "Hey, by the way, I was misquoted."

"You didn't wish Justin luck?"

"Oh, I did. But the complete quote was: 'I wish him luck, and go fuck yourself.' "

I had to laugh, and to my relief Vic was laughing, too.

"You watch the game last night, Joey?"

"Some of it," I said. I wasn't about to tell him I'd actually gone to the ballpark with Justin's mother.

I could hear Vic sigh, the pleasurable sigh of a bone-weary man slipping into a warm bath.

"That swing," Vic said, in a dreamy voice I'd never heard from him before. "What a swing that kid has. I tell you the truth, Joey, that is one sweet swing."

Chapter Twenty-seven

The Seattle Mariners had three more games with the New York Yankees, and Justin hit the hell out of the ball in all of them. In his final turn at bat he crashed a fastball 450 feet into the center-field bleachers.

I was watching the game at home with Eddie Everything, who went out of his skull over that home run.

"Jesus, man, what'd this kid do, make a deal with the devil?"

"He's just a natural, Eddie. It happens."

"Yeah, sure it happens, maybe once every million years. Mariners gonna have to rob Fort Knox to lock this kid up!"

Justin jogged around the bases with his head down, as if he were ashamed of the way he'd made the pitcher look bad, while the TV commentator ran out of superlatives to describe his performance against the Yankees.

"Man," Eddie said, having drained a long-neck bottle of Budweiser in two gulps, "Rose must be so proud of that kid."

If he was prompting me to reveal something about Rose, he was wasting his time.

"Must be," I agreed.

"She gonna be sayin' bye-bye to the Laundromat any day now."

To that I had no comment. I hadn't heard from Rose since our night together at the ballpark. I'd called her once and left a message, asking if she was okay, but never heard back.

It was a strange time for her. I could appreciate that. Maybe she needed to be left alone for a few days, or for the rest of her life.

Eddie guzzled another two beers before staggering out into the night. I went to bed soon after he left and was up the next morning even before the chickens. It was a crisp dawn, perfect for a run around the reservoir at Highland Park. I fed the chickens, pulled on my running shoes and shorts and went outside to stretch on my stoop.

I had my back to the street when I was grabbed from behind by someone who wrapped his arm around my throat, cutting off my air supply as he literally lifted me off my feet. Struggling to breathe, it dimly occurred to me that I'd never expected to get mugged while going out for a run. Who would mug a jogger for the dollar or two he might be carrying in his shorts?

Suddenly I was released. I pitched forward, throwing my hands out to break my fall on the brick steps, then dared to turn and face my attacker.

Justin Wilson stood there grinning, wearing shorts and a Seattle Mariners T-shirt that fit his muscular torso like a coat of paint.

"Okay if I join you?" he asked. The very words he'd spoken the first time we met.

"Jesus!"

"Aw, you can just call me Justin."

I offered my hand to shake with him, and he stunned me by pulling me into an embrace. He seemed a little bigger than he was before he'd left to play ball, but every pound he'd packed on was pure muscle, and the sparse moustache he'd grown was a reminder that this incredible athlete was still just a kid.

"We runnin' or what, Joe?"

"Let's do it."

We set off at an easy trot on our same old route. The streets were empty at that hour, the shops beneath the elevated train line shuttered and gated. A garbage truck was coming our way, and the driver beeped his horn twice before sticking his head out the window and shouting: "Hey Justin, you *rock*, man!"

Justin smiled and waved at the man, who beeped his horn twice more.

"You know that guy?" I asked.

"I do now."

"I know you get sick of hearing it, Justin, but what you're doing is amazing."

"That ain't true. I don't get sick of hearing it."

We both laughed. As we circled the Highland Park reservoir he told me that his agent was working with the Mariners to sign him to a long-term deal. He'd come home the night before to talk it over with his mother, and slept in his old room. He had an afternoon plane to catch with the rest of the Mariners back to Seattle, a city he'd come to love.

"It's beautiful, man. You been there?"

"Never."

"Nice people, clean streets. Not like this shithole. No offense."

"None taken."

"Got a real-estate agent lookin' at houses for me. Gotta get her to come with me."

My heart dropped. "Your mother's moving to Seattle?"

"Hope so. Wanna get her outta here, Joe."

I was suddenly out of breath and slowed to a walk.

"Hey, man, you okay?"

"Little cramp," I lied. We were only a few blocks from Shepherd Avenue and walked the rest of the way.

"I got a favor to ask you, man. Wanna fly my mom out to see Seattle next week, and she ain't never been on a plane. Think you could take her to the airport for me, walk her to the gate? 'Cause I know she's gonna freak out if she goes alone."

I lifted the front of my T-shirt to wipe sweat from my face, and maybe a tear or two.

"I'd be happy to take her, Justin."

"Hey, man, don't know how I can thank you. And listen, I'm sorry it didn't work out between you and my mother."

I felt my heart drop. "She told you about us?"

"Yeah. I acted like I didn't already know."

"What did she tell you?"

"Well, when I first asked her to move to Seattle she got all funny about it, sayin' she was datin' a nice man here. Of course I knew it was you, and she finally admitted it *was* you. Then last night she told me it wasn't workin' out, so maybe she'd come out west with me after all."

He put a supportive hand on my shoulder. "The age thing, right?"

"Huh?"

"The age thing. That was the problem with you and my mom."

I nodded numbly. "Yeah, Justin. I'm just too old for your mother. We couldn't overcome that one."

* * *

I was actually quaking when I went inside. The idea of life on Shepherd Avenue without Rose was jarring to me, even though I couldn't imagine any kind of a future for us together.

Or could I?

I waited until I knew Justin was gone before phoning her, expecting to get voice mail, and I was startled when she picked up. I could tell she was at work from the pounding of washers and dryers in the background.

"Shouldn't call me when I'm at work, Jo-Jo."

"Are you moving to Seattle?"

"I ain't movin' anywhere. I'm gonna visit Seattle, if I can make myself get on that plane."

"I know. I'm taking you to the airport."

"That's very nice of you, but you don't have to bother."

"Justin asked me to do it. He's upset about our breakup."

"What?"

"He told me this morning how sorry he was that it didn't work out between us."

"Oh God! Jo-Jo, this is a mess!"

"It sure is. I've known all along that Justin knew about us. What I didn't realize was that we'd broken up."

"Whoa, whoa, whoa! You knew he knew *and you didn't tell me?*"

"He made me promise to keep my mouth shut, so I did."

"You been holdin' out on me, Jo-Jo! I don't like secrets!"

"I don't like them either, but I had no choice! And then you go and tell him we broke up!"

Silence, and when she spoke again she sounded like a scared schoolgirl confessing her sins to a priest.

"Jesus," she whispered, "my son must think I'm a whore."

"Wrong! He thinks you're a human being, made of flesh and blood. We haven't been doing anything wrong, have we, Rose?"

I could hear a Laundromat customer calling to her. She yelled something back, then returned to the phone.

"Goodbye, Jo-Jo," she said in a voice like steel. "And I mean forever."

The phone went dead. I threw it aside and jumped in the shower, as pissed off as I'd ever been. I was actually shouting at the water as it splashed against my face and accidentally swallowed some, and then a little got into my lungs and I fell to the tiles, choking like a lunatic. BROOKLYN BRIDGE CLIMBER DROWNS SELF IN SHOWER, the *Post* headline would have read, and while I was still choking the phone rang. I ran to answer it, expecting an apologetic Rose on the other end, but it was a male voice I didn't recognize.

"Is this Joe?"

I fought a coughing fit to ask: "Who's this?"

"Kevin. Remember me? Taylor's friend?"

It was my daughter's significant other, sounding extremely distressed.

"What's wrong? Is Taylor all right?"

"Well, actually, no. She's drunk." His voice broke. "Do you think you could come over? I don't know who else to call."

When it rains, it fucking pours.

An hour later I was climbing the creaky stairs to a fourth-floor apartment in a weather-beaten brownstone on West Seventy-Eighth Street, my daughter's home, a place I'd never been. Kevin had buzzed me in and was waiting outside the door up there. His eyes were red from crying but there was a smile on his face, the brave smile of a shy kid about to board the bus to sleepaway camp.

He shook my hand. "Thank you, Joe."

"What happened?"

"I came home from teaching a spinning class and found her drunk. She must have started early this morning, right after I left. Her office has been calling. I told them she was sick."

"Why'd she do this?"

"I don't know. Things have been good—I *thought* they've been good."

He covered his face with his hands and wept silently. I put my hand on his shoulder.

"Take me to her."

Taylor was sitting at a little table in the kitchen, her eyes at half-mast. She was barefooted and wore a gray sweatshirt with matching sweatpants. The air reeked of vodka, but there was no bottle in sight. The smell came from her breath, which was audible in that silent room—long lungfuls in and out, as if she'd just run a hard race. In her hands she cradled a cup of coffee, which she had not yet sipped. She brought the cup to her lips, took a sip and made a bitter face at the taste.

"Christ, Kevin, how many spoonfuls did you put in this?"

Then she saw me standing there. Her eyes momentarily widened and then she shut them, as if I were a bad dream she could wish away.

"How'd *he* get in?" she asked, as if I were a clever pet who'd slipped past a barrier intended to keep me off the good furniture.

"I called him, Taylor."

She muffled a belch. "Not the best idea you've ever had."

"I was out of ideas."

"Obviously."

"Taylor, he's here. Talk to him. And drink that coffee."

Kevin left the kitchen. Taylor forced herself to sip the coffee, shuddered at the taste and looked at me. "Well, have a seat already, if you're staying."

I sat down. Taylor stared at me with glassy eyes. "If you want coffee, the kettle's on the stove. All we have is instant, which sucks."

"I don't need coffee."

"Suit yourself." She slumped down a bit in her chair. "So. How's life in Brooklyn?"

"Well, my girlfriend just dumped me."

"You had a girlfriend?"

"Yeah, I had a girlfriend."

"Why'd she dump you?"

"Some other time. How drunk are you?"

"Not drunk enough."

"Am I allowed to ask why you did this?"

"Go ahead."

"Why did you do this?"

"To stop it."

"Stop what?"

She hesitated. "The free fall."

"Taylor, I don't understand."

"Of course you don't."

"I'd like to."

"Bullshit."

"Taylor. Talk to me. What have you got to lose?"

She tilted her head back and seemed to be searching the ceiling for answers, as if it were a starry sky. "Ever since my mother died, I have no connection. To anybody. I'm just out there, free-falling."

"You've got me."

"Oh, please."

"You've got Kevin."

"Yeah." She smiled. "But he's not blood. I chose him. He chose me. But . . . who *am* I? What am I connected to? Mom didn't have any family, so after she died . . ."

She couldn't finish the sentence. She sipped more coffee, made another face. "God, this tastes like shit."

"You don't consider me your family?"

"Do you really expect me to? I was an accident. Nobody wants an accident."

"Not true, Taylor. Penicillin was an accident. That one worked out pretty well, don't you think?"

She rolled her eyes. "I stand corrected. Me and penicillin. Proof that accidents can be wonderful."

I let my head fall, put my hands over my face. "I should have gone to your mother's funeral."

"Oh, this is deeper than that. I know your mother died young, and how hard that hit you, and your father was sort of a lunatic, always running all over the world, but . . ."

She sighed, weary with it all. "This is stupid, but I guess I wish I'd gotten to know my grandparents. That would have been nice." She pointed at me, almost accusingly. "Even *you* had grandparents."

"I sure did."

It was crazy, but somehow talking it out made Taylor seem younger by the moment, the little girl I'd taken to the playground so long ago.

Suddenly I had an idea. "Hey. Want to hear a story?"

She perked up, actually sat up a little straighter. "A story?"

"Yeah. You loved stories when you were a little kid. This one's pretty good."

Her eyes narrowed. She drained the rest of her coffee and set the cup down. "What's it about?"

"Oh, I think you'll like it. It's about your grandparents, and the day we went out to buy a Christmas tree."

Chapter Twenty-eight

My mother loved the holiday season—the lights, the decorations, gift-giving, everything about it.

Not my father. As a true-blue adman he saw Christmas as an opportunity for all kinds of rascals to make money, and nothing more. If they made a pill that knocked you out on December 20 and kept you unconscious until January 2, my father would have happily swallowed it.

To his credit he respected my mother's Christmas wishes, grumbling all the way. One of her annual wishes was for a real Christmas tree, and he always went to get it on Christmas Eve, knowing he could bargain the price way down on merchandise that would be worthless the next day.

That year he did a weird thing. He turned to me as we were putting our coats on and said, "Don't you think it's stupid to bring a dead tree into the house?"

I was nine years old, a quiet kid, the type of kid who kept his opinions to himself.

"The tree is *dead?*" I asked.

"Of course! It's been chopped down. It has no roots. How could it be alive?"

"Sal," my mother said, "calm down."

He kept his gaze on me. "So what do you think of this tradition, Joey?"

I shrugged apologetically. "I like Christmas trees."

My mother kissed my forehead. "That's my boy!"

A devilish grin came to my father's face. "You both like how the tree smells, right?"

We nodded uneasily. Something was up, and then from his coat pocket my father whipped out a green aerosol can with a drawing of a Christmas tree on it.

"Just so happens my agency did the ads for this wonderful product!" he said. "See? Forest In A Can!"

He held the can high over his head, his finger on the nozzle. "A few spritzes of this stuff all around the house, and we won't need a tree! Or we can get a fake tree, and soak it with this!"

He was in his full sarcastic mode, and we'd played right into it. My father always scared me a little when he sounded this way, but my mother remained calm.

"Sal," she said softly, "give me the can."

She was like a cop, urging a bad guy to drop his weapon. She held out her hand while I stood there, holding my breath.

"Come on," she urged, "give it to me."

My father's eyes glowed with false glee. "It's made with ten percent real pine sap, Elizabeth!"

"That's wonderful." She wiggled her fingers. "Give it to me. Please."

Her hand remained outstretched. His hand remained high over his head, out of her reach. Was he going to start spraying that stuff or not? The tension was killing me. After what seemed like years my father at last lowered his hand and gave my mother the can.

"Ahh, I wasn't going to use it," he said.

"I know," she said. "You just like to be a bad boy this time of year. Let's hope Santa Claus was too busy to see what you did."

"Funny."

"Look, it's dark already. Better get our tree before it's too late."

He turned to me. "Come with me," he said. "Someday you'll be wasting money of your own on a Christmas tree. Might as well see how it's done."

I'd already seen how it was done several times with my old man. For the past few Christmas Eves he'd taken me with him to the Roslyn Christmas tree lot, across the street from the local diner. There was a different tree salesman every year, but they all looked the same. They wore red hunting hats and too many layers of clothing. Drops of mucus quivered from their nostrils from those endless hours in the cold, and their breaths reeked of takeout coffee and whiskey. Cigarettes dangled from their lips, and when they heard my father's lowball offers their jaws would go slack and the cigarettes would dip straight down.

"You kiddin' me, or what?"

Then they'd argue back and forth before settling on a price, usually closer to my father's original offer than theirs.

But this year was different. We got to the lot and there wasn't a soul in sight: just a dozen or so trees, half of them lying flat on the ground, blown down by the wind. My father called out for the salesman. No answer.

I figured we'd be going home without a tree for the first time ever, until my father walked over to a tree that stood tall and straight against the fence, a prom queen of an evergreen.

"You like this one?"

Before I could open my mouth he hoisted it onto his shoulder and began the short walk to the car. I couldn't believe it.

"Dad!"

"Don't worry about it."

"But—"

"I said, don't *worry* about it."

But I was worried, all right, and a little sick to my stomach.

Did I know my father? I thought I did. Until this moment he'd been the most honest guy I'd ever known—but he also loved a bargain, and this was one hell of a bargain.

We didn't talk on the way home. My mother actually gasped at the sight of the tree, which looked even better indoors than it had on the lot.

We set it up in the metal stand, and even the trunk was perfect—it slid right into place, straight and true, with no need for my father to trim it with a hatchet. He fluffed out the branches.

"My God, Sal, this is the best tree you ever bought!"

"He didn't buy it!" I cried. "He *stole* it!"

My father glared at me. My mother glared at him. I looked down at my shoes, then up at my parents, and that's when it became really interesting.

There was no shouting. My mother's glare had dissolved into a look of wonder, as if a stranger was standing in my father's shoes. He looked like a little boy, scared and defiant at the same time.

"I didn't steal it," he said. "I just took it. The salesman wasn't around. Maybe he ditched the rest of his trees and went home."

My mother nodded. "Or maybe he didn't."

"Elizabeth—"

"Shhh, shhh," she said, pressing a finger to his lips to silence him— a tactic that, to my surprise, actually worked.

"Salvatore," she said, "take Joey with you, and fix this thing."

Fix this thing.

My father and I put our coats on and headed for the Christmas tree lot, where sure enough a salesman was sitting on an upended garbage can. He looked like a terminally ill man waiting to see a doctor.

His beard stubble was white and his nose was rippled with broken capillaries. He didn't look happy to see us.

"Look around," he said lamely. "Not much left."

"I already got my tree," my father said.

"So what'd you come here for?"

My father cleared his throat. "I took the tree from your lot. I'm here to pay for it."

The salesman's yellow eyes widened. "You *took* one of my *trees*?"

My father spread his hands. "Hey, you weren't here. I looked all over for you."

"I left to take a piss." He gestured at the nearby diner. "They let me use their toilet, long's I keep buyin' coffee. Makes me piss even more."

"What do I owe you?"

But the salesman's mind was blown. He was shaking his head in wonder. "I can't believe this. You took a tree and you came back to pay for it!"

"What do I owe you?" my father repeated.

The old man got to his feet. I heard his knees creak. "Well, now, that's a tough question. I didn't see it, did I? So how do I know what to charge you?"

My father put his hand on my shoulder. "Ask my son, here. You can trust him, because he's an honest man."

It was the first time my father had ever called me a man. I could feel my shoulders widen, and for a moment it felt as if I might sprout wings. The salesman turned to me, solemn as a priest.

"Was it a good tree, son?"

I nodded. "Best one you had." I held my hand up over my head. "About that high."

He rubbed his chin. "Twenty ought to do it, then."

It was a friendly price, a real break for my father in light of his honesty.

My father took a step back. "Twenty?" He gestured at the empty spot where the tree had stood. "For *that*?"

The salesman made a snorting sound, half-laugh, half-disbelief. "Mister, it ain't even there!"

"Come to my house. See it for yourself."

"I ain't leavin' the lot again!"

"I'm telling you, twelve bucks would be more like it."

"Nineteen!"

"Thirteen!"

I stood there in the cold, listening to them argue about a Christmas tree that wasn't there, wondering if I was going to behave like this when I was a grown-up. I wished my father was the kind of man you could hug, so I could give him a hug. That wasn't such a big deal, though. The big deal was the return trip to the lot. That was my father's way of hugging me, by doing the right thing.

At last they settled on a price. My father paid the man and we left the lot.

That's when a curious thing happened. My father's eyes were brimming with tears as he got in the car. He rested his forehead on the steering wheel and sat there in silence. He was starting to scare me.

"Dad? Are you okay?"

He sat up straight, as if jolted from a dream. He had to clear his throat before speaking.

"That mother of yours," he said. "She's one in a million." He started the car, revved the engine. "Hear me, Joseph? One in a million."

Taylor hadn't quite sobered up by the time I got to the end of my story, but I had her full attention, fuzzy as it might have been.

"Sounds like my grandmother was quite a woman."

"She was."

"And my grandfather was a lunatic."

"Not really. That was a bad day for him."

"Yeah. Because he had to spring for a Christmas tree."

"No, no. It turns out that the day before, my mother had been di-agnosed with the cancer that killed her a few months later. My father knew about it. I didn't. He told me about it years later."

Taylor let her head fall, exhaling long and hard.

"He was angry about that. He never really got over his anger about her illness. And he was baffled by her, because no matter how sick she got, she never complained, never asked why this was hap-pening to her. Brave lady, my mother."

"Jesus."

"Funny you should mention him. She believed in Jesus, with all her heart. She believed Jesus was looking after her."

Taylor lifted her head and rose unsteadily to her feet. I thought she wanted to hug me, but the move she made in my direction turned out to be a loss of balance, which she quickly corrected by grabbing the edges of the table.

"I'm going to get some sleep now," she said, more to herself than to me. Ignoring my outstretched arms, she released the table and shuffled toward the bedroom without another word.

"You're a chip off your old grandfather," I said to her back. "He wasn't much of a hugger either."

Chapter Twenty-nine

At least Kevin was grateful for my visit. He embraced me on my way out and thanked me for coming over.

"Come and see me, the two of you," I said. "Like I've said, you can stay over if you want. I've got a whole apartment upstairs, waiting for you. Total privacy."

His eyes were still red but he forced a brave smile. "We may take you up on that someday, Joe."

As I left I realized that if I was going to make good on that offer, I'd better get some furniture up there. As soon as I got back to Brooklyn I called Eddie Everything and asked him if he could get hold of a van. Of course he could.

The next morning we were off to IKEA, where I bought a king-sized bed, a mattress, a couch, a wooden table with two chairs and a bedside table. I also bought sheets, pillows. blankets, dishes, cups, glasses, cutlery and a couple of lamps.

Eddie drove slowly back to East New York, the fully packed van clinking and rattling all the way.

"So let me get this straight, boss," Eddie said. "You're stickin' all this stuff upstairs, but you ain't gonna rent out the apartment."

"Correct."

"I don't get it."

"My daughter may be coming over to visit, and I want her to have a place to stay."

"She may visit?"

"That's right."

"So you ain't sure she's comin'?"

"No, I'm not sure. Truth is, she'll probably never come over. But I want to be ready, just in case."

Eddie's eyes widened. He shook his head and chuckled.

"No offense, boss, but you are one crazy white man."

"I've been called worse."

We carried everything upstairs and worked together to assemble the furniture through Swedish instruction sheets with pictures but no words, cursing all the way. I cut my finger while putting the bed together and Eddie jammed his thumb trying to assemble the couch.

"Jesus," he said, "these Swedish fuckers don't make it easy, do they?"

At last everything was assembled, the cupboards were filled, and even the bed was made. The second floor of my house looked like a cozy little bed-and-breakfast.

Eddie reached out to shake my hand, and then it hit me why he was doing such an unusual thing.

Because all the work at 207 Shepherd Avenue was now complete. My house was finished.

"Been great workin' for you, boss," Eddie said, and his voice actually cracked as he spoke. "You wanna do anything else, you wanna change anything around, you know where I am."

"Thanks for everything, Eddie Everything. I'll leave the eggs on my front stoop from now on, okay? Pick them up whenever you want."

He startled me by pulling me into a quick embrace and patting my back. I paid him for the day and he pocketed the cash without counting it.

"Anything else I can do for you before I go?"

I hesitated, then decided to go for it. "I could use your advice, Eddie."

"Shoot."

"Justin wants Rose to visit him in Seattle, and he asked me to take her to the airport. But she's mad at me, never mind why. Think I should take her?"

Eddie's face softened. "Man, you don't need my advice this time. Rose is *gone*. Saw her get into a limo last night with a coupla suitcases. I'm sorry, man, I thought you knew."

That's when I fell into a kind of a dreamlike state. I had my book to write and illustrate, but it was an impossible task. Just couldn't settle on a home or a permanent living situation for little Sammy Suit-case.

In the midst of it, a happy bolt from the blue: Taylor phoned to thank me for coming to see her. She sounded awkward and formal, and I had a feeling she made the call at Kevin's urging, but I was grateful anyway.

"Call me any time," I said.

"Will do," she replied, and I allowed myself to believe that she meant it.

Otherwise, I lived my daily stations of the cross: run in the morning, feed the chickens, gather eggs, try to work on the damn book, walk the neighborhood.

Visiting Nat was usually the highlight of my day. The old man knew everything I was up to, everything that was happening, and he was never judgmental.

"You're better off without that Rose for a while," he said. "Young woman like that could put you in an early grave."

"It's a little too late for me to die young, Nat."

"Ahh, nobody's diggin' a hole for you yet."

"You either."

"Maybe not, but I shiver every time I see a shovel. Remember that night you tried to run away, with all that money I paid you for those bottles?"

That's what a conversation with Nat was like. He could jump from the present to 1961 without breaking stride.

"Crazy night," I said.

"Yeah, well, some people blamed me for what you did."

"People like to place blame."

"I didn't know you were gonna use the money to run away! You told me your father was comin' to take you home."

"Sorry I lied to you, Nat."

"Ehh, we all lie a little. Gets you through the day."

"Anyway, I tripped and fell before I could escape."

"No, you didn't."

"I didn't?"

"I say you fell on purpose. Go ahead and make faces. I've been thinkin' about it. You run up and down that block a million times all summer, and all of a sudden you trip and fall? Come on. Maybe your head was tryin' to run away, but your feet had other plans. You were safe here. We all need safe, no matter how bad it is."

"No disrespect for your theory, Nat, but I'm already seeing a court-appointed shrink."

"Yeah, well, what the hell does *he* know? I don't care *where* he went to college!" He stamped his foot on the stony sidewalk. "He can't beat what I got. My degree came from these streets."

"And Auschwitz," I said. It was a thought that had somehow turned into spoken words, which I immediately regretted. Nat stared at me long and hard, his hands clutching his knees. My head pounded as a fifty-year-old echo sounded in my ears. *He escaped from Hitler, but he don't like to talk about it . . .*

I dared to touch his bony shoulder. "I'm so sorry, Nat."

He nodded forgivingly, then relaxed his hands and spread them wide. "These streets," he whispered. "A picnic, compared to that."

Rose was gone, all right, but for how long? I went to the Laundromat, where her replacement, a short black woman with a fierce face, was stuffing a mountain of sheets into the biggest washing machine in the place. I asked her when Rose would be back and she made a snorting sound.

"Nobody knows. She just said she hadda leave town for a while."

"She didn't say how long?"

"What's the matter, you don't understand English? She said she be gone for a while. You got a dictionary at home? Look up *while*. Meantime, I gotta work these fuckin' double shifts."

"Sorry."

"Yeah, I'm sorry, too. Sorry I ain't got no son in the damn Major Leagues, makin' a million bucks."

The days passed. No word from Rose, no word from Taylor. My agent nagged me about the new book, and I told her it was coming along slowly but surely.

Lying to an agent isn't a sin. It's an expectation.

Meanwhile, Justin Wilson's agent came through for him, big-time. He'd finished up the season with the Seattle Mariners without faltering, and the story in the *Daily News* said he'd signed a five-year guaranteed deal with the team for an estimated $20 million. Not bad for a kid who'd just turned nineteen.

I was working at my desk in the front room when Vic phoned me. "You see how much your friend is getting from the Mariners?"

"Yeah. It's unbelievable."

"Sure is. Especially if the pitchers find a hole in his swing."

"A hole?"

"A flaw. It could happen. Kid only played a month in the majors, and they're layin' this kind of a bet on him? They're all nuts."

I had to laugh. "You said he had a sweet swing, Vic."

"He does. So did Kevin Maas."

"Who?"

"Look him up. Kevin Maas, *M*-double-*A S*. Played for the Yankees about twenty years ago. Came to the big club and for the first few weeks, every ball he swung at went over the fence. He was gonna make everybody forget about Babe Ruth and Mickey Mantle. Then the pitchers figured him out, and the word went around the league, and he couldn't hit his weight. Bye-bye, Kevin Maas."

"I doubt that'll happen to Justin Wilson."

"So what if it does? It doesn't matter. He's got twenty million bucks comin' to him, no matter how badly he fucks up. It's a crazy world, Joey, that's all I'm sayin'."

I said goodbye to my uncle and looked out the window. A little kid was walking past in a red one-piece outfit, wearing devil horns and carrying a trident, followed by a girl dressed like a ballerina and another kid dressed like a cowboy. What the hell was *this?*

It was Halloween! I ran out and bought a bag of Milky Ways, hoping I'd get some trick-or-treaters. I also got a pumpkin and carved a scary-face jack-o'-lantern, lit a candle inside it and put it on my front stoop.

They began arriving at dark, mostly with their parents right behind them. I recognized some of the parents from the block, and we nodded politely to each other.

Maybe this would help break the ice, I figured. They'd stop wondering about the weird white guy living all alone in that big house all these months, and have a conversation on the street with me now and then.

Then again, maybe not.

Bertha Washington appeared at my door with her two little boys, both in skeleton suits. I'd seen those kids coming and going to school but this was the first time we were face-to-face.

"This is our neighbor, Mr. *Am-bro-zee-oh*," she told the boys, who studied me with wary eyes.

"I like your chickens," the smaller one said.

"I like my chickens *fried,* " the bigger one said. Bertha tapped the back of his head but I couldn't help laughing. I gave the Washington brothers two Milky Ways apiece.

After the last of the trick-or-treaters left I tossed the seeds and the gooey innards of the pumpkin to the chickens, who tore into the mess. I turned in early and got up early, and when I stepped outside to go running I found that someone had stomped my jack-o'-lantern flat on my front stoop.

That was depressing enough, and then I remembered that I was due at Rosensohn's office that afternoon for my next-to-last session. I wasn't in the mood for it, especially the way things were going.

So I scraped up the pumpkin mess, took a trot around Highland Park and put in a few fruitless hours trying to write my last Sammy Suitcase story when I got a phone call from Eddie Everything.

"How's it goin', boss?"

"Somebody smashed my jack-o'-lantern."

"Little fuckers, they did that up and down the block. Listen, I thought you should know that Rose is comin' back tomorrow."

My heart leaped. "How do you know?"

"I got my sources, man, you know that."

"Is she moving to Seattle?"

"How the fuck should I know that? All's I know is, she's gonna be at the Laundromat tomorrow, which means she's comin' home."

"Thanks, Eddie."

"Hey, no problem. Need anything?"

"Not at the moment."

"Later, man."

I felt rejuvenated. I was ready to face Rosensohn and anything he might want to talk about.

But before I saw him I had another task to accomplish in Manhattan, and time was running out.

Chapter Thirty

Rosensohn looked weary, and I was nervous. I had this session and one more after it to wrap up my probation period. If he didn't sign off on me, I could actually face time behind bars.

Or so they wanted me to believe. It was ball-breaking at its best, but it worked. I just wanted it all to be over. Why was it taking so long? I was a guy who'd had a bad day and climbed to the top of the Brooklyn Bridge to scatter his dead father's ashes at a time when the whole city was on edge, fearful of the next terrorist disaster. It was an unbelievably stupid thing I'd done, no question, but I hadn't hurt anybody.

"Am I in trouble?"

I hit him with that question before I even sat down. He looked at me over the tops of his glasses, the way a teacher looks at a student he suspects of having farted.

"How are you today, Mr. Ambrosio?"

"Wondering if I'm in trouble."

"For what?"

"Look, we meet one more time after this, and then you provide the authorities with some kind of evaluation of me, is that right? I just want to know where I stand."

"For starters, why don't you stop standing and sit down?"

That I could do. I sat down and for a few moments we just listened to each other breathe, while Rosensohn consulted his notes. He didn't look happy.

"What do you do, make out some kind of a report card on me?"

"I guess you could call it that," he said, keeping his eyes on his notes. "I see you missed gym class quite a few times."

"Don't fool around, Doc. On top of everything I'm paying for this, so what the hell is my grade?"

He put his notes aside, looked up and offered me a funny smile. "Incomplete."

I could feel the pulse in my throat. "What are you talking about?"

"We're missing a key element here. Do you remember what I said to you, the very first time we met?"

I remembered. I saw where he was going. I'd been fearing this all along, without ever putting the fear into words.

"You said you suspected that my bridge adventure had more to do with my mother than my father."

He pursed his lips. "That's what I said, all right."

"What am I supposed to do about that?"

He shrugged. "Prove me wrong, or prove me right. It's time to really talk about your mother, Mr. Ambrosio. Don't just tell me she died young. I already know that."

I clasped my hands together to stop the shaking. "Ask me what you want to know."

"It doesn't work like that. Tell me what you want to tell me. Tell me *anything* about her."

I licked my suddenly dry lips. "Want to hear about the last time I ever saw her?"

Rosensohn smiled, shrugged. "Nothing like an ending for a starting point. I'm listening."

It was at the hospital. I knew something troubling was up when my mother asked my father to leave the room. She'd never done that before. We were a team, the three of us, and we'd drawn even closer as her illness progressed, and suddenly here she was asking for a little privacy with me.

My father seemed stunned by the request. "You sure?"

"Just for a few minutes, Sal. You can get me a Coke."

My father detested sugary, carbonated soft drinks—doubly so, because he'd been forced to do ads for a few of them—but at this point Coca-Cola was the only thing my mother could keep down. So off he went to the Coke machine, two flights down. He'd be gone for a few minutes: My mother's precious window of time.

"Come here, Joey."

She patted the bit of mattress beside her hip, and even that little motion seemed to pain her. I obeyed, sitting on the edge of the bed. She ran her hand up my forehead to smooth back my hair, a hand that was little more than skin and bone.

"You need a haircut, young man."

I nodded. She was smiling and friendly but I was actually afraid of the way she looked: pale as milk, and so drawn that her eyes seemed to be floating in their sockets.

But the eyes themselves shined with the same inextinguishable life and love I'd always known.

"Why'd you make Daddy go away?" I asked, aware that my voice was trembling.

"Well, there's something I have to tell you, Joey."

"You're going to die. That's it, isn't it?"

"Yes, that's true, but it's not what I wanted to tell you."

What was this? Could there be bigger news than the fact that my mother was admitting the end was near? I was so stunned I couldn't even cry.

"Mommy. You're scaring me."

"Oh, no, Joey, don't be scared! It's a wonderful thing! Want to hear it?"

I nodded. She put her lips to my ear.

"We're going to *meet* again!"

I pulled away from her. She was smiling, her teeth looking longer than usual and her gums as gray as rain clouds.

I was baffled. "How?"

A truly blissful look came to her face, as if she'd just been injected with morphine. "In heaven, Joey. We'll be together again in heaven."

"You mean, after I die?"

"That's right." She rolled her eyes toward the ceiling. "I'll be up there, waiting for you."

"Heaven is in the sky?"

"Yes. Way up beyond the clouds."

It was a lot to absorb, and I had to absorb it before my father returned. It was as if my mother had read my mind.

"Don't tell Daddy. He doesn't believe in heaven, but he's wrong. He's going to heaven someday, too."

"He is?"

"Yes. It'll be a wonderful surprise for him. It's the place all good people go when they die. Nobody ever gets sick in heaven, and everybody's happy forever."

I swallowed. "Even Daddy?"

It was stunning to hear her laugh, but that's what she did, maybe the last laugh of her life.

"Yes," she said. "Even your Daddy will be happy in heaven."

There was the thump of approaching footsteps, and moments later my father appeared carrying a bottle of Coke and a straw.

"One Coca-Cola, as ordered. A nurse had to get me a straw. Only took her about half an hour. Must be a union job."

He popped the cap, stuck in the straw and put the bottle in my mother's hands, cocooning his own hands around hers.

"So, did you two finish your secret meeting?"

"It wasn't a secret meeting, Sal. Just a moment with my son."

She put the straw in her mouth, sipped the soda and gave me a quick wink. Visiting hours were over. We kissed her cheek and left.

On the drive from the hospital my father approached it cautiously.

"Anything I should know?"

"About what?"

"Whatever it was your mother had to tell you."

"No."

"You sure?"

"Yes."

"So you have a secret."

"It's not a secret."

"But you don't want to tell me."

"Daddy—"

"Ahh, go ahead, keep it to yourself." He gripped the steering wheel as if he meant to strangle it. "Fucking *secrets.*"

He was upset and he was exhausted. His face reddened and it looked as if his head might explode. I couldn't stand it.

"She told me she loves me," I blurted.

He looked at me, eyes wide. "That's it?"

"Yeah." I looked out the passenger window. I wasn't much of a liar at that age and figured my eyes might give me away.

But I got away with it. My father believed me. "Christ," he said, pulling into the parking lot of the diner where we always ate after hospital visits, "why the hell'd I have to leave the room for *that?*"

Her condition worsened that night. I wasn't allowed to go to the hospital anymore. A week later she died, and I never told my father the truth about her last words to me.

Rosensohn sighed deeply when I finished talking, as if he'd been holding his breath for the duration of my story.

"My father totally flipped out when she died. It's as if the moment her heart stopped beating, the world made no sense to him. He had to escape from his own life, wipe it clean. Quit the job, sell the house, hit the road."

"And dump you off on Shepherd Avenue."

"Yeah, well, he saved me for last. That was considerate of him, I guess."

"Under the circumstances, maybe that wasn't the worst thing in the world. He hardly seemed capable of taking care of you himself, but your anger toward him is totally understandable."

By this time I'd actually grown fond of Dr. Rosensohn and I was reluctant to contradict him. But he'd left me no choice.

"Doc," I said, "the one I was really angry with was my mother."

"That also makes sense. When she died, she abandoned you. How else would a ten-year-old be expected to react?"

"*No!*"

Rosensohn was truly startled.

"What am I missing?" he asked after a long moment.

I leaned forward, gripping the edge of his desk. "She lied to me," I all but snarled. "Fucking *lied* to me about meeting again, with that bullshit story about heaven."

"But perhaps she believed it!"

"So what if she believed it? *I* don't believe it. Do *you* believe it?"

"Me, personally? No. But I could be wrong! Maybe there is a heaven, or at least some kind of existence beyond this one."

"I wouldn't bet on it."

Rosensohn chuckled. "Don't you see? You *are* betting on it. We're *all* betting on it. Deep down, whether or not you believe in God or heaven or whatever, it's impossible for any of us to imagine not existing. We all have just enough vanity to buy into that idea of immortality. In your mother's case, it took the form of devout Catholicism. Heaven and hell and angels and devils."

"Exactly! Total bullshit!"

"Okay, let's say it is. Maybe you should look at it another way. Maybe your mother didn't believe it. Maybe she just wanted to leave her son with a comforting thought, knowing she wouldn't be there to take care of you."

"In that case, she was lying."

"Oh, Jesus *Christ,* Joseph!"

It was the first time Dr. Rosensohn had ever summoned Christ's name, or spoken my first name. He leaned way back in his chair to make that squeaky, creaky sound he knew I despised.

"You look pale, Doc. Maybe you need a little fresh air."

"And maybe you should think everything through and give that poor woman who brought you into this world a break. Tell yourself she meant well! Give her the benefit of the doubt!"

"You're getting pretty aggressive, Doc."

"Time's running out. This is crucial stuff."

He leaned forward, causing a far deeper, more sinister creaking noise from under his chair.

"It's pretty simple, though. Just grow the fuck up, Mr. Ambrosio. The sooner you do that, the easier your life will become."

The session was over. I rose from my chair the weary way a boxer rises from his stool at the bell for the fifteenth round.

"You'll be happy to hear that I'm about to do an extremely grown-up thing," I said softly. "Something I've never done before."

Rosensohn's eyes narrowed. "And what would that be?"

"We'll talk about it next time," I said, heading for the door. "I want you to have something to look forward to in our final session."

He called out to me but I ignored him. Fuck his final report, fuck his "incomplete" grade! If I was going down, I was going to do it in style.

In the elevator on the way down I reached into my jacket pocket and pulled out a tiny blue box from Tiffany's, tied with a white ribbon.

Rose didn't wear rings. I was hoping she'd make this one her first.

Chapter Thirty-one

I was going to ask Rose to marry me. I'd gone to Tiffany's before my shrink session and dropped more than two grand on a ring that probably would have cost half that much in the Diamond District on Forty-Seventh Street, but I was willing to pay for the dazzle of that robin's-egg blue box.

It was time, I told myself. I was sixty years old and I'd never asked a woman to marry me before. I'd never even *thought* of asking any woman to marry me. A major life experience for most so-called normal people, and I'd avoided it as if it were a tar pit.

But now, suddenly, I felt as if I might fall into that pit if I lost Rose. What if she moved to Seattle? What would life on Shepherd Avenue be like for me without that late-night knock on my door?

If I pledged myself to this woman, really laid everything on the line, she'd let herself go and admit to the love that she'd been holding back from me, I told myself.

What I *should* have told myself was that sentences ending in "I told myself" usually didn't live up to expectations.

But I had yet another "I told myself" nagging at me, and it was this:

Ignore her order to never, ever go to her house! She'll respect you as a man if you bang on her door and ask her to marry you!

Or so I told myself.

The next night I showered, shaved and put on my best shirt. Then I went to the front parlor and sat there with the lights out, keeping an eye on Rose's dark house. Unless Eddie Everything's information was bad she was at the Laundromat, which closed at seven p.m., which meant I'd be seeing her at a few minutes past seven.

Eddie's information was good. Here she came, walking slowly

and looking exhausted in the November darkness. I realized her body was probably still on Seattle time.

Maybe this wasn't a good night to pop the question. A cranky, jet-lagged woman who had just put in ten hours at a Laundromat wasn't likely to be in the most romantic state of mind, was she?

On the other hand, it felt like now or never.

Now or never, I told myself!

I gave her ten minutes to settle in, then left my house and headed for hers like a guided missile.

I knocked on the door and was startled when it opened a heartbeat later. Rose squinted at me, a look that quickly turned wide-eyed. She grabbed me by my shoulders, pulled me inside and slammed the door shut.

"What the *hell* are you doin' here, Jo-Jo?"

I couldn't immediately answer. I was in a state of wonder, looking all around that tiny living room. It was nothing less than a shrine to Justin: trophies on every shelf, photos and plaques covering the walls. Everything from tiny Justin on a Little League team to a poster-sized photo of him swinging the bat for the Mariners.

That last one was not yet hung. It was leaning against the wall, a wall on which I couldn't see another bit of space to hang such a thing.

I turned to Rose. Her arms were folded tightly across her chest—just as they were the first time she came to my house to confront me, six months earlier.

Were we back to that? I refused to believe it. I took a step toward her. She took a step back.

"You mad at me?"

"Little bit."

"Because I came to your door? How else can I see you, if you don't answer your phone and don't come to my house?"

"I was gonna come over tonight."

"And now?"

"Now, I ain't so sure."

I slid my hand into the chest pocket of my jacket to feel the box with the ring, reminding myself of my mission. There it was, shielding my heart. I didn't know much about marriage proposals, but I was pretty sure they didn't have such rocky beginnings. I had to unlock Rose's arms, if I had any hope of getting a ring on her hand. Would a friendly question do it? It was worth a shot.

"How was Seattle?"

She sighed, but the arms remained locked across her chest.

"It's a beautiful city. Never seen nothin' like it. Clean. Nice people. Justin bought a house."

That stunned me. "Already?"

"He seen what he liked, and he bought it. I think he paid too much, but it ain't my money."

"I don't think Justin has to worry about money for a while."

Rose nodded. "Forever," she said softly.

I could see she was exhausted, every which way. But then she startled me by dropping her arms and reaching for me.

"Could I have a hug, if it ain't too much trouble?"

We embraced. I caught a whiff of bleach in her hair and knew she'd been washing restaurant linens. That was always her least favorite task: the heavy white tablecloths, the endless drying time, the complaints from other customers about the way the linens tied up the dryers.

"He wants me to move there, Jo-Jo."

It was the bleach smell more than her words that brought me to my senses. Here was her son, eager to provide her with a brand-new life far from East New York. Rose had an ancient soul but she was still young, young enough for a fresh shot at everything that got messed up the first time around. With a second chance out west she could start again, marry again, maybe even have another child.

What was I offering her? A move across the street on Shepherd Avenue, to live out her days with an aging children's-book writer whose own crazy life was approaching its final chapters. Like it or not, my funky years were looking me in the eye. I wasn't a kid. Anything could happen. I could become debilitated by a stroke or a heart attack. Great life for Rose—the first half protecting an athletic marvel from the perils of the streets, the second half wiping an old man's chin whenever he drooled the soup she spooned into his mouth.

As Dr. Rosensohn had told me, it was time to grow the fuck up. I was willing to try.

Rose suddenly pulled back from the embrace and poked a finger at my jacket.

"Hey, Jo-Jo, what's stabbin' me, here?"

I put my hand over the box bump. "A very bad idea."

"Yeah? You keepin' a bad idea in a box?"

Before I could say another word she struck like a snake, pulling my hand away and reaching into my pocket to pull it out. A nanosecond of puzzlement, and then she realized what she was holding and her jaw dropped.

"Oh my God!"

"I was going to do it, Rose. I was going to get down on one knee and everything."

"My *God!*"

"It was a stupid, selfish idea. I wasn't thinking of you. Not that you would have accepted my proposal, but anyway, you can relax. I'm not proposing to you."

"You don't want me?"

"Oh, I want you. But getting everything you want is for kids, and I'm no damn kid."

Her lips were trembling, as if a winter wind had suddenly blown through the house. "I ain't no kid, either."

"Sure you are. You just did it backwards. You were old when you were young. Now you can be young again."

She smiled at me through fresh tears. "Well, you're makin' it easy, Jo-Jo. I'm gonna do it. Gonna give my prick landlord notice tomorrow, get outta here by the end o' the month."

My heart sank. "Wow. That soon?"

"Yeah. Justin wants me there yesterday, you know? Gonna have Christmas in Seattle. That's what he wants." She made a sound that was half-chuckle, half-sob. "Shit happens fast when it happens, you notice?"

"Sure does."

Suddenly we were awkward in each other's presence, knowing whatever it was we'd had was officially over, and what the hell had it meant while it was happening? I'm not sure either of us would ever really know. But whatever it was, it had been precious.

Rose continued holding the ribboned box in her open hand, as if it were a baby bird she couldn't persuade to fly away.

"Never seen such a beautiful box."

"Open it if you like."

"Really?"

"What the hell. If you like the box, you're going to love the ring."

She pulled the ribbon and opened the box. The stone was square-cut, in a platinum band. Rose brought the box to her face and turned it to see the ring glitter from all angles.

"Most beautiful thing I ever saw."

"Try it on."

Her eyes widened. "I can't do that!"

"Why not?"

"'Cause we ain't gettin' married."

"You can still try it on. Go ahead, I had to guess at the size. Want to see how I did."

She slid the ring on and held her hand out, fingers spread wide.

"You did good, Jo-Jo."

"I got lucky. The woman at the ring counter had hands like yours."

"No kiddin'? She work in a Laundromat too? That's the only way you get knuckles like mine."

"Anyway, I figured if it fit her . . ."

I stopped talking, because Rose was sobbing.

"Jesus, man, you gotta be so fuckin' *nice* about everything?"

She pulled off the ring, set it back in the box and put the lid on. She even tried to tie the ribbon around the box, but her hands were shaking too much.

"Don't worry about that," I said, taking the box and the ribbon and shoving them both back into my pocket.

"There," I said. "Like it never happened."

Rose had calmed down. She wiped her eyes and forced herself to look stern. "You're gonna get your money back, right?"

"Yeah, don't worry about that."

"'Cause I'm gonna be real upset if you don't get your money back."

"Got the receipt right in my wallet. *That* I'm not going to show you."

She giggled. Then she told me Justin would be back in a few weeks to help her pack up, and that her landlord was going to be pissed off by the sudden departure, and all the spruce-up improvements he was going to have to do for a new tenant.

I headed for the door on shaky legs and dared to ask, "Am I going to see you again?"

She shrugged. "Like I said, I'll be here a few more weeks."

"But you won't be knocking on my door, will you?"

She let her head fall. "Can't do it anymore, Jo-Jo. I'm sorry. It'd make me sad, 'cause . . . you know."

"Yeah."

We hugged one more time. She put her lips to my ear. "You were really gonna ask me to marry you, weren't you?"

"Absolutely."

"So what happened?"

Your hair smelled like bleach, I wanted to say.

"I grew up," I said instead.

I broke the embrace, kissed her forehead and stepped outside. The cold air felt good. It helped dry my tears as I crossed the street and hurried to my lair at good old 207.

Chapter Thirty-two

My lair! That's what the house had become. I didn't want to see anyone or talk to anyone. I pulled down the shades on my front windows and almost wished I hadn't had the bars removed.

I quit running in Highland Park, quit walking around the neighborhood. I existed on whatever I had in the refrigerator and the pantry, supplemented by a few quick trips to White Castle for burgers and fries. I watched a lot of stupid daytime TV, took a lot of naps.

I wasn't particularly unhappy. Mostly I was numb. For a full day and a half I forgot all about my chickens, neglecting to feed and water them.

How about that? My grandmother strangled my first crop of birds, and now these new birds were in danger of starving to death! With a jolt I remembered them and ran outside to feed them. Luckily it had rained the night before, so their water bowls were full.

"I'm sorry, girls," I said, tossing french fries and burger scraps around the yard. "Been a little distracted lately."

They looked fine, having gotten by on whatever they were able to scratch out of the ground, and there was a bumper crop of eight eggs waiting to be gathered. My usefulness was diminishing by the moment. Even the damn chickens didn't need me anymore.

My naps got longer and deeper. I frightened myself by falling asleep once as darkness fell and awakening as darkness was again falling. I'd missed a whole day.

Parched and woozy, I got out of bed, staggered to the kitchen and drank straight from the faucet until I thought my belly would burst. Then I went to the backyard and tossed another load of scraps from White Castle to the chickens. The yard looked like hell, streaked everywhere with dung that needed to be raked into the soil, but I was in no mood to do it.

What the hell day was it? I had no idea. I was lost. I needed a shower, a shave and a reason to live. I got as far as the shower when the pounding on my front door jolted me back to reality.

Rose?

I pulled on a T-shirt and hopped into my jeans before rushing to answer the door. My hair was wet and the cold air was a shock, but not as big a shock as the sight of Officer Billy Debowski standing there on my front stoop, looking grim.

"Joe, I'm sorry," he said.

My head was spinning. What day was it? Had I missed my last session with Rosensohn? Would they actually send an emergency-services cop to arrest me for a parole violation?

I held my hands up, as if he had a gun trained on me. "Billy, I didn't miss a session. I'm not due until next week."

"What the fuck are you talkin' about?"

"What the fuck are *you* talking about?"

"Put your hands down, for Christ's sake!"

I did as I was told. Billy took a deep breath.

"You don't know what happened, do you?"

"I've been asleep. What? Something happen to my daughter?"

"No, no, not your daughter!"

Billy put his hands on my shoulders and gave them a supportive squeeze, the way you do when you have shocking news to deliver.

"You know a guy named Nathan Grossman, right?" he asked.

"Who?"

"Old guy, sits on Atlantic Avenue all day?"

"You mean Nat?"

"Yeah. They called him Nat."

Called. Shit. The past tense was almost always bad news.

The headline in the following day's *New York Post* said 98-YEAR-OLD BROOKLYN MAN MURDERED FOR SEVEN DOLLARS. As if the kid who'd bashed Nat's skull in with a hammer knew he had a five and two singles in his pants before he killed him.

Nathan "Nat" Grossman, a survivor of the Holocaust, died where he lived—"on the mean streets of East New York," as the *Post* reporter put it. He'd been seated in his lawn chair in front of his one-time bottle-recycling center when a shirtless fourteen-year-old boy said to be mentally retarded came up to him and demanded money.

Nat being Nat, he told the kid to get lost. Two blows were struck, though the second was probably not necessary. Nat was pronounced dead at the scene, and less than an hour later the boy was arrested at his nearby home by Officer Debowski, who stood on my front stoop barely an hour after that, sharing the gory details.

"This kid is some whack job, Joe. We got word he had guns, which turned out to be bullshit. So we bust into his house and he's sittin' at the kitchen table, with a big bowl o' Cocoa Puffs. He's pourin' Coca-Cola on the cereal—believe that? Meanwhile the hammer's right there next to his bowl, blood drippin' on the table. He looks at us like he's annoyed. We're interrupting his meal. Total psycho. You okay, Joe?"

I wasn't. I felt faint. Billy realized this and led me to my kitchen, where we both sat down. Through the fog in my head something was nagging at me, and at last I realized what it was.

"Billy. How'd you know I knew Nat?"

He reached inside his jacket pocket and removed an envelope.

"This was on the victim's person," he said. "Looks like he'd been carrying it around for a while."

Billy slid the sealed envelope across the table. It was wrinkled and grimy at the corners, and my name and address were printed on it in shaky capital letters.

"It was zipped inside his jacket pocket," Billy said. "Maybe that's why the killer didn't find it."

I looked at it without touching it. "Okay if I open it?"

"Hey, it's your property. I'm just the mailman."

The envelope practically crumbled in my hands, but the single sheet of lined yellow paper it contained was in good shape. It was a handwritten note, all in capital letters. Maybe nobody had ever taught Nat about lowercase letters. I knew his formal education had been brief.

JOEY,
IF YOU'RE READING THIS I'M DEAD. MAYBE SOME-BODY KILLED ME, OR MAYBE I JUST WORE OUT. DOESN'T MATTER NOW. I WANT YOU TO HAVE WHATEVER I HAD. IT'S NOT MUCH BUT IT'S IN MY

ROOM AT THE SENIOR CENTER. ANYBODY GIVES
YOU A HARD TIME, SHOW THEM THIS LETTER. IT'S
MY WILL.
YOURS TRULY,
NATHAN GROSSMAN
("NAT THE JEW")

"Everything okay?"

Billy's voice jolted me. I knew he was dying to know what was in
the letter. I handed it to him. He read it with a furrowed brow, as if it
were a ransom note, then passed it back to me with a shrug.

"Sad."

"That's the word for it."

"So this old guy just hung out all day on Atlantic Avenue?"

"This neighborhood is all he ever knew. He didn't have any relatives."

Billy's face darkened. "I'm gonna wind up the same way, the rate
I'm goin'. Remember that girl I was dating, the one with the kid? She
dumped me."

"I'm sorry, Billy."

"I don't miss her as much as I miss her kid. Who by the way loved
your book."

"I'm glad."

He shook his head. "Fucking relationships, man."

"Tell me about it."

"I mean, Jesus! What am I doing wrong? I got bad breath or
somethin'?"

"It's not you, Billy. The world's insane."

"You got that right. Coca-Cola on Cocoa Puffs. Christ!"

"Not to mention hammer murders."

"That I can understand easier than Coca-Cola on Cocoa Puffs."

Billy had to get back to the crime scene. I walked him to the door.

"By the way, Joe, if anybody gives you any grief, I can vouch
for you."

"What do you mean?"

He gestured at my hand, the one clutching Nat's letter.

"I'm a witness. I took the envelope out of his jacket, and I
watched you open it. What I mean is, I know it's for real, in case anybody contests it."

I had to laugh. "That's what's so pathetic, Billy. Nat was totally alone in this world." I shook the letter. "There's not a person on this planet who'd give a shit about this."

"Yeah? Listen, you never know. Could be his room is full of shoe boxes stuffed with cash. Hoarders. I've seen it happen with old people. Cash their Social Security checks, never spend a dime. Is that senior center he lived in nearby?"

I nodded. Billy smiled. "I'd get there fast if I were you, Joe. The people who work there have master keys to all the rooms, and some of them have pretty sticky fingers."

The next morning I made my way to the senior center, a gloomy yellow brick building with small windows. You walked in and smelled disinfectant, the really powerful piney kind to mask the odor of the dying. All it really did was remind you that people came here to die.

A young black woman who must have weighed close to three hundred pounds sat slump-shouldered at the reception desk, reading *People* magazine. She had the weary look of a person whose job is so depressing that the only way to do it is to exist in a self-inflicted catatonic state.

She looked up from her magazine and seemed surprised to see me. This wasn't the kind of place that got a lot of visitors.

"Help you?"

I cleared my throat. "I'm here to collect Nathan Grossman's things."

Her eyes widened in what seemed to be amusement. "His *things?*"

I showed her the letter. It was startling enough to improve her posture. She was actually sitting up straight by the time she was through reading it.

"I ain't sure this is an oh-*ficial* document."

"It's all I've got."

She shrugged as she handed it back to me. "Guess it's all right. Cops already been and gone." She shook her head. "Funny old man. He finally get a visitor, after he day-id." She pointed down the hall. "Room one-sixty-three."

"Don't I need a key?"

"Ain't locked."

I didn't see a soul on the walk down that gray hallway, though I heard coughing through closed doors, the kind of coughing where you expect to find a lung on the floor. Round landlord-halo lights in the ceiling lit the way, a fitting bit of decor in a place filled with people on the brink of acquiring halos.

I opened the door to room 163 and stepped into what could have been the dormitory home of a college freshman: a narrow cot, a bureau with a small mirror over it and a freestanding clothes closet.

The lone window looked out onto a sooty air shaft. No wonder Nat spent his days outdoors, regardless of the weather. This place was strictly for sleeping.

No pictures on the cinder-block walls, no photographs, no books. The drawers contained shirts, socks and underwear, and in the closet his winter peacoat hung from a solitary hanger, his gloves and woolen hat jammed into its pockets.

No documents of any kind. No printed matter. I wondered where he'd acquired pen and paper to write that letter to me. There wasn't even a table or chair for him to sit at to write!

I sat on the cot and buried my face in my hands. I was afraid that if I let myself start crying, I'd never stop. I struggled to stay calm in that horrible little room.

There was nothing to take here, nothing anybody could possibly want, so why would Nat leave me a letter sending me to this dreadful place?

I had to get out, and when I took my hands away from my face I became aware of a splash of color, a little green glow on the wall opposite the window. I turned to face the window and there it was on the sill, all by itself in the morning sun, like the last soldier standing after a long, horrific battle.

It was an ancient White Rock ginger ale bottle with bubbly raised lettering, the kind they stopped making when aluminum cans came along. There on the label was the winged White Rock girl, forever kneeling on that rock as she gazed into the water.

That bottle had to be at least fifty years old. How many such bottles had I brought to Nat, all those years ago? Maybe I'd brought him this one! Maybe that's why he wanted me to have it!

I took the bottle in my quaking hands and wiped the dust from its shoulders.

"Thanks, Nat."

On my way out I showed the bottle to the girl at the reception desk.

"That's all you takin'?"

"The rest is just clothing. The Salvation Army can have it."

"A damn bottle," she said, rolling her eyes and waving at the ceiling. "Farewell to you, Mis-ter Grossman."

It was crazy, but I felt wonderful when I hit the street, my precious bottle in hand. I'd expected this trip to Nat's room to send me into the deepest depression of my life, but the opposite thing was happening.

True, Nat had led a strange life: all by himself with no property, no descendants. Even his old place of business was long gone, so there was literally nothing, *nothing* to indicate he'd ever walked the earth. That was one way to look at it.

But suddenly, I was seeing it another way. Nat had been like a rocket ship, voyaging ever deeper into space. The rocket didn't acquire as it went; it dropped pieces in stages as it burned out. Eventually Nat was just a capsule drifting in space, until that crazy kid with the hammer came along, and then he was just a tiny point of light, shining through that green bottle on his windowsill.

That's what he wanted me to find. The bottle. The light. The little bit of hope we all need to get out of bed tomorrow.

Suddenly, I knew what I wanted to do. For the first time in a long time, I knew exactly what I wanted to do.

Chapter Thirty-three

Maybe it was what I'd been building toward all along, without admitting it to myself. Everything I'd done to the Shepherd Avenue house, especially the basement, pointed toward the crazy thing I was about to do.

Which was to invite everybody in my life for Thanksgiving, one week away.

I'd always liked Thanksgiving, the togetherness of it without all the bullshit of Christmas. Not that I'd ever actually had a real Thanksgiving as an adult, or ever even attempted to cook a turkey, but the holiday always looked good to me from the outside. I started working the phone as soon as I got back from Nat's room.

Johnny Gallo sounded stunned to hear from me. "Jesus Christ, Long Island, are you serious about this?"

"Absolutely."

"Funny thing is, we just found out our son's going to the Poconos for Thanksgiving with his family. Skiing! You believe that shit? Ain't this supposed to be a holiday you have at home? Instead, they'd rather slide down a fuckin' hill with strangers, on man-made snow. What the hell's goin' on?"

"The world's changing, Johnny."

"Yeah, and it always gets worse. We'll be there. Holy shit, this might even be fun!"

My old friend Mel was next on my list. I hadn't spoken with her since our dinner at her Central Park penthouse, and she seemed a little frosty.

"What's up, stranger?"

"You busy Thanksgiving?"

"I beg your pardon?"

"Well, Mel, I was just wondering—and I know this is a long shot, what with your kids and your grandkids and all your commitments— but anyway, I was hoping you could come over to my house for Thanks-giving, because I'm cooking the bird for some of our old friends."

"Come on!"

"I'm serious." I hesitated, then whispered: "Johnny Gallo's com-ing. Just got off the phone with him."

"Really?" she squealed. The crush she had on Johnny apparently had not dimmed, even after fifty years. "Is he still married?"

"Yes, he is. She's coming, too."

"Oh."

"Look, I realize you have obligations—"

"Obligations?" She made a snorting sound. "My kids live all over the place. I gotta get on a plane to see any of 'em, and when I get there my grandchildren don't even look at me. They sit there and play with their iPods, and the odd one, always singin' those show tunes on his karaoke . . . the hell with it! I'm comin' to your house."

"You mean it?"

"I mean it, Joey. This I gotta see. You weren't bullshitting about Johnny, were you?"

I called Eddie Everything, who was delighted to be invited and promised to bring dessert.

"Best fuckin' flan you'll ever taste!" he vowed. "Gonna make it with eggs from your chickens, boss!"

On an impulse I rang Billy Debowski, figuring he'd be all alone on Thanksgiving, especially after his breakup. He literally couldn't speak for a few moments and when he did, he sounded all choked up.

"Listen, I don't want to interfere with your holiday."

"Interfere? If you hadn't interfered with me on the bridge, I might still be up there!"

"You sure about this?"

"Just be there, Officer Debowski. Bring a big appetite."

Next I called Vic.

"Shame about Nat the Jew, huh Joey? Unbelievable!"

"Yeah, yeah, but that's not why I'm calling, Vic."

I told him about my Thanksgiving plan, and he was shocked to hear that Johnny and Mel were coming.

"I'll be there on one condition," he said. "On Sunday afternoon you have to come with me."

"Where?"

"It's a surprise."

That stunned me. Vic was not a surprise kind of a guy.

"You can't tell me where we're going?"

"Sure I could tell you. But I won't. I'll pick you up at four."

He hung up before I could agree to it. This meant that we had a deal, unless I called him back to tell him to forget it. Which I didn't, because my next phone call hinged on Vic's attendance.

With a quaking hand I dialed Jenny Sutherland's number. The woman who'd broken my uncle's heart apparently never answered her phone. I hung up on five calls that went straight to voice mail before deciding to leave a message on my sixth call:

"Jenny Sutherland, this is Joseph Ambrosio inviting you to Thanksgiving next Thursday at two-oh-seven Shepherd Avenue in Brooklyn. My Uncle Vic will be there, along with a few other people from the old days. Any time after two p.m. I hope you can make it."

I didn't tell Vic what I'd done, and Jenny would have no way of knowing if Vic knew she was being invited. All she could do was show up, and find out for herself.

I could be a bad boy, especially when I was on a mission.

My last call was to my daughter at work. Her tone implied that I'd caught her at a busy time.

"You got a second, Taylor?"

"I haven't."

"You haven't got a second?"

"No, I mean I haven't had a drink. Not since that day."

"Oh, Taylor, that's *wonderful*! Good for you."

"Checking up on me?"

"No, I'm inviting you to Thanksgiving at my house."

Silence, but I could hear her breathing.

"Your Uncle Vic will be there, plus some people I knew when I was a boy on Shepherd Avenue."

"Sort of a *This Is Your Life* deal, eh?"

"No. Just a get-together for some special people. You can stay the night, if you like. Got the upstairs apartment fully furnished now."

Seconds passed. They felt like years, until . . .

"Is Kevin invited?"

My heart soared. "Of course he is. You have to bring him. He knows the way."

"That's true. Okay, then, we'll see you on Thanksgiving."

I was quaking with joy when I hung up. I had just one more invitation to make, but this one wouldn't be through a phone call. I found a sheet of paper and started writing.

> *Dear Rose,*
> *I'm having some people over for Thanksgiving and hope you can join us. If Justin is in town, he's also welcome. Any time next Thursday after two p.m.*
> *Sincerely,*
> *Joseph Ambrosio (Jo-Jo)*

I stuck the note in an envelope, ran across the street and put it through the mail slot in her front door.

Mission accomplished. Now all I had to do was prepare a feast for a crowd, something I'd never done before. No problem.

But first, I had my final meeting with Dr. Rosensohn. I was actually looking forward to it, no matter what kind of a report card he was going to write up for me.

His face was like the face of a kid on a roller coaster as I began telling him of my adventures since we'd last met: going to Rose's house with a diamond ring to propose marriage, then changing my mind and ending it with her for good as she prepared to move to Seattle, and the murder of Nat, and the will he left for me, and the ancient green soda bottle I found on his windowsill, glowing green in the morning sun.

Finally I told him about all the people I was having over for Thanksgiving on Shepherd Avenue. When I was through talking the sudden silence seemed as abrupt as a car crash. There was a glazed look in Rosensohn's eyes. He shook his head, as if to snap himself out of a daydream.

"Well. It hasn't been dull, has it?"

"No, and the adventures aren't over yet. I still have to go to Tiffany's to return that ring."

"But I take it you're keeping Nat's bottle."

"Forever."

Rosensohn cracked a half-smile. "Was there a message in the bottle?"

"The bottle *is* the message."

"And the message is?"

"I don't know, Doc. I just know it made me feel good. Connected, you know?"

"To what?"

I thought about it. "History, I guess. The past. The future, too, in a funny way. I realize I'm not just free-floating in space. I'm a piece of the puzzle. It's all still a puzzle, this freakin' life, but at least I'm a piece of it."

"Did you finish writing your Sammy Suitcase finale?"

"No, and I realize it's because it's too early for Sammy to stop moving. Got to write up a few more adventures for that kid before he settles down for good."

Rosensohn exhaled with what I imagined to be relief, then leaned toward me.

"One last question: Do you promise never again to climb up the Brooklyn Bridge?"

I lifted my right hand, like a good Boy Scout. "Absolutely."

"All right, then, Mr. Ambrosio. I wish you the very best of luck."

He stood up and reached out to shake my hand. I was stunned by the suddenness of the ending, as well as the softness of his hand.

"I take it I'm not going to prison."

"Oh, that was never really an option, as far as I was concerned. We just do that to scare you."

"So this is it? I'm cured?"

"You weren't sick."

"Healed?"

"You've fulfilled a requirement from the City of New York's Department of Probation."

"Not very sexy, is it?"

"Best I can do. On a personal note, let me say that it wasn't ever boring."

He let go of my hand. I was picking up a vibe. Something was wrong. He wasn't himself. He seemed depressed. Could it be he was going to miss me?

"Hey, Doc, are you all right?"

"Not exactly."

"Don't tell me you're sorry because we won't be doing this anymore!"

He took off his glasses and wiped away tears with the backs of his hands. There was a tiny smile on his face, a forced one, the smile of a child trying to be brave after scraping his knee in the playground.

"Actually," he said, "my wife just left me."

Holy shit. So much for his "strong, nutritious" marriage.

He put his glasses back on, adjusted them and cleared his throat. "So forgive me if I've seemed . . . less than professional today."

"Jesus, Doc, I'm sorry."

"So am I."

"Are your kids okay?"

"We don't have children. But thanks for asking."

I felt my face flush. The hours and hours I'd spent talking with this man, and I knew nothing about his life. It was all about *me!* Of course that was the deal in therapy, but suddenly it seemed unfair, especially now that this gentle guy with the butterfat face had been dumped.

I didn't know what else to say, and then, suddenly, I did.

"Hey, Doc. You want to talk about it? Get a cup of coffee or something?"

He did something he'd never done before in my presence: He laughed out loud, a wonderful booming laugh. Then he looked at his watch and shrugged.

"What the hell, I've got an hour to kill before my next loony shows up. Let's do it."

It's always interesting to see professional people out of their element. I'd only ever known Dr. Rosensohn as a guy at a desk with a diploma behind his head. Strolling beside him on this bright autumn afternoon I saw things I'd never seen before: his waddly walk on short, chubby legs, his thick-soled shoes in need of a shine, his fingernails bitten to the quick. Everything about the man made me think he'd gotten a lot of wedgies back in the schoolyard. He was easily fifteen years younger than me, but when we took a table near the window at a Columbus Avenue diner I felt like I was sitting for a duty lunch with a pathetic old uncle.

He was broken. He was lost. He'd been so busy shepherding strangers to safety that he'd lost his own way.

He asked the waitress for coffee and a grilled cheese sandwich, exactly the sort of thing I would have expected him to order. He looked as if he'd been built out of grilled cheese sandwiches.

I told the waitress to bring me the same. When she went away he fixed his gaze on the pedestrian traffic. I struggled for something to say.

"I'm guessing you didn't see it coming."

"Actually, I did."

"But you couldn't do anything about it."

He turned to me. "Her mind was made up, Joseph."

"Are we on a first-name basis now?"

He chuckled. "Yes, now that the meter's off, this is how it works."

"Wow. Philip or Phil?"

"Either way.

"Did you try to talk her out of it, Phil?"

"You can't talk to a note."

"I'm sorry?"

"A note." He made a scribbling motion in midair. "I came home from work last Wednesday and all of her things were gone. Books, everything. Not a trace of her, except for a note she'd left for me."

"What'd it say?"

"Would you like to read it?"

Before I could answer he pulled a folded sheet of paper from his coat pocket and handed it to me.

"Check it out," he urged. "Won't take you long."

I unfolded it, expecting a long, tortured rant, but just three words jumped off the page in large, neat print.

THIS ISN'T WORKING.

"Holy shit," I said.

"That was my precise reaction."

Our food arrived. The doc took a hefty bite out of his grilled cheese sandwich. I continued to stare at those cold, hard words.

"This is amazing," I said. "This is the kind of note you leave in a hotel, for a maid you've never even seen. You tape it to the busted TV set."

"Ha! Or the busted husband."

"She didn't even sign it!"

"No, Evelyn always had a knack for brevity. She's an advertising copywriter. Twelve years of marriage. One word for every four years."

"It could have been worse."

He stopped chewing. "Did you just say what I think you said?"

"What I mean is, maybe there's hope. Consider the tense."

I passed back the note. "She said it *isn't* working, not it *didn't* work. Maybe she's just taking a break."

He folded the note and stuck it back in his pocket. "You realize, Joseph, that you are a closet optimist."

"I'm just saying—"

"My wife is gone for good. I accept it. My marriage is over. The only question now is whether it ever actually got started in the first place."

He gobbled down the rest of his grilled cheese. I hadn't yet tasted mine. I sipped my coffee, considering my next move. I wasn't sure it was the right move, but I was no longer as worried about certainty as I once was.

The doc got to his feet and threw down a ten dollar bill. I shoved it back at him.

"Lunch is on me, Phil."

"Well, thanks. Didn't mean to wolf it down like that. I eat fast when I'm anxious. You stay, enjoy your food. Good luck to you, Joseph."

We shook hands for the second time that day, and when he tried to break the shake I maintained my grip.

What-the-fuck time had arrived.

"Hey, Phil. You busy on Thanksgiving?"

"I beg your pardon?"

"Thanksgiving. Do you have plans? Like I was telling you, I'm doing the bird for some old friends on Shepherd Avenue and I'd love for you to join us."

We were still holding hands. He was truly stunned.

"Is this a serious offer?"

"Of course."

His eyes narrowed, the way eyes do when prompted by an unpleasant memory. "Normally I spend Thanksgiving in Chappaqua, watching Evelyn's control freak of a mother mock her sexually ambiguous husband's pathetic attempts to carve the turkey. One year he nearly cut this thumb off. Good times, I tell you."

He dropped his gaze to his shoes. "Obviously I won't be doing that this year, and I'm grateful for your offer, but I'm not sure I'd . . . fit in, Joseph."

"Tell you the truth, it's my friggin' party, and I'm not sure *I'll* fit in."

It worked. He looked up at me and once again, he laughed that booming laugh.

"Come on," I urged. "You can feed my chickens. Bet you've never fed chickens before."

"There are a lot of things I've never done."

"Well, come to my party and lessen that list by one. Bring a date if you like."

"Maybe next year, Joseph. This year I'm flying solo."

"Does that mean you're coming?"

He couldn't help smiling. "That's what it means."

"Fucking A, that's great!"

"Just one thing, Joseph."

"Name it, Phil."

"Do you think I could have my hand back now? People are starting to stare."

Chapter Thirty-four

I had a lot to do. I had more than a dozen people coming over for a Thanksgiving feast and I'd never before fed more than two.

I took care of the bird first at the Fulton Street butcher shop, ordering a twenty-pound turkey that I could pick up on Thanksgiving morning.

Then I got all the heavy-duty groceries that wouldn't wilt before the big day: beer, wine, whiskey, nuts, chips and ice cream.

I was going to make sweet potatoes and green beans on the day itself, and I was going to attempt a chestnut-stuffing recipe I'd found on the Internet. I bought cloth napkins and wineglasses and something I'd never had before, a decent carving knife.

There'd be plenty of room for everybody in the basement, at the table and benches Eddie Everything had built.

The final touch was a long red tablecloth. I actually felt faint when I tossed it over the table and squared the corners.

And I could have sworn I heard the voice of my grandmother, echoing in that basement where she'd spent so much of her life.

What'd you pay for that long tablecloth? You coulda put two short ones together!

Not this time, Connie. Not this time.

On Sunday Vic pulled up in front of the house in his rusting Chevy and tapped the horn three times. He obviously didn't want to come inside, and when I got into his car I was shocked to see him wearing a white shirt and a tie.

"Jesus, Vic, you didn't tell me to dress up!"

"You don't have to."

"Where the hell are you taking me?"

"Not far."

Vic was clean-shaved and his hair was immaculately combed. It was a look he couldn't quite sell. He looked like a criminal desperately trying to make a good impression on a jury.

I was wearing tattered jeans and a T-shirt under my peacoat. We rode in silence until Vic started talking about his baseball team.

"Got 'em playin' fall ball," he said. "It's a little cold out, so all they can do is complain about how much their hands sting when they hit the ball. Makin' their fathers buy 'em batting gloves. You believe this shit? What the hell is happening to boys? Have they all gone soft?"

"Vic, where are we going?"

"We're there," he said, making a turn into the entrance at St. John's Cemetery, and I knew immediately where we were going: Connie and Angie's final resting place.

"It's her birthday," Vic said, pulling into the parking lot. "She would have been one hundred and five years old today."

"Oh my God."

"Anyway, I do this every year. Didn't feel like going alone this time. You've never been back, have you?"

"No."

"Well, you're overdue. Come on, we won't stay long."

Vic carried a small paper bag on the walk through the cemetery. Here and there a spray of cut flowers put a little color into the otherwise gray scene.

"If I'd known where you were taking me I could have brought flowers."

"What for?"

"It's a nice touch."

Vic chuckled. "Think back. Was my mother the type to appreciate flowers? You can't eat flowers. Did you ever see a single bouquet on Shepherd Avenue?"

"All right, forget I said anything. Just let me enjoy this surprise of yours."

At last we came upon the two tombstones, Connie's and Angie's, side by side. Angie's stone seemed to sag a bit but Connie's stood upright, straight and true.

Vic put a hand on my shoulder. "I appreciate you comin' with me, Joey."

"I'm not crazy about cemeteries."

"Nobody is. But once a year won't kill you."

"You don't come here on Angie's birthday?"

"Nope. This is a two-fer visit. I commemorate both birthdays at once."

"I feel kind of funny coming here empty-handed."

"We're not empty-handed."

From the paper bag Vic removed and unwrapped a cream cheese bagel, which he set atop Connie's tombstone.

"Happy hundred and five, Ma."

Then he took out a pack of Chesterfield unfiltered cigarettes, which he placed atop Angie's stone.

"Sorry I forgot the matches, Pop."

I couldn't believe what I was seeing. "Christ, Vic!"

"You remember how my mother loved cream cheese bagels, and my father with his Chesterfields?"

I remembered. I had to laugh. "Once I hid his cigarettes, trying to get him to quit. This was after you left to play ball. He came into my room and picked me up by my elbows, holding me straight out. What a grip, and his forearms bulging like Popeye's! 'Where'd you put 'em?' he asked me, calm as could be. Me dangling like a kitten who'd just wet the floor, and him not even trembling. Jesus, he was strong! He must have held me five minutes before I broke down and told him the cigarettes were under my bed."

Vic had never heard that story. His eyes were shiny with tears. "How could somebody that strong die so young?" he wondered out loud. "He wasn't even sixty! And poor you, sittin' right next to him when it happened."

I hesitated. "Did I ever tell you his last words, Vic, up on that Ferris wheel? He told me about our name. 'Ambrosio, like *ambrosia*,' he said. 'Nectar of the gods. It's in you as tight as the pipes I put in all them buildings.' Then he promised me that I was going to taste life, all the way to here."

I touched the bottom of my throat. Vic seemed transfixed.

"Then what?" he dared to ask.

"Then he told me Connie wasn't a bad person, even though she killed the chickens, and he made me point at buildings in every direction. Said he'd worked in all those places, everywhere I pointed, and that the neighborhood was his, all his. Then he closed his eyes . . ."

I couldn't speak anymore. Vic stared at Angie's headstone, letting it all sink in. "It's like he knew his time was up. Wanted to give you a little hope before he checked out."

"Maybe."

"Think it worked?"

I shrugged. "I'm still here. So are you. We're Ambrosios, man. Nectar of the gods."

"That's nice, but the gods drink the nectar, not us."

I had to chuckle. "Oh, Vic, how I love you."

The sun was sinking low, and a chilly wind blew brown leaves that rattled across the ground. I wanted to leave, but I also wanted to ask Vic something I'd always wanted to ask him, and this sure seemed like the right time and place. I gestured at the headstones.

"Hey. Think they were happy together?"

Vic shrugged, chuckled. "I'm not sure that's what they were aiming for. They were satisfied with survival, which is maybe why it worked." He smiled. "Your parents—now, *they* were happy together. Which is probably why your father flipped out when he lost her. Love's a dangerous thing, Joey. You probably figured that out for yourself. Come on, let's get out of here."

He turned and started walking so fast I had to trot to catch up with him.

"You're going to just leave the bagel and the smokes?"

"Why not?"

"What would your parents say? It's a waste!"

"Nah, the old gardener here knows me, saw us come in. He'll eat the bagel and smoke the cigarettes. Nice gift to him, huh? Heart disease and lung cancer. Walk faster, Joey, I hate being here after dark."

He drove me home but didn't want to come inside. I got out of his car and he rolled down his window.

"I appreciate you comin' today, kid."

"Great surprise. Thursday's my turn to surprise *you*."

"Yeah? With what?"

"You'll see."

"I don't need surprises at my age."

"What do you need, Uncle?"

He put the car in gear. "A third baseman who can make the throw to first. But I ain't holdin' my breath."

Chapter Thirty-five

I got up early Thanksgiving morning to do the prep work. The vegetables were ready to cook and the chestnut stuffing was mixed. I had bowls of chips and pretzels to go with the drinks and I set the table.

I hadn't heard back from Rose, so I had no idea whether or not she and Justin were coming.

Jenny Sutherland was another question mark. She'd never gotten back to me and it seemed unlikely she'd show. I'd be feeding at least ten people and at most thirteen.

I erred on the side of optimism and set the table for thirteen.

Connie used to say that thirteen was a bad-luck number. Maybe I should have heeded those words.

It was a little past eleven in the morning when I went to the butcher shop to pick up the turkey. The butcher held it up proudly by its neck, as if he'd tracked it down in the woods and shot it himself.

"Is that a turkey, or is that a turkey?"

"That certainly is a turkey, my friend!"

He bundled it up in heavy brown paper before passing it over the counter to me.

"Three hours, cook it slow," he advised. "Keep bastin' it and it'll be the best turkey you ever tasted."

It was so big I had to hug it to my chest with both arms as I walked toward Shepherd Avenue. It was a beautiful morning, cold but sunny, and the shadows through the elevated train tracks made a lovely laddered pattern on the street.

I was looking at that pattern when suddenly two human shadows approached my own shadow at high speed. They were getting close,

I thought, and as our three shadows converged into one, something came down hard on my head. The last thing I remembered before passing out was the turkey being torn from my arms and the sound of gleeful laughter.

I couldn't have been unconscious for more than a few minutes, and when I opened my eyes I was surrounded by half-a-dozen people, pointing at me and chattering in frantic Spanish. A cop car with flashing red lights roared onto the scene, siren wailing, and the next thing I knew they were taking me to the local police station, a place I had never been.

One of the cops was tall and lean, with thick crinkly hair just starting to go gray. His nameplate said SORRENTINO. The other cop, MURPHY, was short and chubby, with a complexion like rare roast beef.

I sat on a wooden bench with Murphy, who had a notebook and pen in hand. Sorrentino stood behind him, looking bored. The only other person in sight was a weary-looking desk sergeant, who yawned as he thumbed through the pages of *Sports Illustrated*.

"We were hopin' for a peaceful Thanksgiving," Murphy said.

I shrugged. "Sorry about that, guys."

"You say they came up behind you?"

"Right."

"Two of them?"

"I think so."

Sorrentino spread his hands. "Black, Hispanic, Asian?"

"All I saw was their shadows. Which were black."

Murphy stared at me. "You a comedian?"

"Sorry. I didn't get a look at them. One of them bopped me, the other took the bird."

"So that's all they got?" Sorrentino asked. "Your turkey?"

"It was a twenty-pounder. You call that *all*?"

"What I mean is, they didn't get your wallet?"

"Wasn't carrying my wallet. I just walked a few blocks to pick up my turkey, which I'd already paid for."

"What about your house keys?" Murphy asked. "If they got your house keys you could be in trouble, down the line."

"Didn't have my keys."

The cops exchanged puzzled looks "That's a little strange, don't you think?" Murphy asked.

"Figured I'd be back in ten minutes, and I couldn't find my keys, so I left the door unlocked."

Murphy made a snorting sound. "That is not advisable in this neighborhood, sir."

"My grandfather lived in my house before me, and he never locked his doors."

"Yeah? When was this?"

I felt my face redden. "Well, he died in '61."

Both cops chuckled. "Different world now, my friend," Sorrentino said.

Murphy was looking at his notes. "Hey," he said to his partner, "this guy lives on Shepherd. Bet he's the one who took the bars off his windows!" He turned to look at me in wonder. "Is that you?"

I was stunned. "You know my house?"

"Sure. It's the matter-o'-time house."

"Huh?"

"Just a matter o' time before someone breaks in."

I got to my feet, a motion that made my head throb.

"Whoa, whoa, buddy," Murphy said. "Where you think you're goin'?"

"Home."

"Sit. We'll have a doctor look you over."

"I'm all right. Got to go, I'm expecting company."

"At least let us give you a ride."

"Thanks, but I need the air."

I got as far as the door when Officer Sorrentino called out to me.

"Want some free advice, Mr. Ambrosio?" he asked. "Lock your doors from now on, and put the bars back on the windows. Sixty-one was a long time ago."

I walked slowly. I seemed to have to instruct my legs on how to operate: left, right. The day had turned cloudy and the neighborhood never looked rattier. I actually saw a rat, darting between cracks in the broken wall of a burned-out pizza parlor.

The elevated train passed overhead, and it seemed to rattle the fillings in my teeth. My head was pounding. Two flashily dressed Puerto Ricans walked toward me, laughing hard. I thought they were going to collide with me but at the last instant they veered around me, like two ships avoiding an iceberg.

Iceberg: Jesus, I felt as cold as an iceberg! I shivered and hugged myself as I walked, the only man in a blizzard nobody else could detect. I had no idea what time it was. I had all those people coming over, and no turkey to feed them.

At Shepherd Avenue I made the turn toward my house and suddenly, it seemed impossibly far away. I couldn't make it. I was out of gas, out of hope, out of everything.

Where was I? Right outside Rose's house. It was only across the street from mine, but that street might as well have been the English Channel.

I climbed the steps to her door and banged on it with my fist, barely hard enough to crack an egg.

The door opened. "Oh my God!" Rose cried, putting her arms out to catch me as I literally fell into her home.

She was strong. She dragged me to her couch and eased me down on my back. Though my head whirled I could see that the walls had been stripped of all that Justin memorabilia, and the floor was covered with big cardboard boxes full of her stuff. Rose was preparing to leave Shepherd Avenue forever.

She stroked my hair, and I winced when she reached the bump.

"What happened to your head, Jo-Jo?"

"Got mugged. Couple of kids stole my turkey."

"Bastards!"

I heard footsteps coming down the stairs and of course it was Justin, who froze at the sight of me.

"He got mugged," Rose said. "They stole his turkey!"

Justin nodded like a sage. "Looks like we're gettin' out of here just in time."

I shut my eyes, hoping that would calm the dizziness, but it didn't. Then I said to the ceiling, "It would have been nice if you'd at least acknowledged my Thanksgiving invitation. Not that I have anything to offer now."

"Jo-Jo, I've been so busy packin'!"

I opened my eyes. "Ro-Ro, that is bullshit."

"Hey," Justin said, "don't talk to my mother like that."

"It's okay, Justin, he's right." She hung her head. "I'm sorry, Jo-Jo. Just couldn't handle sayin' goodbye to you."

"When are you clearing out?"

"Tomorrow."

She turned to Justin and ordered him to fill a plastic bag with ice cubes for my head. When he hesitated she screamed at him, and that multimillion-dollar ballplayer hustled to the kitchen like a little boy trying to avoid a spanking.

In the midst of all this craziness came something I had to ask, the question that had unconsciously nagged and plagued me since I was a boy, running up and down Shepherd Avenue. It was a question I'd never asked a friend, a cop, a shrink or a parent. I was going to unload it on Rose, this special person I'd known just a few months, and would probably never see again.

The dizziness was fading. Rose's face was just above mine, old and young at the same time.

"Hey, Rose. Can I ask you something?"

"Shoot."

"It's important, so if you don't feel like hearing it . . ."

"How the hell can I know if I don't feel like hearin' it until I hear it?"

"Right, right."

I shut my eyes again and felt tears leak down my cheeks. Rose stroked my hair again, careful to avoid the bump.

"Justin! Bring the goddamn ice, already!"

I heard him hand her the ice bag. She held it gently against the bump, and a sense of sweet relief did battle with the sting of the cold on my scalp. The relief was well worth the sting.

"Feel good?"

"Oh yeah."

"Ask your damn question, already."

I opened my eyes. Justin was standing behind her, hands folded like a penitent. Rose held the ice bag steady on my head.

"Guess it's pretty simple," I said. "I was just wondering, do you think anybody . . ."

"Come on, spit it out, Jo-Jo!"

I cleared my throat. "Do you think anybody *really* loves anybody?"

And there was no answer to my question, or if there was I didn't hear it, because as soon as my words were out I passed out as if the turkey thieves had conked me again.

Chapter Thirty-six

When I opened my eyes I felt as if I'd been asleep for years. I'd been covered with a blanket and Justin was standing over me, looking at me the way I expected God to be looking at me on Judgment Day, had I believed in God or Judgment Day.

"I care about your mother, Justin."

"So do I."

"You're making the right move, both of you."

His face softened. "Hope so."

I hesitated. "If I were twenty years younger . . ."

"But you ain't, so don't sweat it." He smiled. "You know, you run pretty good for an old man."

"Oh, I've got a few miles left in me. Where's your mother?"

"Kitchen."

"What time is it?"

"Little after one."

"Jesus, I've got to go home! They'll be here in an hour!"

I tried to get up but Justin pressed down on my shoulders, turned his face toward the kitchen and shouted, "Mom, he's awake!"

Rose appeared with a mug of tea. I sat up and she held it to my lips. I took a long, sweet swallow.

"You can't be makin' no Thanksgiving dinner," Rose said.

"It's too late. They're all on their way."

"What you gonna do, Jo-Jo?"

"I'll improvise. Got everything but the turkey."

I got to my feet and started for the door with Justin and Rose at each elbow, ready to catch me if I faltered. But I was okay.

"Good luck in Seattle," I said, turning to shake Justin's hand. Then I offered my hand to Rose, who ignored it.

"What are you, stupid? We're comin' with you! Justin, get your jacket."

Just like that, the three of us made our way across the street to 207. And a weird thing happened between Rose and me during that short voyage, something that hadn't happened since our magical trip to Rockaway Beach.

We held hands.

Rose took over once we were inside, cooking the vegetables and the stuffing and ordering Justin to fill bowls with nuts and chips. She'd never been down to the basement and was impressed by the table and benches.

"Jesus, Eddie did a nice job down here!"

"He's coming. Promised he'd bring a flan."

"Yeah, that's real nice for dessert, Jo-Jo, but what we gonna do about that turkey you ain't got?"

"I don't know. White Castle's open today, isn't it?"

Rose's eyes widened. "Burgers?"

"Don't have much choice, do I?"

Justin laughed out loud. "Damn!" he said. "That's somethin' I've been missin' in Seattle! Burgers from the Castle!"

I turned to Rose. "I'll be right back. And when they get here, don't tell them I got mugged."

Justin joined me on the walk to White Castle. We were the only customers in sight, and if the sleepy-eyed girl behind the counter thought she was in for an easy shift she had a rude awakening when I asked her for eighty burgers to go.

"What are you feedin', an army?"

"Just some family and friends."

The fry cook got to work on the order, and as the burgers popped and sizzled Justin told me about the place he was buying in Seattle: a waterfront house with an outdoor pool and a heated garage.

"You can visit us, Joe," he said. "Got plenty of room."

"Thanks Justin, but I think my traveling days are pretty much behind me."

"Were you really gonna ask my mother to marry you?"

"Yeah."

"You're a brave man."

I had to chuckle. "Actually, Justin, the brave part was when I changed my mind."

He shook his head. "You bought the ring and everything. Damn."

"Got a feeling it won't be the last time a man buys a ring for your mother."

We carried the burgers back in two giant sacks. Rose said I'd gotten too many, but they were only three bites apiece, and people had a way of gobbling them like salted peanuts, and anyway, it was Thanksgiving! A day made for excess!

Rose piled the burgers onto the biggest metal tray I had, set the brand-new oven on warm and shoved them in there. As soon as she was done with that I heard a knock on the door, and I went upstairs to let Johnny Gallo and Nancy in.

They hugged me and followed me down to the basement. Nancy had brought a big platter of homemade cookies, which I set on top of the refrigerator. I introduced Rose and Justin to them as "my neighbors." The Gallos weren't baseball fans and obviously had no idea who Justin was. Then again, if the President of the United States had been there, they probably wouldn't have recognized *him*. They were totally distracted and dazzled by their return to the Ambrosio basement, looking around in wonder like a couple of kids at the planetarium.

"We had our engagement party right in this room, fifty years ago," Johnny told Rose. "You believe that?"

"Fifty years in September," Nancy said.

"And you're still together," Rose said.

Johnny nodded and shrugged. Nancy rolled her eyes. Justin laughed.

Another knock at the door, and this time it was Mel DiGiovanna, in a fur coat and an Armani dress. Behind her I saw a long black limo pulling away from the curb.

"Let me in before I get shot!" she said with a laugh as she entered the hallway. "Oh, my *God*, this place hasn't changed! In case you were wondering, that's not a compliment."

"Good to see you too, Mel."

"You know I'm kidding! Here, take these." She handed me two ice-cold bottles of Dom Pérignon. "Is he here yet?"

"Downstairs."

"Ah, we're dining in the basement, are we?"

"I think you know the way, Mel."

She thundered dangerously ahead of me on high heels, and when she saw Johnny she put a hand to her chest as if she'd just spotted a movie star.

"Hiya, Johnny," she all but whispered. Johnny stared at her in wonder.

"Remember me? I used to live on this block." She touched her nose. "My honker was a lot bigger back then."

Johnny squinted, then smiled. "Are you little Mel?"

"Yeah."

"My God! Little Mel!"

He took her in a long, soulful embrace, and I knew that no matter what happened for the rest of the day this trip to Shepherd Avenue would have been worth it to Mel, who turned to me with a thirty-two-tooth smile.

"Crack that champagne, Joey, we're celebrating!"

I did as I was told with the Dom Pérignon, pouring for everyone in the room. As Johnny and Mel talked over the old days Nancy sidled up to me, looking concerned.

"Who's that *putain* with my husband?"

"She lived here the same summer I did. She had a big crush on Johnny."

"Looks like she still does."

"I think she's just glad to see him."

"Why? He's an old man!"

"Maybe, but those eyes of his are still pretty amazing, aren't they?"

Nancy sipped her champagne, trying to hide a smile. "They worked on me, that's for sure."

Another knock on the door, and this time my Uncle Vic was standing there in his usual shabbily comfortable attire, holding a large wooden box filled with three dozen clementines. I knew he'd gone to his favorite produce market in Astoria for the fruit. He loved buying in bulk, a funny thing for a guy who'd lived alone most of his life.

"Sure feels funny to knock on this door."

"It wasn't locked, Vic."

"I didn't know that." I stepped aside to let him in. He handed me the box. "You like clementines? They're nice. No seeds. And I like the color."

He headed down to the basement, where Johnny greeted him with a shout. They stood apart with their hands over their hips, like a pair of gunslingers with no guns.

"Vic, you got so fat!"

"Johnny, you got so bald!"

A true Shepherd Avenue greeting. Then they embraced in a beautiful bear hug.

Then I introduced Vic to Justin. They shook hands, regarding each other like rival gunslingers.

"I hear you could play," Justin said.

Vic nodded. "I hear you're pretty good, too."

Eddie Everything arrived with his promised flan. He was blown away when Billy Debowski showed up minutes later with a box of contraband cigars.

"These are illegal Cubans," Billy said.

"So am I," Eddie dared to reply, and the cop and the handyman both got a kick out of that.

I was stunned when I answered the door to find Dr. Rosensohn standing there in jeans and a flannel shirt, carrying a good bottle of red wine.

"Hardly recognized you in your casual clothes, Doc."

"This is how I dress when the meter's off."

"Come on in."

He followed me down to the basement. I introduced him all around as "my friend Phil," and nobody needed to know more than that.

Only Billy Debowski knew who he was to me, and I took the two of them aside for a moment to show them something that had been delivered to me a few days earlier, from Nat Grossman's retirement home. It was a small metal urn containing his ashes.

"Just wanted to promise you guys I won't be climbing the bridge to dispose of these."

Billy—already giddy from the champagne—slid a friendly arm across Phil's shoulders.

"That's a relief, huh, Doc?"

"I should say so," Phil said, sipping his own glass of bubbly. "Strictly for professional purposes, I must ask you, Joseph: Where will you keep these remains?"

I placed the urn up on the windowsill, which was level with the driveway. Beside it was my precious White Rock bottle.

"My father's ashes were high in the sky. Nat's will stay at ground level. Guess it all evens out."

Justin had eased naturally into the role of bartender, keeping everyone lubricated, while Rose kept an eye on the burgers and the vegetables. Mel sidled up to me, pointed at Rose and whispered, "This woman you hired is doing a good job."

"Actually, Mel, she was my girlfriend until a little while ago."

"Oh. Wow."

"You should know there's no such thing as a maid on Shepherd Avenue."

Mel studied Rose. "I see you went for a younger model, in a darker shade."

"Hey. She's not a car."

"I'm sorry, Joey . . . what went wrong with you two?"

"It's complicated, Mel, but what the hell isn't?"

I was relieved to get away from her to answer the door once again. This time it was my daughter and Kevin, standing on my front stoop. Taylor carried a bouquet of red roses and Kevin had an economy-sized bottle of ginger ale.

My daughter never looked more beautiful. It was as if a line of tension across her brow had finally eased, allowing me to see what she looked like when she wasn't frowning.

I don't know if she was happy, but I suspected she wasn't unhappy. And Not Unhappy was a lot for anyone with Ambrosio blood to be thankful for.

I embraced them together, one on each arm. The noise from downstairs was rich with shouts and laughter. I knew I wouldn't be missed for a few minutes.

"Ready for the tour?"

Kevin had only been to the upstairs kitchen that time he'd come over. I showed them my bedroom and my name under the windowsill. Taylor laughed at the sight of the chickens strutting around in the backyard, and then I took them upstairs to see the empty flat. The maple tree in front of the house had lost its leaves, so the light up there through the bare branches was brighter than I'd ever seen it. Taylor seemed enchanted.

"This would be, like, four thousand a month on the other side of the river."

"Consider this your home away from home. Nothing like a sleepover in East New York to help you unwind."

I brought them downstairs and introduced them all around. Vic was delighted to see Taylor, and he made a fuss over the roses.

"First flowers in the history of this house under the Ambrosios!" he declared. "Hey, Joey, you got a vase or what?"

I didn't have a vase. A plastic bucket from under the sink would have to do.

Kevin suddenly looked pale, staring wide-eyed across the room. I was worried about him.

"You okay, Kevin?"

He nodded, swallowed. "Is that *Justin Wilson?*"

"Yeah, he's a friend of ours," I said casually. "Go introduce yourself. He's a hell of a nice kid."

Rose shook Taylor's hand when I introduced them, a gesture that morphed into an awkward hug. Then Rose hurried back to the stove to make sure the burgers weren't burning.

"You're working too hard, Rose. Take a break."

"I'm okay. We better eat these babies before they're ashes. And listen, I really do."

I was confused. "You really do what?"

"I really do love you, Jo-Jo. In answer to your question about the L word. I think you knew that."

I swallowed hard. "Well, I do now. And I feel the same way about you."

"Too bad God has that funny sense o' humor, huh? Keepin' us apart, first with the years, now with the miles."

"Damn, Rose. You wait until now to let me know you're a poet?"

She laughed, a sound that coincided with a knock at the door. Still tingling from Rose's words, I went upstairs to answer it and there stood Jenny Sutherland in jeans, a peacoat and a wool cap, clutching a big glass jar of nuts and raisins.

It was probably the way she would have dressed on Thanksgiving fifty years earlier, and she undoubtedly would have brought the same gift in 1961.

Same clothes, same gift. Same girl? Who could say? I was so stunned to see Jenny that I couldn't speak. I just stood and stared.

"Kinda cold out here, Joey," she said, prompting me to let her inside.

"I'm sorry, Jenny. I'm kind of shocked. Really didn't think you'd show up."

"You did leave that message, didn't you?"

"Of course."

"Is he here?"

"Downstairs."

"Does he know?"

"No, he does not."

She looked for a moment as if she might turn and flee. I wasn't going to let that happen. I put an arm across her bony shoulders and led her down those echoey stairs to the basement.

And there stood Vic in the middle of the floor, demonstrating his old batting stance to Justin, Billy, Kevin and Dr. Rosensohn. His feet were wide apart and his hands were as high as his head, the same stance I remembered from a long-ago game for Franklin K. Lane High School, when I saw Vic hit an impossibly long home run. Back then, I thought my uncle could do anything. Maybe he still could.

"Hey, Vic. An old friend wants to say hello."

He turned to look at me, hands still held high, and then he saw Jenny and his hands fell to his sides, like the hands of a puppet whose strings have suddenly been cut. He was breathing hard as he regarded her from head to toe, as if she'd just beamed down from outer space. She inched toward him. For what felt like forever all he could do was breathe and all she could do was giggle nervously, as if she didn't know whether to expect a kiss or a slap.

But neither of those thing happened. They just gazed at each other in wonder as the room fell silent, the way it does in Western movies when the villain enters the saloon. The guys backed away from Vic, leaving him and Jenny alone in the middle of the floor.

Jenny took off her cap and shook her hair the way she had as a kid, when the world was nothing more than a shiny ripe apple, just inches from her grasp.

"Well, Victor. Did I wreck your life?"

He actually chuckled at the question. "No. I didn't need your help to wreck it."

She dared to touch his cheek. "Still handsome."

"I'm old and I'm fat."

"I'm old and I'm skinny."

"You still painting?"

"No. Never had a real talent for it."

"Kind of like me with baseball, huh?"

"Could be."

They'd run out of words, standing there like two ancient kids at the prom, too shy to ask each other to dance, and then Rose, bless her raging heart, stepped in behind Vic.

"For Christ's sake, give her a hug!" she cried, and with that Rose literally shoved Vic into Jenny's arms, which opened just in time to catch him in the most beautiful embrace I'd ever seen, as if they were sharing one heart and breaking apart would have meant death for them both.

Jenny was giggling through flowing tears, her face buried in Vic's shoulder, and Vic's eyes were shiny as he rocked her in his arms. He caught my eye and spoke just two words, smiling as he said them, and you really had to know my uncle to know he meant them with affection.

"You prick."

We all laughed and the room came back to life. Good old Dr. Rosensohn, fuzzy from champagne and red wine, took me aside to ask me what the deal was with Vic and Jenny. I told him their backstory, and what I'd done to get them together.

He seemed impressed, even though his eyes were at half-mast. "In my racket, we call that shock therapy."

"Actually, Doc, it's just a reunion of two old friends."

He shrugged. "You may be right. On the other hand, *I* may be right."

"Or maybe we're *both* wrong, and it's just a fuckin' party to celebrate the fact that we're all glad to be alive."

"I'll drink to that," he said, toasting me with his glass before draining it and turning to Justin for a refill.

"Jo-Jo, the food!" Rose called to me from the stove. I raised my hands to get everyone's attention.

"There was a mishap involving the turkey this morning," I announced, "so the main course will feature burgers from White Castle instead. Please sit wherever you'd like."

Rose set the platter of burgers in the middle of the table, then set out the vegetables and the stuffing. Everybody piled onto the benches, laughing at the sight of this bizarre feast.

"What's this?" Johnny Gallo asked, pointing at the stuffing.

"Chestnut stuffing," I said.

"Yeah? Can you call it stuffing when it ain't stuffed into anything?"

"Good question."

We ate, we drank, we laughed. We'd hit that magical stride at a gathering where everybody seemed to be having a good time, and nobody was left out.

Vic and Jenny were cocooned at one corner of the table, talking softly as Jenny nibbled on the nuts and raisins she'd brought.

Would anything come of this reunion? Who the hell could say?

Taylor and Kevin sipped their ginger ale and dug into the burgers, and so did everybody else. I thought Nancy would be annoyed by the attention Mel was paying to Johnny, but Nancy was laughing her head off over something Eddie Everything was telling her, while Justin seemed fascinated by whatever Dr. Rosensohn was telling him, and Billy Debowski had everyone's attention when he stood up to prove that a White Castle hamburger can indeed be eaten in a single bite.

Rose and I sat together, saying little as we held hands under the table like a couple of schoolkids.

"Good Thanksgiving, Jo-Jo."

"Thanks, Ro-Ro."

She gave my hand a squeeze. "I ain't gonna forget you."

"You'd better not."

"Oh, Jesus. I'm happy and sad at the same time. What the hell does that mean?"

"Means you're an intelligent person, Rose."

When the main meal was over, out came Nancy's cookies, Eddie Everything's flan and Vic's clementines, and then Billy broke out his box of Cuban cigars. All the men lit up, even Justin and Kevin. The basement air went blue with smoke.

"Hell, I might as well breathe my own smoke," Mel declared. "Give me a cigar!"

Everybody laughed as Mel lit up and puffed away.

Wonderful as it was, I needed to get away for a few minutes—from the heat, the noise, the smoke. I also had to feed my chickens, so I grabbed the remaining five hamburgers and slipped out through the furnace room to the backyard. I'd promised Dr. Rosensohn he could feed the birds but he was feeling no pain, so I let him be.

Darkness was falling, though it was barely five o'clock. I tore the burgers into bits and scattered them, and my chickens were upon them. It was a comforting sight, watching them feed. They were safe here and they knew it. Down the block, the bells tolled at St. Rita's Church, and I wondered why. Bells on Thanksgiving? I'd never heard of that. It was a real riptide of a sound, as sad as it was joyous.

I didn't kid myself. I was in for a difficult time. Rose was moving away, and she'd never be back. I hoped she'd meet a decent man in Seattle, a guy who was up to the challenge. I'd like to think I did pretty well for a sixty-year-old, but I never had my full game to give.

Maybe if I'd been a younger man . . . but then I would have had the strength and the fury to fuck it up. It takes a long time to become gentle, and by the time you get there, your toolbox ain't what it used to be.

So there I was, shivering in the growing darkness with a bunch of wonderful oddballs warm and happy in my grandparents' old basement because of me and nobody else, giving thanks for whatever they had, or *thought* they had, or used to have.

And still I wondered: What was it all about? Why had I done this crazy, crazy thing, and returned to Shepherd Avenue?

"That is a peaceful sight."

The words jolted me. I turned around to see Taylor standing behind me, clasping her bare elbows against the chill. She gestured at the chickens.

"They don't have a worry in the world."

"Yeah, they've got it pretty good."

"Are you all right?"

"Not bad. You?"

"Just needed a little air."

"Yeah, me, too."

"It's solid cigar smoke in there. Do you believe Kevin, Mr. Fitness himself, is smoking a cigar?"

"It's all part of the fun."

"That cop is some character."

"He's the guy who brought me down from the bridge."

"You're kidding!"

"He's a good guy. So's the bearded man. He was my shrink."

"Was?"

"Yeah. I've fulfilled my parole requirement. I'm officially sane. Now he's just a friend."

"And Rose? Is she just a friend?"

I watched my chickens devour the last of the burgers. "A very good friend who's moving away."

"You okay with that?"

"I will be . . . listen, I have to tell you, the reason we didn't have a turkey today is because I got mugged carrying it home, and two kids ran off with the bird."

"My God, are you all right?"

"Yeah, I got hit on the head, no big deal. But now I'm thinking, it's getting dark, and I know I keep making this invitation, so here goes, one more time: Why don't you and Kevin stay over? Fresh sheets and towels upstairs, and a brand-new bed."

I gestured at my hens, already starting to roost for the night, their heads tucked into their feathers. "Plus, thanks to these guys, I can make you the best scrambled eggs you've ever had for breakfast."

Taylor smiled the way she did when she was a kid, before anything hurtful ever happened.

"Sounds good to me."

Sometimes you aim for what you want in this crazy life, and sometimes it falls into your lap, and sometimes the path is so long and twisted you forget that it's a path at all, until something happens to make you realize there's actually a destination at the end of this mad journey, something you've been striving for all along.

My destination took me in a sweet embrace, the first one she'd ever initiated as an adult. She kissed my cheek, put her lips to my ear and spoke.

"You're a funny guy, Joe."

It was a start.

Don't miss the story of how it all began. . . .

SHEPHERD AVENUE

CHARLIE CARILLO

An American Library Association Notable Book of the Year

*From acclaimed author Charlie Carillo comes a poignant, darkly
funny, coming-of-age story set in the heart of Italian-American
Brooklyn, New York, and the heat of one eventful 1960s summer . . .*

Ten-year-old Joey Ambrosio has barely begun to grieve his mother's
death when his father abruptly uproots him from his
sedate suburban Long Island home, and deposits him at his
estranged grandparents' house in boisterous East New York. While
his dad takes off on an indefinite road trip, Joey is left to navigate
unfamiliar terrain. Besides his gruff Italian grandparents, there's his
teenage Uncle Vic, a baseball star obsessed with the music of Frank
Sinatra; a steady diet of soulful, hearty foods he's never tasted, and
a community teeming with life, from endless gossip and arguments
to curse-laden stickball games under the elevated train. It's a world
where privacy doesn't exist and there's no time to feel sorry for
yourself. Most of all, it's where Joey learns not only how to fight,
and how to heal, but how to love—and ultimately, how to forgive.

Keep reading for a special excerpt.

Chapter One

I never saw my father with a newspaper in his hands. You hear about people in aboriginal tribes who live without ever seeing a written word or hearing the story of Jesus Christ's life, but Salvatore Ambrosio traveled from Roslyn, Long Island, to midtown Manhattan each weekday to earn his living as an advertising copywriter. It was a long ride, more than an hour each way. I guess he looked out the window. It's not likely that he talked to anyone.

When he got home from work his dress pants, jacket, and tie came off and were replaced by frayed work shirts and pants. He was never casually dressed, my father. His clothing was either impeccable or absolutely shabby.

My father's aloofness toward the outside world didn't do me much good when I'd ask him to help me with current-events homework. Without batting an eye he'd say, "Just tell your teacher that people are worse than ever, and do as many terrible things to each other as they can get away with."

"Nice thing to say," my mother would comment. Then she'd trim an article out of *Newsday* and read it aloud to make sure I understood it, while my father watched with amusement as the two of us "swallowed that bilge they print in the paper."

My mother read the paper front to back. "Somebody in this house should know what's going on," she used to say. She knew in her heart that my father *cared* about people, but that he couldn't hide his disappointment in most of them.

One thing that never disappointed my father was his garden. He loved to spend hours tending it slowly, treating our plot of land as if it were a giant jewel that needed daily polishing.

I got to know him best working beside him in silence. The big rectangles of lawns all around ours were tended by professional land-scapers, men who jumped off trucks, unloaded machines, and, in fu-rious clouds of noise and gasoline, cut lawns so fast it was like rape. My father used a four-bladed push mower. The neighbors mocked him behind his back, I'm sure.

I got an important glimpse into a secret chamber of my father's heart when I was nine years old. It was an October afternoon. We had just raked the lawn and put down fertilizer. The job done, I lay on the browning grass and fell asleep. When I awoke he was standing by our hedge, leaning against his rake just hard enough to bend the tines. A honking flock of geese flew overhead. He let the rake drop and did a perfect slow motion pantomime of their wings, flapping his arms and walking in their direction on tiptoes, backlit by the dull or-ange sunset. It was a startling imitation. I was sort of surprised when he didn't get airborne.

And I knew he wasn't just a nut. Something was bugging him, urging him to tear away from the circumstances of his life—some-thing he fought internally all the time. I didn't know what it was, but I sensed that somehow I stood in his way more than my mother did. I pushed the lima beans around my plate and hardly touched the meat loaf that night.

It all came down when my mother became sick with cancer the following year. We used to visit her at the hospital early in the evenings. *She* would make *us* feel better, believe it or not.

"You guys got it backwards," she explained. "The visitors are supposed to cheer up the patient. See?" After about an hour she'd chase us out of there.

"Go feed the dog," she'd say.

"We don't have a dog, Mommy."

"Go feed the cat."

"We don't have a cat," I'd giggle.

"Go feed the ostrich."

We'd leave in laughter, then eat our dinners in Northern Boulevard diners, watching cars whiz past as we forked down cheeseburgers, french fries, and cole slaw. My father knew the rudiments of cooking, but I don't think he was able to bear the thought of a meal at our home without his wife.

She stayed at the hospital for all of April and half of May 1961. In the second week of May, he stopped taking me with him to visit. I was just ten years old but he left me alone in the house those nights and came home with take-out food in foil-lined bags.

It occurs to me that I never had a baby-sitter. Wherever my parents went—to restaurants, the movies—I came along, a son treated like a miniature adult.

Elizabeth McCullough Ambrosio died in the hospital on May 13. That night my father came home and filled a big aluminum pot with water, shook salt into it, and put the flame on full blast under it. He began opening a can of tomato paste.

"We're having spaghetti," he said as he cranked the can opener. I started to cry because I knew she was dead.

They buried my mother without a wake the day after she died. The only ones present at the cemetery were my father and me and a priest from a nearby Catholic church we'd never attended. My father was alternately sharp and polite with the priest, who didn't dare to ask my father why he'd never seen us in church.

We lived an awkward month in the house before my father put it on the market. He hired a stranger to run a garage sale and sell every stick of furniture we had.

All my mother's clothing and all his dress clothes went into a big Salvation Army hopper at a nearby shopping center. My father held me by the hips as I dropped three big bundles down the dark chute. For an instant I had a vision of him pushing me in after them.

Everything that could possibly tie him down was now gone. We lived those final June days in Roslyn like raccoons that break into summer homes through the eaves. With the rugs gone the aged oak floors groaned at every step, and even with the windows down little currents of air puffed in crazy directions.

The only thing we couldn't get rid of was the four-bladed push mower, which my father left behind in the barren garage.

He didn't let me in on his plan until our final night together in the house. We slept on a pair of cots dragged close together in the living room, a courtesy of the moving company that was to bring the new owner's stuff in the morning.

I hadn't asked a single question about where we were going during the scuttling of our possessions. I just sat up in my cot, waiting for him to start volunteering information.

He swallowed. He was hesitating, like a kid reluctant to tell a parent about a broken vase. "I quit my job," he said through a dry throat.

"I figured *that* out," I said, irritated. He hadn't been to work for two weeks. "So where are we going tomorrow?"

He seemed disappointed that I wasn't startled by his announcement. "I have to take off for a while."

I felt my heart plummet. I was being disposed of, too—he'd only been saving me for last!

"What do you mean? Where am I gonna go?"

"You're staying with my parents in Brooklyn."

I was stunned. "I thought we hated them," I said. "How can we stay there if we don't even *visit?*"

"We don't hate them!" my father boomed. "There have just been years and years of misunder*standing.*"

I was disgusted. "Yeah, sure, Dad."

He said weakly, "My parents are good people."

"I don't even know them!" I rolled over on the cot so I wouldn't have to look at him. Not even sure I wanted to be with him anymore I said, "Why can't I go with you?"

"Because you can't, Joseph."

"W*hy?*"

"Because *no*body can," he said in a way that made it clear the matter was beyond his control, as if a demon inside him were calling the shots.

Puzzled, I rolled onto my back. Oddly, I felt my anger melting. I started thinking about how miserable this past month with my father had been. Maybe we both needed a break from each other. Somehow, I sensed that losing both parents might be easier than losing one.

"For how long?" I asked roughly.

The fact that I was talking inspired my father. "A few weeks, no more."

"And then what?"

"I don't know," he admitted.

"Where are you going?"

"Across the country in the car."

We were silent. The wind picked up, making the ancient window panes jiggle and creak in their loose putty jackets.

I felt him grasp my elbow. "Joey, don't hate me," he begged in a voice I'd never heard him use. Desperate.

"I won't," I said. I didn't take his hand but let him hold me for a few minutes before rolling onto my side and falling asleep.

Almost everything we loaded into our Comet station wagon the next morning belonged to me. My father packed one bulging canvas sack for himself, filled with shirts, pants, and underwear. That and his shaving kit were all he'd take across the United States.

When we were on the road I said, "You have to sign my report card." I dug it out of my pile of stuff. "We're supposed to mail it back to school. Maybe you don't have to if I'm not going back."

"Give it to me," he mumbled. At a red light near the Long Island Expressway he glanced at the card, hastily scrawled on it, and handed it back to me.

"Take care of it," he said, knowing I had a stamped, addressed envelope the school had provided.

I looked at the card. Through the first three marking periods Mrs. Olsen, my fifth-grade teacher, had written tiny but stinging notes in the space provided for comments. "Joseph should participate in class more often... Joseph needs to be more outgoing... Joseph holds back during sports."

And beneath each comment was my mother's light-handed, almost fluffy signature, "Mrs. Salvatore Ambrosio." She barely pressed a pen when she wrote.

I looked at the space for the last marking period.

"I suspect he can do better," Mrs. Olsen had written of my straight-B performance.

"I suspect we all can," my father wrote back before scrawling his fierce signature. It violated the boundaries of the dainty white box, and I could feel his lettering through the back side of the card, like Braille.

"There's a mailbox," I said just before we reached the entry ramp to the expressway. He braked the car. I got out and mailed the report card, sort of surprised that he'd waited instead of roaring away.

"Put your seat belt on," he said, and that was the extent of our conversation for the rest of the trip to the East New York section of Brooklyn.

He slowed the car to a crawl when we made the turn down Shepherd Avenue. We drove beneath an elevated train track structure that left a ladder-shaped shadow in the late afternoon light. Rows of sooty red brick houses, fronted with droopy maple trees that seemed to have given up trying to grow taller.

My grandmother and Uncle Victor were waiting for us on the porch. I knew them only from photographs.

Clumsy introductions outside the car door: your grandmother, your uncle. No kisses. My father clasped his mother's hand.

"Long time," he said in a neutral voice. She nodded. Victor, after a moment's hesitation, embraced my father.

"What are we, strangers here?"

Embarrassment melted Victor's enthusiasm. He tore himself away to carry my stuff into the house. I stayed outside with my father, who kept his hand on the open car door, clinging to it as tightly as a rodeo rider grips a saddle horn.

My grandmother had planned to feed us, share one big meal together, but my father said he was already behind schedule. She urged him to stay long enough at least to see his father, who was late getting home. My father said he couldn't.

"Not twenty minutes?" Constanzia Ambrosio asked. "What's this *schedule?*"

"I'm very late," my father said. "Believe me, Ma."

How strange it was to hear him use that word, and how anxious he was to get moving, as if a bomb were about to explode inside him and he wanted to put distance between himself and his family to protect us from shrapnel. He stood like a chauffeur, handsome in denim jacket and jeans, misty-eyed, apologetic and arrogant at the same time. At last he hugged his mother, a collision of flesh like two human bumper cars.

"I'm sorry she died," Constanzia blurted.

"Me, too," my father said, his voice like a child's. He let go of her and put his hands under my armpits. I braced myself, anticipating a lift.

But his hands went limp against my rib cage. "No," he decided. "You're too big for that now." He crouched and hugged me, said "See you soon" in a broken voice, and split. I don't know which of us felt more relieved.

Relieved, but not for long. The switch was concise, a changing of the guard.

"You're gonna be livin' here awhile, so forget about that Grandma and Grandpa business," said Vic, my roommate, as he lugged double armfuls of my stuff to his room.

"We decided this morning," he said, breathing hard. "No titles. Just Connie and Angie and Vic."

Vic was eighteen years old, five foot ten, a hundred and ninety pounds. His hair was thick as a cluster of wire brush filaments—when he ran his hands through it, it leapt back into place. His hairline ran straight across his forehead and down the sides of his head, with no scallops at the temples. His eyes were brown, like the eyes of everyone else in the house, including me. Only my father had picked up blue eyes, through some errant gene.

Every pair of Vic's pants looked tight on him but he insisted they were comfortable and kept wearing them, despite my grandmother's warning that "They'll make you sterile." His hard belly bulged slightly, like an overinflated tire. His rump bulged in the same way. From time to time he patted his buttocks, rat-a-tat-tat, as if they were bongos.

Vic's room was sparsely furnished: a horsehair mattress on a platform bed, an army foldout cot (for me), a crucifix on the wall, a photo of the *Journal-American*'s 1960 all-star baseball team ("I'm third from the left—that guy's hat hides my face"), a Frank Sinatra record jacket tacked to the wall, and a Victrola.

"Put that down," he said. I'd picked up his athletic cup and put it against my nose, thinking that was where it was worn. He took it from me and gestured with it.

"Listen. If we're gonna get along we can't be messing around with each other's stuff, okay?"

I nodded. "What is that thing?"

He blushed. "You wear it here," he said, holding it in front of his pants. "In case you get hit with a baseball. You like Sinatra?"

"I guess."

"You *guess*?"

"I don't listen to music much."

Shaking his head, Vic put on a record. "If you hang around here, you gotta like Sinatra." Music filled the room. Vic lay on his back, his stiff mattress crunching as he rolled with the music.

"Look," he announced when the first song ended, "I think you and me can get along real good. See, I'm a ballplayer, I need lots of sleep. Most nights I'll probably go to bed earlier than you."

"What position do you play?" I asked politely.

Vic's eyebrows arched. "You *know* baseball?"

"A little."

"I'm the shortstop. I play in between the second baseman and the third baseman."

"Oh."

"Hey, don't go thinkin' I can't hit, just because I'm an infielder. I hit better than all the outfielders on the team. If you can *call* 'em outfielders. Now listen to this part, how he does this," Vic said, leaping off the bed and cranking up the volume on the Victrola.

Down the street the elevated train rode past, partially drowning out the music. Vic muttered "Damn" and lifted the needle off the disc to play the same part again, scratching the record.

"Here it is," he said solemnly.

I forget the song but at a certain point my uncle was jumping up and down on the bed, singing along. When the song ended he stepped to the floor, pink-faced.

"Like, I get carried away," he said.

Connie appeared at the doorway. "I heard you jump, all the way downstairs! You're gonna come right through the floor."

"Sorry, Ma."

"Come on," Connie said. "We'll eat."

When she left, Vic grinned at me. He clasped the back of my neck and led me into the hallway, giving me a slight Indian burn.

On the way in I'd noticed a beautiful dining room where I figured dinner would be served, but Vic surprised me by leading the way to a dark, rickety staircase. Our footsteps echoed as we walked down to the cellar. There were no banisters. I put my palms against the walls for balance, feeling the scrape of rough stucco.

The basement floor was red and yellow tiles. There were windows along one wall, facing the driveway—you got a view of any approaching visitor's ankles. A long table with built-in benches stood under fluorescent lights. My grandfather's oak chair stood at the end of the table.

This was the hub of the home. During Depression years the main floor of the Ambrosio house had been rented out to boarders, so the family had gotten into the habit of using the basement. It was roomy, and always cool in the summertime.

Upstairs, the dining room might as well have been a museum— the mahogany table with its fitted glass top, a buffet table on wheels, heavy long-armed chairs. On the backs of those chairs there were doilies that stayed white year-round, and if you opened a cabinet door in the dining room there was a clicking sound, as if the long-untouched varnished surfaces had welded together. Trapped inside the cabinets were gold-rimmed teacups and saucers with paper tags still glued to their undersides.

But that room couldn't hold a candle to the character of the basement.

For one thing, the floor wasn't level, which Vic demonstrated by placing a baseball on it. The ball was still for an instant, then rolled to the opposite wall.

"Enough with that trick, already," Connie said.

The ceiling was a network of pipes and cables, painted white. There were upright poles at strategic locations, supporting the house above us.

A bowl of spaghetti sat in the middle of the table, steam rising off it and disappearing into the fluorescents. Connie worked it with a pair of forks.

A cameo portrait of her would have displayed a slender woman. Most of her two hundred and twenty pounds hung way below her breastbone. She was fifty-five years old but her hair was black, save for a pair of white-gray stripes at either side of her part, like catfish whiskers.

Those fleshy arms rose again and again over the spaghetti, curtains of fat dangling and dancing from her upper arms. I was reminded of the flying squirrel pictures I'd seen in my science book.

Her guard was all the way up that night. "You hungry?"

"Yes," I said.

"You didn't eat so good when you and your father lived alone." A statement.

"Sometimes we ate out," I said.

"Mmmm." She was confirming her own thoughts. She put a bowl of spaghetti before me. "You remember the *last* time you ate here?"

I hesitated. "I never ate here before."

"Ah! You don't remember!"

Vic bared his teeth tightly. "*God*, Ma, he was a baby. Why do you bring that up?"

Connie ignored Vic as she loaded his dish. "That was some fight," she said. "I still get knots right here when I think about it." She made a tight fist and held it near her stomach.

"Forget the knots, let's eat," Vic said, winking and squeezing my knee.

Eating noises. Connie pointed at my side dish. "He don't like it."

I was poking my fork into something I later came to love: bread, raisins, capers, and cheese, mixed together and baked into half a red pepper. It reminded me of a little coffin and was too sharp a taste for my first day.

"You don't like it, don't eat it," Connie said, as if she didn't mind.

"This food's gotta grow on you," Vic said. "Eat a mouthful tonight, next time eat two. Before you know it you'll love it."

I held my breath and swallowed a mouthful without chewing. It went down like a giant slippery aspirin.

"I promise it won't taste so bad next time," Vic said. Already I was chasing it with a forkful of spaghetti.

"You talk like my food's poison," Connie said.

"Ah, quit acting hurt, Ma."

Connie pointed at him with a fork. "You. Don't eat so fast."

She had a point. Vic ate with the speed of an animal fleeing predators. He held his fork in his right hand and a piece of Italian bread in his left, which he used to shove food onto the fork. When the bread got mushy with sauce he took a bite off it, then resumed work with the dry bread.

"You'll bite a finger off," she warned him. "Gonna get fat."

"Ah, I burn it off fast," Vic said, a crumb flying from his mouth. He elbowed me, and I found myself smiling and nearly echoing, "Yeah, he burns it up fast," but I stopped myself. Why make an enemy of Connie when I barely knew Vic?

The rest of the meal was quiet, save for low, muffled belches out of Vic. Connie picked up a bit of food that had flown from Vic's mouth and crushed it in a paper napkin.

"Now don't go thinkin' your father don't love you," she said.

A direct hit; my eyes welled with tears. Vic stopped chewing and shot a searing look at her. Then he softened and looked my way, prodding me with an elbow.

"What team do you like, the Yankees or the Dodgers?"

I'd never even heard of the Dodgers. "Yankees."

"Me, too. My father likes the Dodgers, he's ready to kill O'Malley for sendin' 'em out west. Listen, if I make the majors, I'm gonna play for the Yanks."

"Big shot," Connie said, getting up to clear the table. The meal had lasted barely ten minutes.

Vic ignored her. "Only thing is, they got so many good players that hardly anybody gets to play every day, except for guys like Mantle and Maris." He wiped his mouth with the back of his hand. "See, I don't wanna warm some bench when I get there."

It never occurred to my uncle that he might not make the major leagues, but only that he might get cheated out of valuable playing time once he arrived.

He folded his big hands behind his head. "The big dough's in New York. You set yourself up nice, and then you can get into, like, broadcastin'. That's how come I'm takin' a speech class in school. They remember who you are when you play in New York."

"They forget," Connie said above the thumping of hot water into the sink. "You'd be surprised how fast people forget."

Again he ignored her. His eyes narrowed suddenly. "Who hit more homers last year, Hank Aaron or Mickey Mantle?"

"Mickey Mantle," I guessed.

"Wrong!" Vic roared joyfully. "They both hit forty! See? Here's a guy hittin' homers all over the place and nobody knows about it, 'cause he doesn't play in New York. Poor guy's stuck in Milwaukee."

"Shut up already," Connie said. "Every night we hear this."

She finished washing the dishes. We climbed the stairs to the front parlor and watched TV for a while. Not once had my grandfather's absence been mentioned.

They set my cot up next to the bedroom window, which was open all the way. Warm air puffed through the screen, but you'd be exaggerating if you called it a breeze.

The sheets were stiff, having been hung to dry in the dead air of the basement because it had rained earlier in the week. Getting into bed was like climbing into an envelope.

It wasn't dark and it wasn't quiet. Light filtered in from the street lamp. Two or three radios played somewhere. There were bouts of distant laughter and the screech of brakes on Atlantic Avenue.

"Vic?"

"Yeah?"

"Is there a party going on somewhere?"

"Whatsamatter, can't you sleep?"

"Too much *noise*," I complained. "Is it always so bright in here?"

"Are you crazy?" He hated being awakened. "Here, sleep on this side," he said, rising.

"It'll be the same over there," I whined.

"The *same*," he mimicked. "Roll over and close your eyes."

"I already did."

"Well, just shut up."

I heard his irregular breathing across the room and imagined him hating my guts. Now and then he sucked in his breath and socked the pillow with his fist.

I had to break the silence. "My father cried when he left."

"I saw him cry once before," Vic said, startling me with his friendliness. He sat up, propping his head up with his hand.

"The time Dixie died, a long time ago. You never knew Dixie. Swell pooch. Well, anyway, he made him a coffin out of an old desk drawer and stuck him in a pillow case. Buried him right out in the backyard."

Vic flipped onto his belly. "Didn't make any noise when he cried, though. Cried and cried until his eyes got red, but . . . funny." He looked at me. "Didn't he cry when? "

"When my mother died," I said, completing his sentence. "No. Not around me, anyway."

Vic let it sink in. "Weird guy." He reached around under his mattress. "Want a Milky Way?"

"We just brushed our teeth."

"Ah, it's all right, you just rub the chocolate off with your tongue. Here."

He tossed one at me. It landed in the sheets, near my knees.

"Dixie," Vic said through a mouthful of candy. "Once in a while my mother still chucks a bone out in the yard for her, where your father buried her. You can't touch the bone, either. It has to sit on the grave till it rots."

His voice grew serious. "So if you see a bone in the yard, don't touch it, 'cause it's for Dixie."

"Okay," I said.

"Especially if my mother's lookin'."

"I won't. What would I want with a dumb bone, anyhow?"

He flipped onto his back. "I'll tell you this—your father's all right. He was good to me when I was a shrimp."

I let his remark go without comment.

"But he was always a little crazy," Vic continued. "Remember when he got married, and everybody told him . . . jeez, do you believe this? I'm expectin' you to remember your father's wedding!"

"What did everybody tell him?"

Vic sighed. "All right. When he got married nobody was marryin' Irish girls. That's the truth. I mean it's no big deal now, but to my mother . . ."

"What?" I said. "Say it."

Vic licked his lips. "My mother thought she wasn't good enough for Sal," he said. "She apologized a million times since then," he added quickly.

The news hit my heart like dull daggers.

"God, I shouldn't have told you that," Vic said, pummeling his bedding. "Why the hell couldn't you fall asleep?"

Vic rolled away from me. I saw the black back of his head, suspected he was nowhere near sleep. I was right. When he rolled to face me again his eyes were wide open.

"*No*body could ever tell your father what to do," he said with fierce pride. "If he had his hand on a hot stove and you told him to take it off he wouldn't. A rock head. Now it's the same thing. He wants to drive away, he drives away. Understand this? Joseph?"

"Joey," I corrected. "No, I don't."

"Want another Milky Way?"

"Yeah."

This one landed on my navel. "They got married real young, they had you right away. He's makin' up for lost time, I figure. Few weeks and he'll be back, guaranteed."

The bedroom door opened. Connie's form filled the doorway.

"Talk soft."

"Sorry," Vic said, wincing.

She looked at me. "He keeping you awake?"

"No," I said, "I'm keeping him awake."

"Lie down and shut up," she instructed, pulling the door closed. It was shut nearly all the way when it opened again, suddenly.

"You ain't foolin' me," she said to both of us. "I find the candy wrappers in the morning."

The door closed for good. Vic's breathing became rhythmic with sleep. I ran my tongue over my teeth to get rid of the last traces of chocolate and caramel.

The night that had given Connie "knots" was still a mystery, but that was all right. I could wait. I certainly wasn't going anywhere.

"Nowhere to go."

I hadn't meant to say it out loud. Vic rolled over.

"What'd you say?"

"Nothing."

He pushed a thick knuckle against one eye. "Aw, c'mon, kid, get used to this place and sleep, already."

Queens-born **Charlie Carillo** was a reporter and a columnist for the
New York Post before becoming a producer for the TV show "Inside
Edition." His first novel, *Shepherd Avenue,* was named a Notable
Book of the Year by the American Library Association in 1986. He is
also the author *of My Ride with Gus, Raising Jake, One Hit Wonder,
Found Money, God Plays Favorites* and *The Man Who Killed Santa
Claus: A Love Story.*

Charlie now divides his time between New York City and London,
England, where he works as an independent television producer. He
is a frequent contributor to the *Huffington Post.* Visit his website at
www.charliecarillo.co.

Lightning Source UK Ltd.
Milton Keynes UK
UKOW01f2224070817
306873UK00001B/84/P